Kenneth Sinclair

Pantolwen
Press

Published in Great Britain
by Pantolwen Press

This edition is available through UK bookshops printed digitally by Gomer Press, Llandysul, on carbon balanced paper; or set digitally, print-on-demand, from various sources worldwide.

Copyright © 2024 Kenneth Sinclair
All rights reserved

Kenneth Sinclair has asserted his right to be identified as the author of this work in accordance with the Copyright, Designs and Patents Act 1988.

This is a work of fiction. The names and characters of the protagonists are the product of the author's imagination. Any resemblance to actual persons, living or dead, is entirely coincidental.

First edition 2024
www.pantolwenpress.com

A CIP catalogue record for this book is available from the British Library.

ISBNs
Hardback: 978 1 7393623 3 1
Paperback: 978 1 7393623 4 8
eBook: 978 1 7393623 5 5

Edited by Gillian Paschkes-Bell
Cover based on a design by Karl H

Body text typeset in Source Serif Pro 10pt

In memory of my beloved Irish Red Setters
Max, Jamie and Mia
who accompanied me through the time of writing

I thank my dear friend, Gillian Paschkes-Bell, for her astute, sympathetic, and meticulous editing—sometimes over coffee and croissants.

Contents

Chapter I   1
At night Scheherazade sent for me
The long oars of the Greeks drip diamond drops

Chapter II   12
I explore a network of little alleys
The scratch of a feather pen

Chapter III   23
Candles shed their gentle light
Dante stands in a dark wood; the sun is silent

Chapter IV   33
An antique wooden globe set spinning
We no longer stand at the centre of the universe

Chapter V   45
We enter on turbulent times
Michelangelo creates God, stretching out a finger

Chapter VI   55
Shakespeare leaves Stratford-upon-Avon
Scattered deep red roses shed their scent

Chapter VII   68
The old storyteller rests beneath a palm tree
The little Infanta is faintly surprised

Chapter VIII   81
The cry of the peacock: the hour of the tale
Watteau's couples on their tender quest for love

Chapter IX   91
Candide sets out on his adventures
A pale blue ribbon falls from a closed grey volume

Chapter X   101
Turning the corner to come upon Farquharson's
Mozart dances with his beloved Constanze

Chapter XI	114
The apartment is lit by soft globes of silvery light	
The novel is a mirror travelling along a highway	
Chapter XII	127
Alone in my cell, reveries return me to Wiltshire	
Flaubert sets out his ideal	
Chapter XIII	140
Late afternoon in the courtyard	
Amfortas raises the Grail cup	
Chapter XIV	159
A soft-stepping youth has entered my dusky cell	
Max Planck formulates quantum theory	
Chapter XV	178
Gardeners with long rakes slowly advance	
No war, asserts the young man from Freiburg	
Chapter XVI	191
The old storyteller sits cross-legged as before	
The train from Chartres stops at Illiers-Combray	
Chapter XVII	207
A scattering of meditatively inclined scholars	
Jazz comes in from Canal Street	
Chapter XVIII	227
Low-lit lamps cast an opaque, reddish glow	
Hitler wipes cream from his mouth	
Chapter XIX	240
Chartres is liberated! The bells ring out	
The Angel of History abandons the Germans	
Chapter XX	256
The white ferry departs the land of the gods	
Messiaen notates the cries and songs of the birds	

I

At night Scheherazade sent for me.

I keep pace by the dark guard who took me from my cell. In the torchlight, glistening drops of sweat on his naked back turn to moist points of dancing fire.

The long corridors—soon to grow so familiar—we traverse at measured pace. Lit at intervals by torches blazing in their sconces, they give way to an extended flight of low wide stairs that I know will lead towards the Princess's apartments.

Gently floating oil lamps cast hushed pools of lambent light. Before me, by an open terrace lies Scheherazade. Clad in white silk, she reclines on a low juniper couch like a leopard taking her ease, a cornelian on her finger brought to gleaming life by the burning torch of my unknown guard.

I feel its warmth leave my side.

We are alone.

Her searching eyes burn like dark stars. When she speaks, her voice is deep and rich, redolent of layers of meaning, of question and suggestion, reverberating through me as she falls silent.

—We are approaching the end, in the reckoning of your time, Gabriel. The *fin-de-siècle* will soon be upon us. Another millennium beckons. Another thousand years.

A faint trickle of water sounds from the starlit garden.

—You are going to entertain me, are you not, see me through the nights—those interminable nights—with a tale. A tale of light and shade, of wonder, advancing through the ages.

She inclines her head.

How to respond.

I am a man encumbered with the limitations of my temperament and time, Princess …

A faint smile touches her lips.

—Indeed.

Then—where shall I begin.

A slight breeze blows the fountain notes off key, causing the palms to rustle, shadows flit and dance.

Her voice.

—Begin with the speck of gold in the blue, the sun in the sea.

She turns her ring.

—There. Do you not see. The long oars of the Greeks drip diamond drops …

Then—shall I be free.

—Free, Gabriel …

My name, like rich red wine upon her lips.

—Is freedom what you want …

Her dark eyes rest on me.

—To return to your misty island …

The piercing cry of a peacock calls from the starlit garden.

—Time to begin, she said.

And so that night, the black hulls of the Greeks already on the blue Aegean, bound for Troy. The long sea oars drip diamond drops that flash in the noonday sun. In all beginnings there is a magic force.

Underway.

My blue pen poised over an A4 pad.

Max waiting for his walk.

Night.

The hollow ships, stern first, pulled up along the shore where, by firelight, a youth plays sweetly on a clear-toned lyre. And the gods: far-shafting Apollo, Apollo of the silver bow; the bright-eyed Athene, grey-eyed Athene, draw near, pace soundlessly along the flickering shadows' edge.

—When the gods still walked among us, murmurs Scheherazade.

I incline my head.

Zeus raises his golden scales, catching the ascending light. Achilles' spear flashes. And Hector, glorious Hector, pride of Troy, falls. He is dragged in the dust as Andromache, his wife, watches the maid return from drawing water for the evening meal.

White columns, warmed by the circling sun. A vermilion butterfly frolics round a flat stone. Light shines through grapes, turning the green fruit gold.

Below in the underworld, Orpheus, now on the homeward path towards the light, turns—to see his beloved Eurydice, her mouth open in a soundless cry, vanishing back into darkness.

Dark blue swallows dip and cut through the air. A laurel leaf trembles. Athene is near—bright goddess of radiant action. The scent of wild thyme and rosemary clings to her robes. The old pine gently creaks, sways.

Underway.

Wet ropes hauled on board.

Sails unfurled.

My blue pen moving along a pale grey line.

Land slipping from sight ...

Wonder at the heart of philosophy. Thales of Miletus inquires into the nature of things. Heraclitus holds that all things are in a state of flux. Parmenides believes Time to be an illusion.

Sappho sings of Hesperus, loveliest of stars, who brings back all that the radiant dawn has scattered. The bleating sheep to the fold, the goats to their pen, the child back to his mother.

She waits.

Her lover, Anactoria, may return perhaps, to lie with her. I'd sooner see her lovely walk and the moist glow on her face than all the horse and arms of Lydia.

Love, limb loosener. Yet what a bitter-sweet creature she can be.

Scheherazade rests her eyes, now slightly abstracted, upon me.

I lower my gaze.

Agamemnon steps on the crimson cloth Clytemnestra has caused to be laid out to greet him on his return from the plains of Troy. Blind Oedipus, on reaching white Colonus, extends a trembling hand and bids farewell to his weeping daughters. Dance-drunk Dionysus leads the Bacchae in furious frenzy.

From the cooling shade of the olive groves at Academus Plato aspires to the pure world of forms. Epicurus, touching an oleander in his fragrant garden, teaches that we must be free to pursue the natural aims of happiness and tranquility.

Others cling to the senses. The smooth motion of an oiled hand over a yielding body. Yet concern that, after lying on the beach, Greek youths cover their evocative imprints in the sand—not to distract the lightly-clad soldiers who will come to exercise after them.

Our tale wings South.

We arrive at Alexandria, that magical city set on the confines of East and West, where Callimachus saw three verities.

—The decorative surface of the world. Study. And the joys of love, observes Scheherazade.

I incline my head.

Scent of santal, odour of perfumed soap, invade the markets. Eye-shadow is carefully applied in the bed-chamber. Aristarchus suggests that the earth might be revolving round a motionless sun. As cool of evening descends, men stroll along colonnades, passing through bands of light and shade, or stop to admire oiled youths exercising in the gymnasium.

Night advances. I see Orion commencing his descent. The emerging Roman empire. Scheherazade's dark eyes.

Augustus wears the laurel wreath. Virgil is master poet. A blue-winged swallow weaves through deserted colonnades, skims out over fly-hung pools. Ascanius, out hunting, looses a swift arrow—the decisive moment held in amber on Claude Lorrain's last painting—and the stricken deer brings on another war.

Virgil crushes a laurel leaf between his fingers.

Leaves the *Aeneid* still with a few stepping stones—as he called passages to be replaced. Maybe a certain weariness, a sadness. Are there not tears ... tears, at the very heart of life. Taken ill, he turns back from his voyage to Greece, where he wished to take up the study of philosophy. He dies at Brindisi, within sight of the sea.

Water trickles faintly from the dark garden.

Scheherazade slides a slender finger down her cheek.

—And so ...

And so, as Virgil prophesied, a new cycle of the centuries unravels. A still, six-pointed star shines over Bethlehem. Three shepherds leave their bleating flocks, three kings their silken courts. An ox and an ass turn their quiet eyes away ...

—Knowing there is little to hope for. The world is not for them.

I incline my head.

A moist star silently enters the dark mirror.

Walking by the Sea of Galilee on a windless day, Jesus bends and picks up a tiny pale blue stone.

And walks on.

The Emperor Tiberius is in close retirement on the island of Capri. Pretty boys vie with one another to pleasure him as he floats on his back in the bath.

In the dark garden of Gethsemane Jesus kneels. Alone. Afraid. But bound to his mission.

He looks up.

Thy will be done.

Pontius Pilate turns from the baying mob. A certain respect for the bleeding prisoner brought again before him mingles with relief at escaping the flies and the suffocating heat.

Sentence has been passed. Crucifixion. Normal punishment for non-Romans found guilty of sedition.

In a cool inner room Pilate turns his sardonyx ring, sips a little red wine. But why, he wonders, did the prisoner not answer his question. What is truth.

Night.

The palace garden.

Caligula stares up at the sky. Spats of rain fall on his livid, powdered face. Now that he has become a god he requires Clitus to bring him back the moon. The man has not yet returned.

Caligula shivers. Stamps his foot.

How much longer will he have to wait. The pale disc floats free, untroubled, among oyster-shaded clouds. The Emperor's pointed, painted nails press into his soft palm.

Nero peers through an emerald—such a good idea—to enjoy the spectacle of muddy green lions devouring pale green Christians. He'll retain that image when climaxing on the couch with Lucius.

Scheherazade's dark eyes flash.

She leans forward.

Low and resonant, her voice pervades the room:

>—A cool morning in Alexandria. Hypatia, inspired teacher, has given what will be her last lecture on Euclid and is returning home when she is pulled from her carriage, dragged along the street, flayed, then torn limb from limb by a mob of Christians.
>
>Zenobia, fabulous queen, assumes the imperial diadem in the oasis-city of Palmyra, seeking to bring all of Syria, Egypt, Persia and the dim lands beyond, under her sway. But the stars are doom-laden and she is borne to Rome. Her desert capital—its temples, its theatres, its terraces—abandoned to the sand and wind.

An oil lamp flickers.

With a wave of her hand, I am invited to continue.

By flickering lights in his camp on the northern frontier Marcus Aurelius writes his meditations. He struggles to preserve the empire; looks out with eyes that are disillusioned yet serene, as mist drifts silently over the impenetrable German forest, so far from the pomp and ceremony of Rome.

The chaste Julian attempts to revive the fast-fading gods. They return at his bidding in one last, low glow; flicker fitfully, on the brink of their eternal night.

An oil lamp dips and gutters.

We are silent, still ... until, with a slight toss of the head, her voice:

>—Our tale sweeps East. To former times. For in Time Present is contained Time Past.

From the Indus valley to vast plains where Ganga meanders, the laws of karma are applied to all who wander, bound to the ever-turning wheel of birth and rebirth, awaiting liberation.

The Buddha said,

> *I consider the position of kings and rulers to be like dust motes; the teachings of the world, the illusion of magicians. Its judgement of right and wrong, the serpentine dance of a dragon. And this universe, no more than a juggling picture show.*

He turns his gaze upward.

The serenity.

On his westward journey Lao Tzu arrives at Han Ku Pass. At the request of the innkeeper, Kuan Yin, he writes the *Tao Te Ching*.

> *A man is supple and weak when alive, but hard and stiff when dead. Thus the hard and strong are companions of death, but the supple and weak are companions of life.*

Kuan Yin remembers him. In his movement he was like water, in his stillness, like a mirror. In his response, like an echo.

Summoned to appear before the Emperor, the artist Chuang Tzu is asked to draw a crab. He bows, and asks that he be granted seven years, a country house, and seven servants. His request is granted.

Seven years pass.

The Emperor summons Chuang Tzu to appear before him. He bows. Asks for a further seven years. It is granted.

Seven years pass.

The Emperor leans forward. Chuang Tzu takes up his brush and, with a single stroke, draws a crab. The most perfect ever seen.

A peacock screams from the dark garden.

Scheherazade draws herself up.

> —A princess attached to the Han court is married against her will to the ruler of a northern kingdom. Setting a face like jade against the whirling sands and windswept clouds, she composes music on her lute to console her. The jade princess falls into a fever and dies in exile. But her music reaches her homeland, where delicate-fingered girls master it in serene inner chambers, unable to imagine the sallow skies and yellow clouds at the end of the world.

She lies back. Turns her ring.

I am to continue.

The poets of the late T'ang flower.

Li Po climbs Blue Cloud mountain where tigers roar and dragons roam. Waterfalls plunge three thousand feet, raise white rainbows. Here a cloud princess—a pale pearl iridescent, glimpsed through mist and vapour, vanishing in fading candle smoke by the edge of the bed—where the poet finds but pillow and quilt, wind sighing in the bamboo.

Tu Fu contemplates autumn. Glistening drops have not yet fallen from fir needles as the evening mists rise. Tangled in bushes, mountain berries. Some scarlet, cinnabar red; others black lacquer. Splashed by rain.

Shadows of clouds float on the ground. The washing blocks pound. A purple haze fills Han Ku Pass all the way to the stars. On a still lake, at the end of the world … one bent old fisherman.

Fluttering white butterfly.

In a moonlit room, cold blue candle flame. Raven hair hangs loose. Damp perfumed silk slips silently to the floor. A jade comb falls. Li Shang-yin begins to close his eyes.

A faint fragrance of musk hangs in the air. Threads of gold shorten. How long before the heart's threads, all cares gone, float free as gossamer.

As the last-lit lamp goes out, releasing a whiff of greyish blue smoke, Scheherazade, with a faint sign, indicates it is time for me to go.

II

For many nights Scheherazade does not send for me. I watch shadows retreat and lengthen along the dusty ochre walls of my cell.

Silence fills the nights and spreads out through the days.

I had arrived alone, travelling light, at this orient city. A sense of expectancy, excitement: my future uncertain, dark as jade. And on that first night, leaving my hotel and tossing a last Camel away (its red glow flaring and dying) I set out to explore.

I entered on a network of little alleys—narrow, intricate—giving out in all directions: a maze of white walls, receptive to every shadow that floated, tinged with blue, under an amber moon that hung low in the sky.

The air was sweetened with the scent of santal. Men walked gently, hand in hand. From the shadows came the sound of laughter, smothered, low. Turning a corner, I found myself in an empty square. A fountain trickled faintly releasing a thread of water flecked with silver. All was quiet. Yet there seemed more moving shadows ... A slight sound. Sudden. Rapid. A bird's wing. Then—darkness.

Now the key grates in its iron lock and Yusef stands before me. In his dark hand, a burning torch.

For a second time we advance slowly along the flickering corridors towards the broad, wide stairs I now recognise as those that lead towards the Princess's apartments.

Scheherazade reclines on her juniper couch, quiet as a coiled spring. Tonight she is clad in a pale ivory silk, a milky opal firing a slender finger. Bronze mosque lamps cast intricate shadows, floating pools of limpid light. Her dark eyes rest on me.

Yusef silently withdraws.

We are alone.

Her low, rich voice.

—Time, Gabriel—we are so little out from land—time to take up our tale, our fabulous voyage.

Unfastening a clasp, she shakes her hair loose. It falls like raven's wings. She fixes me with an enigmatic gaze.

—Our tale of wonder, to beguile the night ...

Time to begin again.

And so ...

Waves break. White foam rushes over rocks. The grey sea rises; rises and falls, batters the dark cliffs.

Raised at the court of Elffin ap Gwyddno, a Cumbric-speaking bard proclaims:

I am old. I am young. I am Gwion. I am universal.

Taliesin, of the radiant brow.

In a beechwood near Wye, a young monk stands still. He has halted after a spring fall of rain, drops glistening, dripping from the green leaves. A blackbird sweetly sings.

Scratch of a feather pen.

On the edge of an illuminated manuscript an Irish monk pauses in his copying. Writes,

> *Pleasant is the glint of sun today on these margins. It flickers so.*

Lashed by the grey North Sea the Venerable Bede likens our life to a bird that, on a winter's night, passes from window to window across a brightly-lit hall.

Imprisoned in Pavia, Boethius is visited by the Lady Philosophy who tells him of Providence's simple and unchanging plan, Fate's ever-changing web. From the shores of the Mediterranean, under a resplendent North African sun, Augustine cries,

> *Thou hast made us for Thyself, O Lord, and our hearts are restless till they rest in Thee.*

Scarcely rustling palm leaves.

The Princess takes up the tale. Her low voice.

> —The universe is an immense book. According to our sages, one who has no history inscribed upon the heart cannot discern, in life's alloy, the gold.

On Mount Hira, Muhammad has his vision. Whoever believes in One God and the Hereafter should speak what is good or else remain silent. He desires three things from the world: sweet scent, tender sex, and prayer. Declares:

> *The coolness of my eye has been caused by prayer.*

It is given to Bilal the Abyssinian to be first to call the faithful to prayer; to the Arabian goatherd, Kaldi, to discover coffee.

Banners unfurl. Silk over sand. We attach leaves from the Koran to the tips of our lances. They prove almost invincible.

Having raised the flag of Muhammad high above the walls of Alexandria, Amr dictates a letter to the Caliph Omar: *I have taken the Great City to the West.* Yet the sands run through our fingers; they trickle silently from our grasp. We close our hands on empty air. As Amr lies near to death a friend addresses him: *You have often remarked that you would like to find an intelligent man on the point of death, to ask him what his feelings are. Now I ask you that question.*

And Amr, conqueror of Alexandria, turns his dark eyes glowing on his friend for one last time, and grips his hand: *I feel as if heaven lay close upon the earth and I between the two, breathing through the eye of a needle.*

The Princess lowers her eyes. A breath from the world of deep space and dark stars reaches us. She continues.

—Over these my own lands, tents are being lowered, fires kicked out, last rugs strapped to camels' backs. The caravan, with its tinkling bells, moves off. At the first encampment the blind *takshif* calls out. He asks for some sand to be given him, that from its scent he may discern the route.

A day's journey unfurls in a single glance towards a shimmering horizon. The walls of Petra give way to those of Ctesiphon—where once Greek philosophy sought refuge—and beyond: to Persia, where the Grand Vizier, Abdul Kassim Ismael, unwilling to be parted, when travelling, from any one of his collection of one hundred and seventeen thousand volumes, had them carried by a caravan of four hundred camels, trained to walk in alphabetical order.

Frankincense, which Melchior bore, comes from the Yemen. Snow, to be sipped in sherbet, travels from the Lebanon. Silk leaves Chang'an, the Chinese city of Perpetual Peace. The caravan skirts the Taklimakan desert where demons roam, mirages and strange sounds lure, enticing the unwary into the shifting sands of the high dunes. After many days and nights the caravan crosses the two parted friends, Tigris and Euphrates. And journeys on, to white-walled Antioch.

Secrets of paper-making, wrung from the Chinese, reach Samarkand, appear in Baghdad and, as a hundred years pass slowly by, travel westward, to Cairo. Still following the sun and another two hundred years they reach Fez where, slipping silently across the narrow strait, they arrive at last in the Land of Vespers. Spain.

Water trickles faintly from the fountain.

Scheherazade lets fall an arm. Long fingers dangle. Dark eyes shine. Resting them on me, she waits.

I am expected to resume.

༺•༻

The chant of plainsong rises.

Clouds of incense billow out. Flickering golden lights advance.

The feast of All Souls is being celebrated for the first time at the abbey church of Cluny.

It is 998.

St Benedict lays down his rule. The four monastic virtues are formulated.

It is further observed, at Cluny, that during the hour of silence a monk may request a book by the gesture of turning over pages with his hand.

Scheherazade smiles.

Kenneth III is King of Scotland. Gerbert of Aurillac has become the first French Pope. As the millennium approaches, anxious faces are turned towards the skies for the first signs that will herald the end of the world. A day when sun and moon will be devoured by wolves, a ship made from the fingernails of the dead depart from realms of ice and snow or, while shrill angelic trumpets ring, a day when the dead will rise. Then ... then ... through a rent in the clouds ... Christ is seen, coming in glory.

A few flakes of snow start to fall.

A thrush ruffles his feathers.

A sorrel horse gently settles on the cold ground.

❦

Her resonant voice.

—Now, as your millennium breaks, the poet Firdausi laments the passing of Persian kings and heroes. He glories in the colours raised by the sun at dawn, the purple dust kicked up by elephants' feet, clouding the heat of battle; the moon-cheeked attendants that console at close of day.

During the still watches of the night, when impressions are strongest and words most eloquent, Scheherazade—a name not unfamiliar to you— captivates her Sultan; holds him prisoner, for a thousand nights and one.

She tells him the adventures of a poor scholar who falls in love with the youngest daughter of the King of the Jinns. Her jasmine-pale body, the wind-dancing arakha tree; her hair, a winter's night; her mouth, a rose; her teeth, hailstones in the sun ... Passing by a high tower, he encounters three old men with long silvery beards sitting upon a many-patterned carpet surrounded by myriad manuscripts. Leaving them behind, his quest takes him to a perfume-laden hall where the eldest daughter of the King of the Jinns appears, attired in a robe of shimmering white silk on which is embroidered a golden bird with curved emerald beak and claws. Her sisters demurely follow, clad in cyan, apricot, dust-rose, lemon, watered green. Till, at the last, his beloved—like starlight on a dark sea.

She tells of a caliph who retires to make observations of the moon and disappears for ever. Or, delightfully, of a lady who loved the Cadi's daughter and escaped with her to a villa by the Nile, near Tantah.

Water faintly trickles.

Scheherazade narrows her black eyes.

Or, perhaps more to your taste, tells of a beautiful youth—a letter-writer who sets out to trace a mysterious manuscript. On entering an unknown city he finds all fall beneath his spell: those who cut silk pause with their heavy scissors poised in the air, such is the eternal call of beauty. She tells of two usurers (one fat, one thin) who tremble on Al-Sirat, the Bridge of Breath, narrower than the thread of a famished spider; sharper than the edge of the finest sword. Of a certain tailor who for forty nights sought to pleasure forty beautiful maidens, till on the forty-first night— But *ziq*, that is another tale.

The Princess pauses ... swiftly resumes.

—So ... of the philosopher who insists on explaining his system of the workings of the world to a distracted merchant, as they cling to the legs of a giant roc that bares them out over the dark and menacing ocean.

Her dark eyes become abstracted.

—And then, that mystical, numinous night a thousand years ago, when the stars seemed to stand still in the sky and the water in the jug tasted sweeter, as the Sultan, amazed, absorbed, heard Scheherazade unravel a tale to a Sultan, amazed, absorbed, listening to a sweet succession of tales ...

A thousand years ago. A time of conjurors, carpet-beaters, jugglers of seven-coloured balls; of darrats, dung collectors, water diviners; of bath stokers, barbers, masseurs and dealers in oils, in unguents and bottles of scent; also, of astrologers, candlemakers and menders of nets; makers of candied fruit or embossed trays; dyers of cloth, sellers of knives, of water, books, bread, peppermint, of frankincense and myrrh; letter-writers and story-tellers; readers of old manuscripts, reciters of poems; shadow-theatre players, singers, dancers, treasure-seekers, breakers-in of horses, and falconers ... All emerge from fleeting shade, from spangled dreams. They walk, as in bright day.

The lamp casts intricate, trembling shadows.

Scheherazade lies back. She turns her opal ring.

The serrated points of light patterning the floor become a pale disc, silently floating among mother-of-pearl clouds, towards Japan.

Faint rustle of silk.

Sei Shonagon, a lady attached to the Heian court, is writing her *Pillow Book*.

> *Things that make my heart race. Sparrows feeding their young. A mirror that has become a little cloudy. A night when one is expecting a visitor. Plum blossom, flecked by snow. A pretty child eating strawberries. And clouds. I love to watch purple and black rain clouds driven by the wind. To see a delicate wisp drift across the moon.*

A screen is pulled back.

> *Broken threads of raindrops hang on spiders' webs like strings of white pearls. Later, when describing to the court ladies how beautiful it all was, what most impressed me was that they were not at all impressed.*

The screen is replaced.

> *Elegant things: two ladies seated at a Go board.*
>
> *Splendid things: grape-coloured silk. And purple, be it on wisteria, thread, or paper.*
>
> *Rare things: a cunningly wrought silver tweezer, good for plucking out hairs. And trying to avoid ink stains: not making a single blot.*

Sei Shonagon looks up.

> *The tiger moth is very pretty and delightful. When sitting close to a lamp while reading, I see it often flutter prettily before the scroll.*

She waits.

> *During the summer months it is a great delight to sit on the veranda enjoying the cool of evening and observing how the outlines of objects gradually become blurred. To hear, from*

one side, the low notes of the lute. The players pluck the strings so gently that even when the murmur of conversation ends one can barely make the music out.

Things that are near, though distant ... Paradise. Reflections on water. Relations between a woman and a man.

A clear moonlit night. Her Majesty sat by the edge of the veranda.

—Why so silent, she asked. Say something. It is sad when you do not speak.

—I am gazing at the moon.

The Empress smiled faintly.

—Ah, yes. That is just what you should have said.

Clear shadows.

The rustle of silk recedes.

The moon is climbing a sea of sky.

Clouds drift across the silver disc ...

Ono no Komachi, a beautiful and imperious courtesan, has refused a rendezvous to an infatuated nobleman until he has undertaken to spend a hundred nights beneath her window. But as the ninety-ninth night advances—blurred stars appearing behind the falling snows—she looks down from behind her screen and sees him stand up, place his stool beneath his arm, and slowly walk away. In the dark mirror, on cold white cheeks, a tear hangs, like jade.

The Lady Murasaki appears upon her balcony. She is composing *The Tale of Genji*.

It is night.

Prince Genji visits the cloistered Emperor at dusk. They sit on the veranda quietly recalling days of long ago. A courtier plays a few notes on the flute as the light fades and the bell-insects can be heard in the pines.

Night.

Full moon. A mansion has fallen into a state of neglect. The garden grown wild. In the deep stillness the hours wear on and on. Ghostly wisteria trails from a tall pine, waves gently in the wan light, releases a nostalgic perfume, bringing on reveries.

Outside in the courtyard, a peacock screams.

A lady turns on her mat.

She lies awake.

> *The fire that burns through my body this autumn night does not dry the tears on my sleeve.*

A letter is brought.

He has chosen to write on paper of the palest blue attached to a willow twig. She chooses delicately scented plum-coloured paper for her reply.

Autumn approaches. Leaves drift over the courtyard. Tears well up. The wings of the locust are shed. A summer robe is put away.

The messenger has taken her poem.

We weep aloud.

Alone.

Scheherazade's dark eyes rest on me.

> —Like the mallards on the lake we too are floating on the surface of a transient world. Alone.

III

—Continue, Gabriel, commands Scheherazade from her juniper couch.

It is the third night I have been asked to take up the tale.

She wears cornflower-blue silk, a sapphire shining on a slender finger, a bowl of fruit beside her.

The night is fragrant with the scent of santal. A scattering of stars hangs in an indigo sky. For the first time, candles shed their tranquil light over her apartments.

Time to turn back to a medieval world.

I gather myself to begin.

Peter Abelard, castrated by hired ruffians for his love for Héloïse, has raised a question. *Has God free will.* He also believes phenomena cannot exist in a void, must surely subsist in the encircling air, where the scent of an apple persists, even if the fruit is no longer there.

Scheherazade bites into a ripe peach.

The white-clad knights of the Teutonic Order ride out over the misty plains of East Prussia, claiming them for Christ the King. Merchants, their horses' saddle bags weighed down by heavy gold coins, tremble at the rustling of leaves in the wind as they pass along the edge of a wood.

Vincent of Beauvais writes his *Speculum*, his great mirror, reflecting the divine order now rising in splendour over France. At the cathedral of Naumburg, Uta, Margrave Ekkehart's elegant wife, draws the collar of her cloak over her stone cheek.

The first giraffes to be seen in Europe glide past.

Guillaume de Lorris leads his lover through a garden of delight to find his rose. Richard of Furnival will arrange his catalogue of three hundred books in the form of a garden. Leonardo da Pisa works out a sequence of numbers that can be found in the spiral shell of a snail or on the domes of cathedrals. Dietrich of Freiberg studies tiny glistening rainbows in the dew-drops on a spider's web, before Terce calls him to prayer.

Count Hugh de Vaudemont begins his return journey from the Holy Land. But the way is long, he becomes lost, and he does not reach home for a further fourteen years. A young monk, whom we have already encountered pausing to listen to the sweet purlings of a blackbird, hurries back to the monastery gate—to find that no one remembers him, he has been gone so long.

Chrétien de Troyes places the court of King Arthur in a castle to the West—where the Lord Rhys invites a great gathering of bards. To the best, he gives a chair: the first *Eisteddfod*.

The tuning of harps gives way to the scratching of pens. The four branches of the *Mabinogi* are being written down, the telling and re-telling now caught in amber.

During the long darkness of an Icelandic winter the salt wind howls. Snorri Sturluson realises that his hut is surrounded; the bright sword is about to fall across his worn face—as it fell so often in his saga.

Borne in solemn procession across the desolate steppes, the corpse of Ghengis Khan is carried home. Every living thing that crosses his path is slain with these words: *Depart for the next world and there attend your dead Lord.*

❧

The Sung Emperor, Hui Zong, paints a five-coloured parakeet resting on a branch of apricot blossom.

Marco Polo departs from Venice. East from Acre, he takes the silk route to the court of Kublai Khan. After many adventures he returns to Italy and dictates his memoirs from a Genoese jail. He observes a link between ape and man.

Court jesters tumble, fart, do wild somersaults, hop and skip, prat. Ladies, and gentleman too, discover the delights of standing, or slowly turning, before a long glass mirror.

A grey heron takes to wing and flaps away into the mists now gathering over Lough Conn in County Mayo.

In the scriptorium—the monastery's only heated room—the gentle scratch of goose quills can be heard; a delicate, pleasant sound. But on the margin of a manuscript we read what writing is: *It destroys your eyesight, bends your spine, and makes your whole body ache.* Like the sailor entering port, so the copyist rejoices on reaching the last line. *Deo gratias semper.*

Keen speculation continues on the possibility of an infinite number of angels dancing on the point of a pin. Ladies at their embroidery raise high their brightly coloured threads on sparkling needles.

After travelling as a troubadour through the Auvergne, Guillaume IXth, Duke of Aquitaine, encounters three ladies of noble birth. Believing him to be mute, they invite him to make love to them; he remains with them in service more than seven days.

Bernard of Clairvaux mellifluously believes that tears are the wine of angels. He compares the Virgin to the perfume on a ripe fruit that lingers on the hand long after the fruit has gone.

>—It's true, murmurs Scheherazade, slowly licking her fingers.

Hugh of St Victor admonishes us, even in private when we may imagine ourselves unobserved, not to do anything to offend the sensitive tastes of angels, believed to be very elegant beings.

Scheherazade smiles.

Brightly-clad troubadours bring the *Ars Nova* style from Provence to the courts of Tuscany and Umbria. Guido Cavalcanti remembers everything admirable, beautiful, heart-rending that he has encountered: a wise heart, birdsong, ships in a high-running sea; the quietness on the air at dawn; snow falling without a breath of wind. And his lady, who far surpasses all of these.

As his servants begin to light the lamps, dusk closing in, the disfigured Gianciotto da Rimini comes on his young bride, Francesca, in the arms of Paolo, his younger brother. In a fit of jealous fury he stabs them to death—but they are destined to remain together for ever.

Francis of Assisi—in whom renunciation was a pervading fragrance—explains that for love of Christ it is necessary to endure all contradictions, all sufferings. That is perfect joy. On the dusty road to Siena, an angel appears before him, golden-winged. Francis—who knows the angels are close indeed—faints in an inrush of grace.

Going out into the fields one May morning after Prime, Francis speaks to the birds—birds, to whom all the paths of the world lie open. Then, raising his fingers, he blesses them. The birds respond with a great chorus, take to the air and form a cross in the sky.

Saint Thomas Aquinas reigns supreme in the world of thought. The Angel of the Schools, Aquinas writes a dense, lucid Latin—not unacceptable to certain tastes. The rotund angelic doctor with the broad placid face holds, in his magisterial *Summa Theologica,* that everything, whether it has knowledge or not, tends towards good.

Moreover, the highest felicity of man consists in speculation, seeking knowledge of the truth. He names three things that are required for beauty: wholeness, harmony, radiance. James Joyce was later to realise his ideal, a luminous silent stasis of aesthetic pleasure, bringing an enchantment of the heart. Nor, to touch on an earlier point, can two angels dance on the same space, for confusion of action would result. An angel is where it operates. What we believe, they see.

On 6th December 1273 Thomas lays down his pen, wielded with such effect, after experiencing an ecstatic vision.

> *All that I have written seems as straw compared to what has now been revealed to me.*

Scheherazade rests her cheek on her hand, her eyes, questioning.

Joachim of Fiore had predicted that the year 1260 would bring the third stage in the coming of the Kingdom of Heaven on Earth: the Age of the Spirit. In that year Chartres cathedral was consecrated.

Stone prophets and saints, some with one hand already raised, face West. Deep red hues burn above the altar at Terce; dark violets and blues glow during Vespers.

ॐ

A sapphire flashes.

Her voice.

> —Now let us move away from your grey medieval mists, dank mouldering stones, slow pacing monks. Away from clanking knights, pale-faced creatures languishing by narrow windows, to return to my lands, where coffee makers are pounding pestles against wooden bowls. Spice vendors set out their wares, handling sacks of green cumin, yellow turmeric, red sumac, while coppersmiths beat patterns into shining metal trays. It is the hammering of the goldsmiths in the bazaar of Konya that inspires Rumi to dance and recite. So we dance too, stepping for a moment back into time past, only to spring forward once again, towards a newly-revealed future.
>
> The philosopher Averroes discusses the eternity of the world with the Almohad prince, Abu ya'qud Yusuf. For the language of religion is like the language of poets: a marvellous perfume that intoxicates the spirit, drifts

over the rose gardens of Shiraz, breathes through the pages of Sa'adi, falls from the sweet lips of Hafiz.

In his work, *A Recreation for the Person Who Longs to Traverse the Horizons*, Al-Idrisi divides the Earth, round as if a sphere, into seven climes. Sohravardi teaches that when we gain our own lightness, everything radiates lightness. While beyond lies a realm of wonder, where time and space die.

Black holes, I murmur.

Scheherazade inclines her head. And continues.

—Al Biruni, in one of his one hundred and forty-six books, explores the mysteries of shadows; Alhazen, light and colour. The calligrapher Yaqut al Musta'simi devises the sloping nib. Beyond blues and blacks, inks become the colours of peacocks, of the rose, pistachio, apricot, wine ... and many more subtle shades.

In Damascus, where a marvellous clock fills the nights with its soft tinklings, al-Ghuzuli writes on the pleasures of life: of horses, gardens, the joy of watching birds; of hammams, lamps, chess, and of wine borne in by swaying, liquid-eyed cup bearers; of their fluttering lashes, learned talk with viziers ... and perusing chancery documents.

Ibn Khaldun conceives of history as a great circle. Cities rise and fall, climb and tumble. Peace brings wealth, that breeds indolence, that harbours decay. We are bound to the rim of a turning water wheel that bears us up, dashes us down.

Mansa Musa, ninth and most glorious ruler of the Empire of Mali, undertakes his pilgrimage to Mecca with no fewer than a hundred camels, carrying gold.

This he distributes to the poor. He returns in the company of the Andalusian poet and architect, Es-Saheli. On the long journey, plans and poems pass between them. Ibn Battuta, who traversed the world, passes through Mali, pausing at Timbuktu—destined to become a seat of learning. He retires at last to Fez, where he narrates his adventures to those curious as to the ways of strange lands and the wonders to be encountered on the route.

The journeys of the spirit take place on a different plane. Born in Nishapur, land of turquoise and swords, Farid Ud-din Attar sent his birds, led by the Hoopoe, on an arduous quest to seek the Simurgh, the ruler of birds.

They come on seven desolate valleys which they must cross: Search, Love, Apprehension, Detachment, Unity, Bewilderment, Fulfilment.

The seven valleys loom and fade behind them as the birds, in great jubilation, trace intricate arcs and designs above gently swaying palms and glittering waters. They fly as if one spirit inspires their flight, for they have come to realise that they themselves—being thirty birds—are the Simurgh.

Radiant in narration, Scheherazade smiles. Fine gold threads running from the flames of blue candles touch her throat.

Silently, the birds fly through us.

From the dark garden, a faint trickle.

Her eyes.

In her dark eyes I see the stars appear, inviting me to resume my tale.

❦

In exile, Dante begins his *Divine Comedy*. Long, thin, perfectly formed letters raise his invisible cathedral: *cum pondere et mensura*.

Easter Day 1300.

Dante stands at the mid point of his life, alone in a dark wood where the sun is silent.

The poet Virgil, mild and grave in a long greyish blue gown, approaches to become his guide.

They reach the gates of Hell. Dante reads the adamantine legend: *Abandon Hope All You Who Enter Here*.

They go on.

Francesca and Paolo, swept for ever on the rushing wind, narrate their affecting story.

The poets pass on.

They encounter souls hopping, rubbing, twisting, on scorching sands. Upon them slowly fall broad flakes of fire, like snow descending in windless mountains. Ever deeper, they journey on, find souls weighed down by cloaks of lead, scarcely able to move through the foul and dusky air. The despair of the tortured souls drains the colour from Dante's cheek. In their anguished eyes he sees the desolation of hearts without hope.

Scheherazade's lips draw tight. Her gaze is fixed.

They emerge from the dark and fire of the Inferno to a clear sapphire sky and begin to climb the mount of Purgatory.

Dante is instructed that the human race should be content to understand things as they exist and not attempt to enter into the mind of God.

They reach the Garden of Earthly Delight. Virgil departs from his side. Beatrice breathes his name.

He is ready to leave Purgatorio, to ascend to the stars.

A coolness touches our eyes.

He is ascending; this he sees in Beatrice's glancing smile, ever more joyous; in her eyes, ever more radiant, where all desire finds rest.

At her request, Dante, not without struggle, turns back to see the spheres—their magnitude, their speed, their distance—all holding to their stations. Then to Beatrice—*she who imparadises my mind*—he returns his gaze, to see, beyond the stars, the angels in their angelic orders shining in her eyes.

He has risen to pure light, light intellectual, suffused with love, full of gladness, as the lark at noon soars in the sky, first singing, then silent, content in surpassing joy. Here, a single point of light (on which all creation depends) is more difficult to describe than all the twenty-five centuries that have elapsed since Neptune looked up through the whirling waters, amazed to see the green shadow of that first ship, the Argo, passing by.

Radiance ... beyond all words ... that moves the sun and stars.

God, Dante wrote, *requires nothing of us but the heart.*

I lift my eyes.

Burning in the dark sky, the moist stars.

IV

For many nights Scheherazade did not send for me. Was she travelling within her lands. Taken up by affairs of state. Or did another visitor beguile her nights. All this was dark to me.

I watched shadows extend and withdraw along the dusty ochre walls of my cell; but was allowed exercise within an enclosed, white-walled courtyard where, by one corner, a palm tree gently rustled.

During that long stretch of time I had leisure to reflect on those French writers who might have been attracted to a fate similar to mine. Gérard de Nerval had conjured with a history, mingling memories of his studies with fragments of dreams. And had not Huysmans contemplated the fascinating prospect of writing a novel concentrated to a few sentences, that would open vistas where the reader could muse.

Then, breaking my tender reverie, the key grates in its iron lock, the door swings open, and I see once more the burning torch in Yusef's hand.

I have been summoned.

The tale will go on.

Following along corridors now grown familiar to me, I see tiny points of fire dance on the drops of sweat that run down Yusef's naked back.

Scheherazade greets me with an enigmatic smile. Has she moved since last we met. But then she wore cornflower blue silk and a sapphire shone on her finger. Now she wears grass-green and scarlet silk. A waxing moon races through oyster-tinged clouds, rimming them silver.

Yusef withdraws.

From the terrace, the faint splash of water upon stone.

Scheherazade sets spinning an antique wooden globe, dull yellow and moss green. Continents appear and retreat before our separate gaze.

With a resounding slap, the Princess stops the globe.

Her dark eyes rest on me.

She points to Italy with a carmine-polished nail.

ಽೕಽ

We begin in the wine-growing lands of Tuscany, where Boccaccio is writing his *Decameron*.

A party of seven young women and three young men takes refuge from the plague in a villa overlooking Florence. Here, for ten days, they beguile the time with tales.

One tells of sails that billow out, silken ropes that dangle loose, as a sultan's daughter departs to wed the ruler of a distant land ... Another, of a hesitant king at nightfall, awakening in a great hall and stretching out trembling fingers to feel the beating heart of each sleeping man ... A third, of a falcon who takes to wing at dawn and, on gaining height, looks back to meet the eyes of his adoring master.

Laura, in her light green dress, passes Petrarch by. The sun's rays pale with pity as her lovely eyes dazzle the poet.

On reaching the summit of Mont Ventoux, he opens a little book of Saint Augustine's *Confessions* and reads at random: *Men go forth to admire mountains, only to neglect themselves.*

Twenty-one years later Laura de Sade dies, a victim of the plague, in the same month, on the same day, and at the same hour that Petrarch caught sight of her.

—We are not finished with that name, observes Scheherazade.

Still far in the future, the dim figure of the Marquis de Sade, clad in breeches of grey silk and deep orange, acknowledging the remark, bows.

Lords and ladies, gaily apparelled, go out hunting on horseback. They emerge from the forest where they see peasants at work among the golden corn.

Cold and hungry, François Villon writes his *Testament* in letters wide and brave. At break of day, when freed falcons rise, when wolves eat wind, he is saved from the gallows. And disappears.

William of Ockham, wielding his razor, cuts through entanglements of medieval philosophy. But tentatively hints that God may have hesitated before creating the world. A momentous moment, little explored.

Prince Henry the Navigator watches his ships sail from Sagres, where the salt wind bites your lip. Bound beyond an ever-receding horizon, the scarlet cross of Christ billows on their lateen sails.

Giotto breathes new life into art. St Francis bends, one hand outstretched, the other raised in blessing, to deliver his sermon to the birds, who look up at him from the ground.

Scheherazade smiles.

But not until the Master of Flémalle are angels allowed to dry their eyes with the backs of their hands.

—Hugh of St Victor would hardly approve, she remarks dryly.

Indeed, no.

ॐ

In Italy, the Renaissance takes fire.

Donatello creates a smooth-limbed bronze David, languidly toying with the head of a vanquished Goliath; and a proud horse with raised hoof who bears his grave master, Marcus Aurelius, through time. Over the Florentine sky, Brunnelleschi's dome—the first since the fall of Rome—airily rises.

At San Marco a linnet sings; an annunciation takes place. The Angel Gabriel appears before Mary who sits with crossed arms, receiving the Incarnate Word with quiet joy.

A golden thread of faith runs through Fra Angelico's art. His angels—bands of moss green, crimson and pale lilac-blue on their wings—take each other gently by the hand as they form a circle. They seem about to dance.

On the walls of a cell in San Marco the sublime figure of Mary kneels before the angel, her eye weak with love.

Water trickles faintly.

Scheherazade rests her dark eyes on me.

The candle flames release their threads of gold.

The three graces, portrayed by Botticelli, breathe a sainted air. They turn in a slow trance, lost in thought. Long, slender fingers entwined, their tender feet hardly seem to touch the ground; not a flower, not a blade of grass, disturbed.

Standing on a pale, gold-rimmed shell, the wistful goddess Venus is wafted gently towards the shore by Zephyr and Aura; her attentive lady waits on tiptoe holding out a billowing, blossom-strewn cloak.

The pious and contemplative Pico della Mirandola envisages a mystical ascent through the spheres; invokes the Archangels Gabriel, Michael, Raphael, to his aid.

Her voice is soft.

> —In what forms, perhaps more sublimely beautiful even than those painted by Leonardo, did they approach, appear before him; as once one came to Mary.

I raise my eyes. The moon rims a cloud.

Marsilo Ficino gazes out over the gentle wooded slopes surrounding Florence. He dreams of a reconciliation, a cherished union of Plato with Christ. Believes it possible to draw down the life of heaven; that stellar influence is borne upon very fine air. The stars, he holds, incline, but do not compel.

The higher we rise, the more concise language becomes. We must use words, weak as they are—since we cannot communicate in the way of angels, to whom has been given immediate apprehension.

—Quite a company of angels, then, in the air over Florence.

I incline my head.

Our tale winds South, to the green heart of Italy, where Tuscany touches Umbria and calm reigns over the frescoes and paintings of Piero della Francesca, master of light and line.

An imperious concentration, capturing glints of light on nails, specks of dust as they fall in a band of light. Light is the secret theme of the Flagellation; the same figures are touched both by moonlight and lamplight, while the walls are bathed in cool sunlight.

The lowered eyelids, restrained modesty of his ladies. The grave beauty on their faces. An awareness, a sense of moral confidence; an uncertain hope.

Constantine dreams in his tent on the eve of battle. His melancholy young page, absorbed in his own musings, rests on an arm. Above, unseen by either, an angel extends a slender finger.

The old gods tremble.

Before the Christ child, Mary kneels, her fingers closed in prayer, as angels—delicate bands of pearls, emeralds, sapphires about their throats—touch their lute strings, break into song.

Their faint sweet voices fade on the air as we approach Mantua where, in the course of a long council, Pius II and Nicholas of Cusa have before them a set of cards, depicting Apollo and the Nine Muses, the Ten Firmaments, the Seven Liberal Arts—together with Astrology,

Theology and Philosophy, the Seven Virtues, the Three Cosmic Principles.

Nicholas believes God to be the incomprehensible maximum: not so much an approach towards something, as towards nothing.

   —The universe, my dear Pius, whose circumference is nowhere and whose centre is everywhere.

We leave them to their wine and disquisitions and travel West, towards the land of Vespers: Spain.

※

A faint breeze causes the flames on the scarlet candles to bend.

With the tip of her nail, Scheherazade touches the globe.

We watch the continents pass, the wide seas …

Isabella, far-sighted queen, finances an expedition seeking a shorter sea route to the Indies. Christopher Columbus, at forty-one, sails from Palos aboard his flagship, Santa Maria.

Before the departing ships, the ocean and its empty wastes wait.

They encounter very light winds, very calm seas—as if on the river at Seville. A blue immensity of sea and sky.

   —Sea and sky, breathes Scheherazade, her dark eyes shining.

Silently the sun dips and enters the waters to the unknown West. At the lighting of the ship's lantern, the lilting voice of the sand boy:

> *The watch is set*
> *The glass runs yet*

Dawn. Lanterns are extinguished. Sails released. The sun burns away the clinging mists from the face of the waters.

—Blue, murmurs Scheherazade.

Sea melts into sky. A shimmering horizon, hazy, forever receding, filling men's eyes with reverie and longing.

—Blue.

Vasco da Gama rounds the Cape of Good Hope and arrives off the Malabar coast. On his third voyage, Columbus ventures up the Orinoco river. Amerigo Vespucci and Alonso de Ojrda discover the mouth of the Amazon. Diaz de Solis reaches the Rio de la Plata.

—Blue.

On Catholic seas the sun glints off helmets, shines on gold. Scent of pineapple, stench of vomit, seep from creaking hulls. Columbus sails on his fourth and last voyage. The gay adventurer, Nuñez de Balboa, stumbles on the sands, wades out into the vast sea that stretches to the West and, raising the flag of Castile, claims possession of the ocean and all surrounding lands for Spain.

Ferdinand Magellan sails from Seville with five ships bound beyond the confines of the known world. New constellations of stars swing into view.

A wandering albatross appears, borne on wind currents from Antarctica. His great wings spread, he passes over mountainous grey seas.

It is the Feast of St Ursula. Entering the tortuous strait that now bears his name, Magellan christens the headland—where submerged rocks release a retinue of eternally dancing spray—the Cape of the Eleven Thousand Virgins.

As they progress, sailors toss lines weighted down with lead and sing out the fathoms in a mournful dirge, while priests waft incense into the freezing air.

They finally emerge from the strait to enter on a peaceful expanse of water, which Magellan names: the Pacific.

Only one ship, the Victoria, returns to Spain, becoming the first to circumnavigate the globe. An account of the voyage appears, written by Antonio Pigafetta, who had appealed to Magellan as a cultivated companion who could prove useful with the sword.

—Time now to turn from the sea and its blue enchantments, commands Scheherazade.

Time to return.

Faint splash of water on stone.

Ink stains the fingers of merchants' clerks as they grapple with Fra Luca Paccioli's double-entry book-keeping. Pocket handkerchiefs come into use. Playing cards flash for piquet. The great comet passes.

We seem no longer to stand at the centre of the universe but spin endlessly through dark space, one among many. Nicolaus Copernicus states that the Earth and other planets move around a motionless sun.

Within the Dominican Order, but in love with the pagan past, Francesco Colonna writes his Renaissance romance. His young hero delights in arcane classical allusion; his nymphs protest as a gentle breeze lifts their diaphanous garments. He contemplates inscriptions on gravestones that narrate a life, paint a moral.

Telephone.

—How are you.

—Oh ... you know.

—Can we meet up.

Leonardo da Vinci looks at the stars, shorn of their rays, through a tiny hole made on card with the extreme point of a fine needle and held so as almost to touch the eye. He observes that motes of dust caught in the solar rays brighten as they rise. One ray, the colour of ashes; another, in thin smoke, a most beautiful blue.

Left-handed, he prefers to write as if in a mirror.

Salai waits at his side, a most attractive youth of unusual grace with very beautiful hair, which he wears in ringlets, and which delights his master—hair like that of the ardent angel he had painted some fifteen years earlier, witnessing the baptism of Christ.

He observes (before Impressionism) that shadows caused by the redness of the sun close to the horizon, will often be blue. As dusk descends—his favoured hour—subdued light confers softness to faces in a street; a delicacy ... a liminal beauty.

Candles beat down their threads of gold.

Leonardo rises in the early morning and visits markets to buy caged birds. Then, gently taking the frightened fluttering birds out of their cramped cages—his angels have bird-like wings—he releases them, beating into the boundless blue.

Scheherazade sweeps back a lock of thickly falling hair.

The Renaissance settles over Venice, a golden haze.

The Virgin raises her hand.

Giovanni Bellini's saints stand rapt as achingly beautiful celestial music played by an angelic trio dies away. A unique sensuous piety—deeply spiritual and warmly physical—held in luminous harmony.

An ethereal female saint, lost in contemplation, bathed in a soft warm light that seems to glow from within, gently crosses her hands. A pensive young woman holds up a small hand-mirror to adjust a brocaded scarf around her auburn hair; reflection upon reflection recedes in a round mirror placed behind her. By her side, a narrow note discloses the artist's signature.

Carpaccio gives us a city and its people suspended in a magic stillness. A red parrot has strayed in from the Americas.

Raphael, the tender young master from Urbino, reveals his Saint Cecilia entranced by the harmonies she hears from above, an organetto slipping from her fingers.

Candle flames flicker.

The air is threatening. A storm lurks. A young man leans on his lance, regards a young woman who is feeding her child. Giorgione conceives of painting as expressing an elusive moment.

Moments, held in amber; hushed spells, on the verge of breaking.

A mellow late October light lingers on three philosophers. The eldest is attired in saffron and brown, perhaps an admirer of Plotinus. The one in middle years wears an oriental dress of crimson and pale violet; possibly a follower of Averroes. And the youth, with a gentle, abstracted look, clad in rich dark green and white, holds a sextant. He belongs to the new world of natural philosophy; awaits an auspicious sign that may appear.

I raise my eyes.

A moist star enters the dark mirror.

On the walls of Julius II's private library, the dream of Marsilo Ficino is realised. Poets on Mount Parnassus, among them an ardent Sappho, gather round Apollo and the muses. The Church welcomes the Classical into her widening embrace. The longed-for reconciliation—the passionate desire of Florentine artists and scholars—visibly takes place.

The Sistine Madonna swims into view: a radiant, tender epiphany. The Virgin, showing us the Christ Child as if in response to our *Salve Regina*, comes towards us on soft, swirling clouds, warm and human; a sublime vision, suffused with love.

V

Sand runs softly through the glass.

Dark, honeyed candles gently burn.

Scheherazade wears a restrained deep burgundy and cream silk. Tonight her resonant voice is sombre, low.

—We enter on turbulent times.

I incline my head. Dark and hazel eyes, meeting.

High in the sky Orion the hunter climbs, the constellation of Virgo rises, and lovely Vega burns, a clear blue.

Time again, to take up the tale. We enter the sixteenth century.

Martin Luther bangs up his ninety-five theses. In response, Leo X calls for a five-year peace throughout Christendom.

In vain.

Michelangelo has created God, stretching forth his arm almost to touch—with an extended finger—that of Adam, reclining on the barren ground below.

At Urbino, Castiglione's courtiers are absorbed in discussing divine love and beauty. The rosy light of dawn creeps upon them unawares. But Benvenuto Cellini notices a halo of light that appears round heads when the grass is moist with dew and the sun still low in the sky.

Erasmus writes to his Prior:

> *Whenever I consider the jealousy and lack of learning of the priests—those cold, useless conversations—it is the study of humane letters that alone attracts my spirit.*

Sir Thomas More sees his Utopian dream fade.

Paul III calls the Council of Trent. The mystery of the Eucharist is re-explored—that pronoun *'hoc'* changes the nature of things.

A breathless messenger springs from his snorting sorrel horse, bringing word to Elizabeth—whilst out walking with her ladies in the beechwoods at Hatfield—that she has been proclaimed Queen.

Sebastian of Portugal sets sail with a vast fleet to win Morocco for the Cross. He lands with his soldiers, an entourage of bishops, priests, page-boys, slaves, prostitutes, musicians, coachmen—only to be overtaken by the sands, cut down in battle. A few straggle back to the fleet anchored off the coast and narrate their misfortune.

The tide of enslaved Africans crossing the seas has commenced. They take with them the complex rhythms of their own cultures. But musical instruments must be left behind, for fear they may summon revolt. Those who survive the voyage, in place of bells, interrupt their labours to sound the blades of their hoes.

Asking forgiveness of everyone whom he might have offended, Charles V abdicates, assigning Spain and its territories to his son, Philip II, whose fleet will defeat the Ottoman Empire at Lepanto. In Venice, bells will be rung and a *Te Deum* sung. But coffee, coming from Turkey, will still be sipped. Trade, after all, must go on.

Tulips, Kant's favourite flower, reach Holland. In Spain, Ruy López is playing chess—the pawns are not so cautious as before. Johannes Schöner, cartographer—a friend of Copernicus—sets spinning his globe of the world.

Consulting her magic mirror, Catherine de Medici sees the future of France up to the time of the coming revolution. At a banquet given at Chenonçeaux she is waited on, with a certain delicacy, by two naked young ladies. One is an ancestor of the Marquis de Sade.

Again from the shadows the Marquis, attired in grey silk and deep orange breeches, makes his bow.

☙❧

Our tale veers West, in the path of the sun. The Aztecs have received divine instruction to build where they witness an eagle on a cactus devouring a snake.

This they do.

At the temple at Tenochtitlan, two columns of men, women, and some children, climb the stone steps towards the priests standing by the altars to have their hearts ripped out of their bodies. Some, freed by Cortez, demand indignantly to be sacrificed.

Francisco Pizarro draws a line on the sand with his boot and barks out that those still willing to follow him should cross that line. Thirteen men step forward.

They hack their way through dense, mosquito-ridden rain forests, up mist-shrouded slopes of the Andes, to confront the Inca Empire. The Emperor's wife—after her husband has been put to death—takes the name Doña Angelina and becomes Pizarro's mistress.

Eyes become drunk with brutal feasting, served on gold and silver plate. Constant helpless cries rend the air ... A few manage to survive the slaughter and create Machu Picchu, precious citadel, lost in mist, beyond the reach of Bible or Sword.

But a young soldier, Juan Valverde, falls in love with a native girl and together they run away to her home village, Pillaro, high in the Andes.

Scheherazade lowers her eyes and touches her ring: a pearl set in silver.

Our tale sweeps West, across the Pacific.

She looks up.

Her voice is warm and soft as she murmurs,

　—The sun in the sky, the speck of gold in the blue ...

Her dark eyes seem to gaze on a world beyond.

Autumn.

Bands of mist float in the pines.

The wild geese fly low.

Become specks in the sky.

Winding paths take the eye on a long journey up rocky crags where slender waterfalls fall. Beyond—distant, mist-laden peaks.

On the mountain path, the windswept pine. By the lake, the willow and the bamboo.

Bamboo.

Pliant but resilient, symbolizing the perfect gentleman: he who adapts with the times, but remains true to his inner self.

Ni Zan, a scholar painter impoverished by taxation, has disburdened himself of his remaining possessions to live out the rest of his life on a small houseboat, drifting on the rivers and lakes of south-eastern Kiangsu.

His medium—black ink. Used sparingly, as if it were gold. His subjects—a group of sparsely leafed trees, a deserted pavilion by an expanse of water, low hills rising on the far shore ...

Water trickles faintly from the fountain.

Like Sinbad the Sailor, Zheng He undertook seven voyages.

>   —Eight was too many, six not quite enough, observes Scheherazade, slightly raising an eyebrow.

He sailed beyond the horizon to Malacca, west along the Malabar coast, then on across the Arabian sea, and south to Java. On his last voyage he reached the coast of East Africa and returned laden with giraffes, ostriches and zebras—to the delight of the Ming court.

Yet the purpose of his voyages was uncertain. It was not to develop trade nor to extend influence. And he had no successor.

Her voice:

>   —Perhaps the ocean and its sounds and silences, the immensity of its waters, a tern skimming above the waves, the fire on the waters at sunset, were enough.

Tears of wax run down the dark, honeyed candles.

On her progress to Rye, Queen Elizabeth rests under the shade of an oak, leaving behind a pair of green silk damask shoes.

Nicholas Hilliard portrays her.

The Queen chooses her place to be—an open walk of a goodly garden, no tree near, nor any shade. He captures the fantasy and poetry of that feminine court; at its heart, a Virgin Queen.

Displaying exquisite delicacy, he shows a youth leaning against a tree, surrounded by a briar of wild roses. How carefully the miniaturist must watch the delicate movements of the eyes, mouth and nostrils, seeking to limn these lovely graces, witty smilings, and tender stolen glances—which suddenly, like lightning, pass.

A peacock screams.

Richard Burbage is granted a licence to open a theatre in London. William Byrd and Thomas Tallis are appointed organists to the Chapel Royal. Mary, Queen of Scots, having been denied landing in England, comes ashore at Leith. For the first time, Francis Drake sees the Pacific ocean. Sir Walter Raleigh has arrived off America. To honour his Queen, he names the surrounding land: Virginia.

༺༻

We return to Spain.

My life has been one long journey, declares Charles V.

Having abandoned his palaces, his empire, his oceans, he takes his portraits of Isabella, painted by Titian, and retreats into close retirement at the monastery at Yuste. An amber light in the evening sky is caught in the Queen's hair; the grey-blue on the distant mountains finds an echo in her eyes. He dies, holding in his hand the same wooden cross that once she too had held.

High on a hill overlooking the desolate Castilian plain, Juan de Herrera builds the Escorial for Philip II. His instructions from the King are clear. Simplicity of form, severity in the whole, nobility without arrogance, majesty without ostentation.

The king's mind, in stone.

A fitting burial place for Charles and Isabella, who now must be re-interred in accordance with his wish to be placed: *half-body under the altar and half-body under the priest's feet.*

To Teresa of Avila comes an angel that pierces her heart.

So! The pain—great.

And the sweetness ... passing beyond measure.

She attends the last agony of Mother Genevieve and notices a tear like a diamond glistening on her eyelash. That tear, the last of all she shed on earth, never fell.

I saw it still shining as her body lay exposed in the choir, so when night came I approached unseen with a little piece of linen and gently gathered it.

A night of darkness.

John of the Cross steals forth from his cell, burning like a lover, on fire to meet with Christ.

As scented breezes drift from cedars, I caress Him. With unhurried hand He wounds my neck, consumes my senses ... O living flame of love, how tenderly you wound and sear. O lamp of burning fire, feeding darkness with such splendour.

Ignatius Loyola formulates his Exercises. The Jesuit Order is founded.

He calls on Francis Xavier.

Go! And set fire to the world.

The Saint complies.

Ignatius asks of us to prefer neither health nor sickness; riches nor poverty; honour nor ignominy; neither a long life nor a short one. He writes that the touch of an angel to the soul is as a drop of water entering a sponge, and confides: *I ought to live like an angel for the privilege of saying Mass. With this thought, gentle waters come to my eyes.*

We return to Venice.

In that city of constantly changing reflections—colours running, coming together, rippling, dissolving, as palazzos seem to shift in the waters—Veronese has Cupid approach, holding two fine-bred black and white hounds with lolling pink tongues. The male seems slightly melancholy, while the female has an air of amused contentment.

—Often the way, observes Scheherazade, smiling.

I incline my head.

He gives to *La Bella Nani* a sumptuous dark blue velvet gown, over which floats a diaphanous silvery white veil. She stands, a tender vulnerability shining in her face; a sense of sadness in her eyes.

Shows, in the dark garden of Gethsemane, Christ sinking into the arms of an angel, accepting his mission on earth. A celestial light of pale lemon and pallid lavender pours down, turning the rose and blue of his garments ashen.

We arrive in Rome.

There is no sun in Caravaggio, little daylight and less sky. Figures remain in darkness; appear, coming out of darkness. A face, a hand, the nape of a neck, emerging from the shadows ...

Christ has entered an ill-lit tavern, causing a band of light to fall on Matthew, who sits at a rough table in the company of alert youths.

Darkness.

At Emmaus, an uncomprehending innkeeper and two amazed disciples watch Christ who, without fuss, raises his hand to bless the evening meal.

David grasps the head of the slain Goliath by the hair—a self-portrait of the despairing artist; redeemed, perhaps, in meeting such an end by such a boy ...

Caravaggio is found wandering, delirious, along a beach near Civitavecchia, with a raging fever. He dies, without comfort. Much as he lived.

᎒‍᎒

We journey North.

About to enter his alchemical laboratory Tycho Brahe is staring intently at the night sky. A new star has appeared in the constellation of Cassiopeia.

On the island of Hven, off the Danish sound, he builds an observatory at Uraniborg. Its foundation stone was laid as the sun rose, with Jupiter near Regulus, while the moon in Aquarius was setting. He calls it: The Castle of the Heavens, fashions a silver nose for himself, and continues to pursue his studies.

A candle gutters, releasing a thread of grey-blue smoke.

Wreathed in a pale green light Zeus appears before Giordano Bruno to plead for the existing heavenly images. The Nolan (as he is sometimes called) sees the advent of astral virtues mount once more in the sky. Justice replaces Iniquity in the Corona Borealis. Civility and Concord are found again in the Pleiades, while, as Rapine and Deceit desert Orion, Magnanimity and Union rise. The constellations and their influences are reborn, for all things depend upon this upper world. The proclaiming sign is—the Copernican sun.

It has grown late. An early linnet sings.

Orion has abandoned the chase, Virgo has set, and lovely, blue Vega vanished. Blue to blue.

VI

William Shakespeare leaves Stratford-upon-Avon for London. Giordano Bruno is being rowed along the Thames by two Charons, who have appeared out of the gloom, with strokes that would be dwarfed by the waving of a lady's fan.

The night is warm. Scattered deep red roses shed their scent. The Princess is clad in a light, fine cloth of shimmering nacre, her arm extended, a diamond burning on her finger. Fine as any cobweb thread, a cloudy drop of moisture creeps down her throat.

—Time, then, to remain a while upon your misty island.

Time to begin again.

And so ...

Sir Philip Sidney, the flower of English chivalry, while staying with his sister, the Countess of Pembroke, composes *Arcadia,* his prose romance.

He is cut down on campaign in the Netherlands. The nation mourns.

Voice and viol take up the strain in William Byrd's dark lament:

> *O heavy time that my days draw behind thee.*
> *Thou dead dost live, thy friend here living dieth.*

Mary Queen of Scots is tried for treason, and sentenced. An unseasonable sun that February morning lights the graceful tower of Fotheringhay castle. Mary, clad in red velvet, kneels before the block:

> *Even as thy arms, O Jesus, were spread upon the cross, so receive me into thy mercy and forgive my sins. In my end is my beginning.*

The Duke of Medina Sidonia sails in command of the invincible Spanish Armada—has any sea known such a concert of sails on the blessed expanse. He seeks, according to his king, Philip II, to defend our peace, tranquillity, and repose.

All is lost.

Throughout Spain bells toll. Defeated by foul winds and the English, under Charles Howard. Philip, alone in his study, kneels.

> *Thy will be done.*

Her voice.

—He found he had over-reached.

Her eyes, a brilliant darkness.

The over-reacher Doctor Faustus—ravished, like his creator Christopher Marlowe, by ideas—signs a blood pact with Mephistopheles who appears before him and, in answer to his anxious question, avers:

> *Why this is hell, nor am I out of it.*

After much restless wandering, seeking out the new astronomy and conjuring sweet grapes to appear in December, comes upon Faustus gnawing, gripping fear: the flickering flames ...

Think thou on hell Faustus, for thou art damned.

The clock strikes eleven.

Ah Faustus, now hast thou but one bare hour to live.

The sands run out early for Kit Marlowe, stabbed in a tavern brawl over reckonings, aged thirty.

A peacock screams.

A change of tone.

The joy of words new minted flows from Shakespeare.

Love's Labours Lost—a dazzling display of puns, innuendo and learning, till the dark messenger, Marcade, enters the sunlit park and stills the voices of merriment with news of death. After the joys of Apollo, the words of Mercury come harsh. The scene begins to cloud. The ladies agree to wait for their lords a twelvemonth and a day. Too long for a play.

Sir Francis Drake and Sir John Hawkins leave Plymouth Sound, bound on a last voyage to the Spanish Main. Will Kemp merrily dances, jingling, all the way from London to Norwich.

In a wood outside Athens, Titania, bewitching Queen of the Fairies, turns her languid, violet eyes from ass-head, snoozing Bottom, and calls her elves—Peaseblossom, Cobweb, Moth and Mustardseed—to fan the moon-beams from her new love's eyes.

Back in fairest England, Sir Walter Raleigh has his way with a maid-of-honour against a tree.

Swisser swatter, she cries, closing her eyes, the more to enjoy.

Swisser swatter ...

He secretly marries her.

The Queen confines the couple to the Tower.

Released—but still in hot pursuit—he explores up the Orinoco river in search of the fabulous, legendary land of El Dorado.

In vain.

Scheherazade.

Her eyes, like starlight on the night sea, rest on me.

❧

Edmund Spencer celebrates a double wedding.

Sweet Thames, run softly, till I end my song.

His long narrative poem, *The Faerie Queene,* he called 'a dark conceit.' There, in the garden of Adonis, the Goddess Mutability lays claim to the world; the Lady Una and her knight become lost in the entanglement of a forest deep; a learned sorcerer pursues glittering pages of dark magic and strange enchantments; and the Queen herself appears as Gloriana.

But all that lives must bow before that adamantine law.
All things decay in time and to their end do draw.

At his obsequies, gentlemen of his faculty cast into his tomb funeral elegies, and the pens they were writ with.

Always, before us and to come, the grave.

The Queen dances.

> *Forward they paced and did their pace apply to a most sweet and solemn melody ... forward and backward, upward and downward, forth and back again, to this side and to that and turning round, all together trace ...*

The Queen dances.

Sir John Davis' cosmic harmony of moon and moving stars is palpitatingly alive and on show where the mortal moon, Elizabeth, is surrounded by her starry court.

> *Many an incomparable lovely pair,*
> *with hand in hand were interlinked seen,*
> *making fair honour to their sovereign Queen.*

The Queen dances.

> *Their moving made them shine more clear*
> *as diamonds, moved, more sparkling do appear.*

Dusk is falling over the park, darkening the green shade by the cedars, gathering round the house, the stone mullioned windows and leaded panes where, once, vanished voices murmured cadences of evocation and longing.

From within that vale-like place of lowly height where joy, peace, love make harmonious chime, comes forth to reign a lady crowned with highest merits, on whom the graces and the muses wait.

The Queen dances.

A poignancy: *O care, thou wilt dispatch me!*

A world ever closer to tears.

Scheherazade raises a diamonded finger to her lip ...

And waits ...

In atrocious agony of body, fervent piety of spirit, Philip II dies.

From his desk in the Escorial, he claimed he could rule half the world with two inches of paper.

Now Philip asks that, in the Escorial, ceaseless prayers be said for his soul for two centuries to come.

The chanting begins.

Requiem aeternam dona eis, Domine, et lux perpetua lucat eis.

༄༅

Giordano Bruno, languishing in the prisons of the Inquisition in Rome for more than seven years, holds to the Copernican theory of the universe—that the sun stands still; the earth and other planets circle round. But the Polish astronomer's vision was still bounded by the sphere of fixed stars. Bruno shatters this outer crystal wall and goes on to imagine, beyond, an infinite space where stars—vast, dark, inconceivable—burn.

His writings are consigned to the flames, and he is led to the *Campo di Fiori*—the Field of Flowers—to be burned alive as a heretic.

A peacock screams.

Opera is born.

Orfeo's achingly beautiful pleading charms the ear of Proserpine and enchants the Mantua court.

Claudio Monteverdi slips from the animated, brightly lit hall.

As do we.

Autumn mists rise.

Wild geese descend on the rivers Hsido and Hsiang.

Matteo Ricci SJ, wearing his robe of purple silk lined with blue, proceeds to show the court of the Emperor Wanli how to create a memory palace without wood or stone, where one may glide from room to room, encountering images that release their store of treasures.

T'ang Yin, a Ming landscape painter and poet, seeing his mistress slip from the bed and hold a mirror close to her painted cheeks, hears her ask,

> Which is lovelier, these petals or my complexion.

He gives a hesitant reply.

She gaily laughs and, running a long nail down his naked back:

> Tonight, my dear, sleep with the cherries!

Two cherry petals fall from a spray in a Ju porcelain vase.

❧

A cold wind is blowing off the Danish coast. A nipping and an eager air.

Hamlet, on the heights of Elsinore, sees his dead father walk; the guilty, usurping King rise from uneasy prayer.

Elizabeth delivers her golden speech to Parliament, surveying the achievements of her reign. She speaks of princes, who are set on stages, in sight and view of all the world:

> Though God hath raised me high, yet this I count the glory of my crown: that I have reigned with your loves.

On this late November day she feels creeping time at the gate.

The great reign lasts for two more years.

In winter she liked to listen to William Byrd's lullaby.

> *Lulla lulla lullaby*
> *My sweet little babe*
> *What meanest thou to cry.*

Her mind full of foreboding, cares of state, she would shut herself up in a darkened room in paroxysms of weeping. Still she danced.

The Queen dances.

The viols play, the jewels gleam in the soft candlelight. She dies, almost standing, as she had lived.

The Princess lowers her eyes.

৯৵৶

On Dover beach, as the ebbing tide sucks over each pebble, King Lear stumbles into view and comes on the eyeless Gloucester who kneels before him, crying,

> *O, let me kiss that hand.*

Lear backs off.

> *Let me wipe it first; it smells of mortality.*

Dark clouds scud across the skies as Macbeth, on the blasted heath, encounters three weird sisters, standing hand in hand.

A crow departs from a windswept crag, flapping towards a distant wood.

John Donne meditates on the nature of shadows. Falling upon clay they appear grey, but in a garden, green. Shadows are not utter darkness, but rather a thicker light. Nearer light than darkness, shadows presume light. Shadows could not be, except there were light.

Eochaidh Ó hÉoghusa sings of the wild hare trembling in the long grass; the dark coming to the land of the Gael; courts in flames; the flight of the earls; the loss of the North ...

☙❧

Spain.

A distinguished old soldier in a worn black doublet (one who has taken part in the battle of Lepanto) straightens out a scrap of paper with his left hand.

Miguel de Cervantes has acquired a taste—like Saint Francis—for reading whatever his eye falls on that lies in the street. He sends Don Quixote, Knight of the Sad Countenance, with his faithful squire, Sancho Panza, to take whatever route his old nag, Rocinante, decides. For that way lies true adventure.

Claudo Monteverdi is appointed Maestro di Cappella to St Mark's, Venice, and composes *Vespers of the Blessed Virgin*. Voices seem to float and melt in the surrounding darkness. Just three years before, the German astronomer, Christopher Clavius, attached to the Vatican, had calculated how many grains of sand might be required to fill the vast space between the earth and the firmament.

Galileo Galilei constructs an astronomical telescope and turns it eagerly on the night sky. He is the first to observe the moons circling Jupiter; raising the possibility that, after all, the Earth is not the centre.

—All certainty, undone.

Boatswain!

—Here, master: what cheer.

William Shakespeare watches the shining black ink dry.

Prospero wades ashore carrying Miranda in his arms.

From the shipwreck he retrieves several volumes: *These I prize above my dukedom.* Sea salt swells the pages; encrustments cling to the bindings.

—And, of the volumes, inquires Scheherazade.

A sea-green book of islands, a grey book of ideas, a book showing the paths of migrating birds who seem to fly out from its azure pages ... An indigo book given over to the stars; a dark book of enchantments; a book still releasing fragrances through its dappled, dancing pages, evoking sunlit gardens, green shade, memories, regrets, hopes, longings ... A book of all books: those in existence, lost, abandoned, yet to be written. A rouge book of wines. A vermilion book of sunsets ...

—And, after twelve years ...

Another storm at sea, raised by Prospero's magic art. His high charms work. Miranda is discovered at chess with Ferdinand, checked in love.

On seeing so many men before her, Miranda cries out in wonder.

Prospero's eyes rest on the sinking sun.

'Tis new to thee.

Over coffee.

—How is Max.

—We don't go for such long walks any more.

John Webster witnesses the new philosophy cast all in doubt. Men move and act as in a mist; strive to fashion meaning in a disintegrating world. While great women—Vittoria Corombona and the Duchess of Malfi—like diamonds, radiate through darkness their richer light. A world where Lodovico glories, as he is led away: *I limb'd this night-piece and it was my best.* Where Bosola rails: *While with vain hopes our faculties we tire, we seem to sweat in ice, and freeze in fire.*

Slain, in turn, he bloodies out: *Mine is another voyage.*

Caught by a sudden gust, a honeyed candle gutters.

Walled up for a second time in the Tower of London, Sir Walter Raleigh is granted an infinite melancholy leisure to write his vast, meditative *History of the World*.

Beginning by affirming his fidelity to Elizabeth, his Queen—*whom I must still honour in the dust*—he begins the first volume.

A diamond trails its fire.

Finding the long day of mankind fast drawing towards evening and near at an end, he takes comfort from those beautiful creatures, the stars.

—The stars shine still.

He closes in resplendent darkness. *O eloquent, just, and certain Death ... thou hast drawn together all the pride, cruelty, and ambition of man and covered it with these two narrow words: 'Hic jacet.'* Here lies.

He is released by King James from his cell—but not pardoned—to lead a second doomed expedition to Guiana in search of El Dorado.

> *What is our life.*
> *Our graves that hide us from the searching sun*
> *Are like drawn curtains when the play is done.*

☙❧

We sweep South.

Galileo has been summoned to Rome. The Copernican World System is under suspicion. Walking in the Belvedere, his private garden, as lengthening shadows stretch out across their path, Urban VIII stops to sniff a yellow rose and reminds his friend that God is not necessarily constrained by human logic—may indeed act beyond it. So that arguments from physical evidence, which he no doubt has, are fallible.

They watch a tiny cloud of gnats rise and fall in the ebbing light.

Urban smiles. Galileo remains silent.

In Prague, the sun's last rays fall on dulled panes as Johann Kepler leans over a table covering sheet after sheet with minute figures and calculations, in pursuit of his fabulous prey—the harmony of the world.

He announces his three laws of planetary motion.

The planets move in ellipses, having the sun in focus. As they orbit, the imaginary straight line joining a planet to the sun sweeps equal areas in equal time intervals. The square of the time of revolution of any planet about the sun is proportional to the cube of its mean distance from the sun.

The *Harmonice Mundi,* almost a reality.

A white swan drifts out on a glittering reach of the Avon, dividing the waters in soundless ripples.

William Shakespeare dies. The beating mind is still. What was not achieved, quietly, in a low room with quill and paper.

Man and the Universe still one, as the sun, arrayed in a last glory over Stratford, touches the river with vermilion; fires the mild air of mid-most England.

VII

In the quiet courtyard an old man sits, resting beneath a palm tree. It is approaching noon, the hour of prayer. A fountain releases a fine thread of water, shimmering as it rises and falls through the intense light. The tall palms faintly rustle under an unalloyed blue, casting flickering shade.

At my approach, the old man raises his eyes from contemplating the moving shadows at his feet, and smiles.

—Peace be with you.

I wish him peace, my hand on my heart.

It is the first time anyone other than my guard and I have animated that sequestered spot. I join him beneath the palm. Yusef silently withdraws to the white wall that runs around the courtyard, offering scant shade at this searing hour. High above us, the fronded leaves catch a faint breeze, and pools of dazzling, dancing light float at our feet.

—You appear disturbed, my brother, the old man observes. He seems to await my reply.

A little … uncertain.

> —You sigh, like a young boy caressing himself during our warm nights.

His eyes shine. Perhaps, I think, in fond recollection … or rather, as I am about to learn, he is preparing to quote from his holy book.

> —The Prophet, may peace be upon him, said: Do not look long on beardless boys. Their eyes hold more temptation even than those of the Hur al-Ayn, those peerless maidens who dwell in Paradise.

The old man looks gently at me, then turns his gaze on the flickering ground.

> —The Princess Scheherazade, her eyes are such. Her glances flash like the blades of Isfahan.

Above, incandescent light tears through the dark palm leaves.

He speaks softly.

> —You are a maker of entertainment. A player on the flute of time.

Indeed.

> —To beguile the night.

To beguile the night, as you say.

And, as he waits, to encourage me to go on …

For it is what I must do, if I am to regain my freedom.

He smiles.

> —Ah, yes. Freedom. That Western word.

I feel the sway of Islam.

> —That is a way. If you should so desire. If freedom is what you seek.

Yusef moves his back slightly against the western wall.

—Over our lands there blow two winds. One comes from the Mediterranean; the other from the desert.

He sniffs the air.

—Islam is the desert.

He looks at me keenly.

—I, too, once waited upon the Princess Scheherazade. Was once her teller of tales, you might say.

You, I exclaim.

He seems delighted by my response.

—Indeed.

Was that ... very long ago.

In the quiet of the courtyard I await his reply.

It comes.

—I am the sole survivor from those former times still left here now; an aged falcon, my claws cracked on the perches of repose.

He seems pleased by this remark and rubs his hands.

Have there been many ... tellers of tales.

—Enough to fill the forty jars—as in the famed tale.

He smiles.

—For, you see, I was the first to venture out on those shifting sands.

So ... am I the forty-first.

He does not answer; his dark eyes seemingly intent on the oscillating shade.

And your tale ... of what did it relate, I inquire.

Still he remains silent, continuing to study the pools of light undulating at his feet.

At last he raises his head.

>   —It told of many marvels. Of forgotten texts; of light and shade, colours, stars and webs; of other tales; of other tellers of tales; of the ways of Heaven. And those of Earth.

He rises.

>   —Fix not your hazel eyes on this fleeting world that glides away, a shadow, a wisp of strengthless smoke ... There is no net like illusion. Desire makes everything appear to blossom; with possession, everything fades. Tread softly, as on a silken carpet. Life hangs but by a thread.

He looks at the glistening trickle that rises and falls.

>   —He who sees no portent in a motionless cloud, the swift cry of a bird, a certain fall of light—such a one ... hardly exists.

Rising, he turns back to me.

>   —I have enjoyed our encounter. Maybe, by Allah's grace, we will meet again. But it is not written. The future is as dark as jade. Only the past exercises enchantment ... as I see you have discovered.

Slow, stately, he takes his leave, and I am left with the faint murmur of water, the rustle of leaves, till Yusef breaks his reverie by the western wall and, advancing, leads me back from the light.

༄༅།

The Princess raises an inquiring eyebrow; fixes me with an expectant regard.

I am to begin.

We start and finish with a fine brush-angled stroke: with a *V*, that most magical of letters.

The attentive Princess.

She reclines in a blue watered silk, raised on an elbow. Pale lemon candles shed their gentle glow. A pearl earring gleams.

Velazquez has been appointed court painter to Philip IV of Spain.

The King with his sad gaze.

In restrained harmonies of black, silvery grey and rose, the royal children stand in their stiff braided dress: pale, vulnerable. The Infante, attired for the hunt, holds his glove negligently, by a finger. The little Infanta, attended by her maids of honour, turns her face expectantly towards her parents. They appear mistily on a distant mirror, having their portrait painted by Velazquez, who is shown—long, slender brush in hand—poised in thought by his canvas.

An earring gleams as the Princess, raising her head and gesturing with her long elegant fingers, remarks:

> —Or, perhaps the mirror may reflect the canvas, the King and Queen absent, and the little Infanta, faintly surprised, becoming aware that she is at the heart of the painting.

Moist stars appear, trembling on the dark mirror.

I incline my head. And move on.

It is decreed that plans set out by the Count-Duke of Olivares to channel the waters of the Tagus over the plains of Castile should not be implemented. The Church finds he sins against Divine Providence for seeking to improve what She, for inscrutable motives, had wished to be imperfect.

I pause.

Valdes Leal issues a sombre warning.

The fingers of a skeleton reach out to extinguish a candle flame, bringing down darkness and oblivion on scattered gold; on crowns, books—all attributes of wealth, power and learning.

※

Our winged way bends North, to England.

Sir Francis Bacon finds that the pencil of the Holy Ghost labours more actively in describing the afflictions of Job than the felicities of Solomon; that atheism is rather on the lip than in the heart.

He essays forth on travel—what may be seen and observed. Ruins and libraries; money-markets and warehouses; displays, stables, churches, treasuries of jewels and robes. Nor should triumphs, masques, feasts, funerals, comedies, capital executions, and suchlike shows be neglected.

But the purest of pleasures, the greatest refreshment to the spirit, is to be found in gardens.

Nothing is more pleasant to the eye than green grass kept finely shorn. To have shaded alleys, there to walk, if you be so disposed, in the heat of the day. The breath of flowers floats, sweet in the air, where it comes and goes, like music.

Robert Burton remains ensconced in his dark tower of books: *I have lived a silent, sedentary, solitary life ... never travelled but in a map ... sequestered from those tumults and troubles of the world.* Sir Thomas Browne turns at the end of a shaded cypress grove. Sombre sonorous cadences fall from his pen: *Our hard entrance into the world, our miserable going out of it, do clamorously proclaim we come not to run a race of delight ... 'Tis too late to be ambitious. The great mutations of the world are already enacted.* And hopes for eternity, studied through enigmatic epithet by antiquaries, are cold consolations.

He explores causes of common errors: of the unicorn's horn, concerning the ring-finger, the beginnings of the world. Of the forbidden fruit, the three kings of Collein, the cessation of oracles and the lake Asphaltites.

His dark disquisitions: on the sun as the dark simulacrum, on the created world as but a small parenthesis in eternity—for our longest possible life is but as a winter's day. Yet: *We carry within ourselves the wonders that we seek without.*

The Princess seems triste as we abandon the Norfolk fens and cross the North Sea, where a revolution in thought is taking place.

ೊ

René Descartes, closeted in his stove-heated room, is on a dramatic voyage of discovery: *I am a being whose whole essence is to think.*

Blaise Pascal joins the community of Jansenists at Port-Royal.

But God is hidden.

Night.

Faint crackle of a candle.

He writes: *The eternal silence of these infinite spaces fills me with dread.*

Spinoza sits at his bench, grinding and polishing lenses.

In his austere *Tractatus* he maintains that all things always think. There can never be any lapse—not for the stone Sphinx, forever gazing out over the sands; nor for the giddy butterfly approaching a sprig of buddleia.

Scheherazade extends a long, supple toe.

Skaters are out on the frozen rivers of Holland. On a dank rock off Copenhagen a mermaid appears, causing some confusion as to the shade of her sea-green eyes. But all concur, she had a forked tail.

An earring gleams as she moves.

—Which waved gently at all the attention she received.

Returning to England, a chivalrous highwayman, Claude Duval, seems to rob a bewitchingly beautiful siren of her jewels. But he scorns to take them if she will but dance with him there, on the roadside, by the flickering carriage light.

The lady agrees.

Sarah, Duchess of Marlborough, thoughtfully dips her red feathered pen in some agreeable blue ink: *The Duke returned from the wars today, and did pleasure me while still in his top-boots.*

She sighs.

As does Anne, Countess of Winchilsea, wandering, late, round her moonlit park.

> *In such a Night let Me abroad remain,*
> *Till Morning breaks, and all's confus'd again;*
> *Our Cares, Our Toils, our Clamours are renew'd,*
> *Or Pleasures, seldom reach'd, again pursu'd.*

We cross the Sea of Japan.

Matsuo Basho is re-threading dark blue cords on his bamboo hat before setting out on the narrow road North to Oku. He is halted on his journey—by a motionless cloud alone in the sky, by glistening raindrops suspended along a spray of fern, by mist drifting among blue pine needles ...

A faint trickle comes from the fountain.

André le Notre lays out the park and gardens at Versailles.

The sun passes through the King's bedchamber and out into the surrounding gardens; past the urns, the trimmed hedges, the beckoning statues, the pools; along avenues and canals; across nymphs and tritons, swept by a constant spray of foaming water; finally to set—lingering, vermillion—on the low, western horizon.

Molière pounds the stage with his stick. Those three imperious thumps thrilling as any signal come from Mars, according to Marcel Proust.

Passion burns at the French court.

Racine invites a select audience to witness Bérénice and Titus act out their tragic destiny. He loves and forswears; she loves, and flees.

Phaedra runs love's every fury in controlled, burning lines; believes sunshine cannot be purer than her heart.

In a lighter vein, Mme de Sévigné, writing to her daughter, observes that many people deprive us of solitude without affording us company.

—How true, exclaims Scheherazade.

Driving back to the station.

We are quiet.

Spots of rain dance on the windscreen.

☙❧

We reach Rome.

Among the silent evocations of the ruins, Nicolas Poussin is drawn back through time—the Golden Age gone; not to return, except in his paintings. Everything breathes regret for that lost world and its serene delights.

Diana—a crescent moon adorning her hair—takes quiet leave of a distracted Endymion as the horses of Apollo, led by Aurora, begin their surge across the sky.

A shepherd traces with his finger the poignant legend, *Et in Arcadia Ego*, cut into the stone tomb on which his fleeting shadow falls. The swift years pass, and Poussin returns to the theme. Now stiller, more spacious, a shepherd bends before the tomb under a subdued evening light. His questioning glance is answered by that of the goddess: her gentle, compassionate response.

A candle flame flickers.

A mellow Italian sun sets over the Campagna.

Soft, idyllic light bathes Claude Lorrain landscapes where Virgil seems to breathe again. Slanting sunlight falls on warm stone walls. Fleecy clouds drift over slow-flowing rivers. Trees darken against an amber sky.

A mysterious castle by the sea. A wistful Psyche, contemplating her fate. Graceful green-dark trees rise to a pale-blue, grey-streaked sky.

His last painting returns us to Virgil. Dusk approaches. Hues of violet tinge the distant hills. Ascanius, follower of Aeneas, has drawn back his bow. The stag stands unafraid, believing himself protected.

A few seconds remain before the swift arrow will bring on the coming war.

৵৽৽

We linger in Rome.

1661. A triumphant year for the Immaculists. Alexander VII reaffirms the Blessed Virgin's immunity from original sin.

In the Church of the Gesù, the movement is always upward, aspiring, soaring. Over billowing clouds, Jesuit saints and martyrs follow Christ as he bears the cross towards the Empyrean, where dazzling light will envelop them, where the sacred name of Jesus burns as the blinding sun at noon.

Apollo is in hot pursuit of Daphne, carved out of marble by Bernini. As the toes of the nymph take root, terror clings to her lips; desire, to those of the god.

He changes the thin jet of water issuing from Rome's fountains to an exuberant, Baroque spray—gushing, foaming, tumbling in cascades.

—You are rich in water, observes Scheherazade.

Throws a wide, Doric colonnade round the *Piazza San Pietro* to establish a majestic repose, embracing Catholics in love and peace, inviting agnostics to venture to approach, encouraging those who have turned astray to return to the True Faith.

We wing our way North—cross the glistening Alps—to arrive at the Low Countries, where painters are affected by the fall of a shadow, entranced by a shaft of sunlight, almost mesmerised by the vast sky ... We enter the still, serene rooms of Vermeer, forever suspended in light.

A limpid light passes along a white wall, over a faintly crinkled map. It touches the studs of a chair, throws reflections on a glass, falls on colours he made his own: blue, lemon-yellow, pearl.

His quiet rooms, where truth and harmony dwell ...

A young woman wearing a blue wrap clasps a letter close to her as she reads with slightly parted lips. A lady looks up from her letter writing. Has a sudden thought occurred, and she is uncertain how to proceed. Another young woman holds before the glass two yellow ribbons attached to a pearl necklace. She seems stilled by poignant reflections.

The artist is seen in his studio painting a young woman attired as Clio, Muse of History. She wears a laurel wreath, which time has tinged blue. Light falls on her lowered eyelids, on a thick yellow-bound volume which she holds, on the sleeve of her blue dress. These colours appear in most perfect harmony in the *Girl with a Turban*, a pearl softly gleaming below her ear as she turns her dark eyes tentatively towards us: a consoling star in a vast night sky.

A lady is gently touching the virginals, releasing restrained notes. Light varies an inscription on the instrument from ochre to blue A gentleman stands near, following the music: *Thy fingers make dead wood more blest than living lips.*

Now the last drops of rain have fallen on his *View of Delft* where, as yet unseen, breaking through a cloudy sky, the sun casts shadows on the water. *Little patch of yellow wall*, murmurs Bergotte, Proust's fictional novelist, as he dies.

Little patch of yellow wall, as slips away, for ever, all he sought to achieve.

Scheherazade turns her gaze away. A glistening tear clings to her soft cheek.

VIII

Pale blue candles burn.

The scent of sandalwood hangs in the air.

It is the hour of the tale. The Princess Scheherazade has commanded me to come to her apartments.

She wears a grey blue silk with pale raspberry stripes. A waning moon of mint drifts among nacreous clouds.

The cry of the peacock rises.

I draw up a low seat that has been left for me.

☙

The Age of Reason is come upon us. In its cool, clear light mystery fades, the adventuring spirit falters. We move towards a more enclosed propriety.

Writing his essay concerning human understanding, John Locke sees himself as an under-gardener charged to clear the ground and remove some of the rubbish before him—much as I, Princess, do omit the same such stuff.

Her dark eyes flash.

The mind at birth is a blank tablet, Locke maintains. No one is born with ideas. All our notions come from experience, via the senses. So begins empiricism, running flatly before us.

Isaac Newton, after leaving his Lincolnshire garden, picks up a tiny blue-veined pebble, sea-washed from the edge of the shore. Brings in his law of universal gravitation. Back in the Fens, John Ray picks a sprig of peppermint and inhales deeply.

In Scotland, glasses will soon be raised to the little gentleman in black velvet who will unseat the King. Now ladies, and some gentlemen too, fix black beauty patches to their rouged cheeks. We arrive at the eighteenth century.

—Hurrah! cries Scheherazade.

༺༻

A pale moth with an amber bar flutters near a candle flame.

Ladies and gentlemen, freshly powdered and patched, step gracefully out into the park and down the long vistas where, forever, Diana and her nymphs greet Actaeon and his hounds. They arrive at a dark lake, where stars burn.

Watteau is master of this fleeting, fragile world where ladies and their gallants shimmer in silk. See there, with an air of indecision, intrigue—a graceful figure restraining the amorous advances of an admirer.

A poignancy, a sense of loss; an elusive, delicate moment as, under the benevolent gaze of Venus, his couples prepare to take their leave of the enchanted Isle of

Cythera. Mist is gathering on the waters, beginning to veil the trees; a pair of lovers still linger. The gentleman assists his lady to rise. Standing apart, another looks back, with a wistful smile.

Assembled in a park, we come upon a little group of ladies in their long, shimmering gowns of rose, white or bronze. As the light fades from the trees, an intimation, a tremor of mortality, near to tears. A young girl stands a little apart by the darkening lake. Across the still water, almost lost in the twilight, two lovers embrace.

The little moth flutters away.

At Gersaint's shop, a lady is examining an area of blue sky in a picture on display. Her companion kneels, the better to observe the charms exhibited by the frolicking bathers beneath. A girl in a rippling pink gown steps lightly up to enter the shop, revealing a pretty sage-green ankle, as her beau offers his hand. The last of Watteau's couples on their tender quest for love.

> —A quest that many follow—dallying, or hurrying after.

Flitting across Scheherazade's face, the hint of a wry smile.

I incline my head.

Chardin instils poetry into the quiet domestic scene. A young mother places a final pin in her daughter's cap as she stands before the mirror, poised to leave for early morning Mass. A maid pauses from peeling turnips; lets one gently slip down her apron, falling from her slackened fingers …

As a servant slowly lights a candle, a lady waits with tender impatience to seal her letter with red wax. A young boy carefully places a card—a breath will destroy all—on the very top of his fragile house of cards …

A plum colours a clear glass. Cherries are reflected on a silver goblet. White bulbs of garlic tinge a tumbler of water. Liquid gleams around olives in a dark glass. As Proust will observe: *From Chardin we learn that a pear is just as alive as a woman; common crockery as beautiful as precious stone.*

Boucher throws a graceful silver and salmon-striped banner above a reclining Venus. She rests, exuberant yet relaxed, surrounded by pale pearl nymphs, borne on the surging, glittering, dark-green, foam-flecked sea.

Diana, after a dip in the cool and yielding waters of the river, allows the sunlight to glow on her pale rose body. Extending a foot, the better to admire, she is lost in tender regard of her delicate toes.

We enter a Rococo dream park where Fragonard's green and lemon-yellow trees merge in a turquoise haze. A girl in billowing pink satin soars on a swing. A pink shoe flies from her tiny foot as a young man in pale green looks on admiringly.

Silently, Scheherazade brings her hands together.

A lady attired in a powder-grey and oyster satin dress leans to one side to accept a stolen kiss, still holding a long, striped scarf that matches her dress and trails over a small table where, from a half-open drawer, pale-blue, pink, and black ribbons dangle.

He brings a last, late, lyrical note to the capricious and wistful Rococo world with his four panels, *The Progress of Love.*

An ardent beau storms the citadel, clambering over the wall of an enclosed shrubbery where pink roses bloom, precipitating a startled gesture from his love.

The young man proffers a pink rose as the girl trips coquettishly away.

We arrive at the declaration—the couple have reached a stage of tender intimacy as she dwells lovingly on a billet-doux...

Last scene of all, the happy lover is about to be crowned with a garland of flowers by his sweetheart, who looks away—while an eager young artist leans forward to sketch the scene. Cupid, apparently no longer required, has fallen asleep on his pedestal.

A candle releases a wisp of blue smoke.

※

A certain Lord Petre snips a ringlet from the unwilling head of a Miss Arabella Fermor—fit subject for an epic by Alexander Pope.

His heroine, Belinda, cries:

> *Oh, hads't thou, Cruel! been content to seize*
> *Hairs less in sight, or any hairs but these!*

Sailing down the Thames, James Bradley notices a little pennant on a mast change direction. This helps him in his calculations of the speed of light. John Harrison sets sail with his marine chronometer—the first clock capable of keeping time at sea. Now longitude can be known. Captain Cook, benefitting, punctures the Aboriginal Dreamtime.

William Kent has freed the English garden from restraint. Plants grow in profusion and are not cut back. Yet a Mr Vernon chases a blue butterfly for nearly nine miles, before netting him.

Jonathan Swift considers that modern writers spin books out of their entrails, producing dirt and poison instead of honey and wax.

—What difference today, inquires Scheherazade.

I hesitate, before continuing ...

Samuel Richardson falls in love with his heroines, Pamela and Clarissa. He sheds bitter tears as he plots their fate. As flakes of snow spot his dark blue cloak, a masked highwayman reigns in his snorting horse. Inside the stationary coach, her heart madly thumping, a silk-clad lady peeps out—her eyes, that wan blue the English call grey.

Camellias arrive in France. Ladies are sipping chocolate quite late in the morning; dab eau-de-cologne behind their ears. By not quite kissing, but breathing their lips' closeness, practised young lovers experience new delights.

Using lemon on their skin, ladies pursue a fashionable, pale look. At Bellevue, Madame de Pompadour arranges a midsummer garden of spring and summer flowers—all made from porcelain. Taking her soft chalk pastels to France, Rosalba Carriera captures Watteau, his face slightly in shade, and, back in Italy, the melting gaze of a young lady of the Leblond family, with her limpid, smoky-blue eyes.

Bonnie Prince Charlie, defeated at Culloden, flees to France. He leaves behind sorrowing Jacobite ladies, who each retain a treasured lock of their chevalier's hair. As shades of evening creep on, a pensive Thomas Grey silently meditates among the tombs of an English churchyard.

The fourth Earl of Sandwich, wishing not to abandon the gaming-table, instructs his servant as to the making of a snack. Louis de Lacaille presents to the Academy of Science his map of the stars of the southern hemisphere. It shows fourteen new constellations, all named by him.

Scheherazade remains silent, still.

☙❧

Falling snow.

Japan. The depths of winter.

Forty-seven samurai gather outside a fortified mansion, bound by a moral code that forbids they live beneath the same skies as the enemy of their dead lord. After avenging his death, they commit ritual suicide by his grave.

Wind tears at their green and red banners.

In a last letter to his mother, one among them, Shiyo, leaves a haiku, his death poem:

> *Snow on the pines*
> *So breaks the power*
> *that splits mountains*

Motoori Norinaga defines Shinto as belief in *kami*: found in the bud of a rose, a blade of bending grass, the swirling wind; on a chrysanthemum, an old cypress, snowcapped Mount Fuji. The gods, if they come, do not descend from the sky, but appear on the far horizon.

Chiyo-ni looks out, after the loss of her only son, on the departing mists.

> *How far*
> *My hunter of dragonflies*
> *Would have roamed today*

Buson watches:

> *A camellia*
> *As it falls, spills water*
> *From last night's shower*

Across the western seas, in Cao Xuegin's novel, a vision of beauty is seen approaching. Her fluttering sleeves release a fragrance of musk and orchid. With each rustle of her lotus garments, jade pendants tinkle. The curve of her slender waist is snow, whirled by the wind. Soon her delicate shadow falls on the veranda.

Who can she be.

A flame flickers on the dark mirror.

Scheherazade turns her ring.

༄

In a candle-lit salon overlooking the Grand Canal, Vivaldi raises his violin. At the Opera, a minister of state is tapped upon the nose by the long fan of a notorious beauty who wishes to rebuff his advances. Bach, summoned to Potsdam and still dusty from the journey, sets Frederick's noble theme in fugal form. This becomes: *The Musical Offering*.

Mozart is born.

—Happy times, exclaims Scheherazade.

Leibniz certainly thought so. *This is the best of all possible worlds.* Though not necessarily, metaphysically speaking.

He assumes we are not destined to attain the beatific vision: our happiness ought not to consist in an enjoyment where there is nothing more to be realised, but rather in perpetual progress towards new pleasures and perfections.

He sends Sophie and her companion to the woods to search for two identical leaves. They emerge a little flushed, and empty-handed.

—Nature is teaching them a pretty lesson.

With a graceful bow to Giordano Bruno, he brings forth his monads, living mirrors of the world. Rather as we, setting out to explore an unknown city, find—at each vantage point where we pause—things can appear quite different: a city within a city.

—You are dazzled by labyrinths, avers Scheherazade.

I was lost in the maze of your city, Princess. Your narrow and intricate alleys ... Now that maze has opened on another.

Her dark eyes challenge me.

—Rather say, you have found a labyrinth within a labyrinth.

And, gesturing with her slender hand,

—Let us catch a coach, South, to Naples. There to greet Giovanni Vico who now bows before us. Sees History (our enchanting tale) as a vast O, an ever-recurring cycle.

James Joyce will take up his theory of corso and ricorso: the same, anew.

Scheherazade inclines her head.

—Language spins its merry way. It is cut in stone, then scratched on paper; agreed upon and spoken in the street. The cycles slowly turn, like one of our great waterwheels. Humanity, crude and severe, becomes more benign; attains discernment and delicacy. Then sinks back into dissipation.

She lets her hand drop. With a slight wave, invites me to continue.

A wisp of smoke rises from a low candle.

From that sad prognosis let us hie ourselves North to the agreeable David Hume, the Scottish laird's son, who lives in high good humour in Edinburgh, the Athens of the North, not acknowledging God's existence and, to all appearances, no worse for that.

Sipping a little red wine in his high-backed chair, he muses by the fire.

Empires may rise and fall, liberty and slavery succeed each other; ignorance and knowledge each give place to each. But still, the cherry tree flowers in the woods of Italy and Greece.

Now we must brace ourselves for a sharp crossing of the treacherous Irish seas, to meet with George Berkeley, seeking to catch him before he becomes enamoured of the beneficial effects of tar water. He requires a metaphysical nightwatchman—God—to keep all things in place, while his nibs—the philosopher—blinks an eye.

A third candle releases its grey-blue thread.

He finds a curious opinion prevailing among men (women may be too sensitive) that mists, mountains, moonbeams, macaroons, money—in a word, all sensible objects—have an existence, natural or real, distinct from their being perceived.

And yet did Berkeley prove that all things are but dreams, which must vanish on the instant the mind but changes its theme.

The dark eyes of the Princess linger on me, till a scurrying cloud crosses the path of the waning moon, and all vanishes.

IX

Candide sets out on his adventures. He passes through High Germany and on to Cadiz, where favourable winds blow him South, across the equator, and on to the thriving city of Buenos Aires. Beyond, the hazy land of Eldorado beckons, where one may dine off gold plate. Did Voltaire's hero wonder at the unknown stars visible in the Southern hemisphere.

On his travels he encounters War, Murder, Deception, Fraud. Can this be the best of all possible worlds, as Leibniz so confidently assures us.

I raise my eyes. Tall turquoise candles shed their tranquil light. Scent of jasmine lingers in the air.

Scheherazade wears a pale grey-green and oyster striped silk. She had been reading. A pale blue ribbon falls from the grey volume set down by her side. An opal adorns the hand with which she invites me to continue.

The first issue of the Almanach de Gotha appears, allowing ancient aristocratic families to look each other up. At Weimar, Goethe, one hand held behind his back, is enjoying the sensation of lightly gliding over gleaming ice.

On the back of a Jack of Spades, Jean-Jacques Rousseau jots: *My whole life has been little more than a long reverie, divided into chapters by my daily walks.* Cards are being cut for whist. A vast opal is found in Hungary.

I glance at her jewelled finger. But Scheherazade makes no sign.

Many more varieties of flowers grace European gardens. From faraway Peru comes fuchsia; from the distant Orient, hortensia and chrysanthemums.

—Beauty is spreading fast, she remarks.

I incline my head.

Choderlos de Laclos, an officer attached to the artillery, writes his novel of letters. A faded blue ribbon is attached to the key of Cécile Volanges: the one delicate drop of colour he allows in his pellucid prose.

Cécile, her fair hair floating over bare shoulders, is a tempting sight to the Marquis de Merteuil. In an unwritten sequel she flees from convent life to join him in Amsterdam, where they pursue further pleasures and adventures.

—We wish them well.

Violins are being raised, and gentlemen begin to bow gracefully towards the ladies gathered in the Assembly Rooms at Bath, soon to be joined by Jane Austen and her heroines. Dr Johnson and James Boswell dance a reel on the summit of Dun Caan. Tam O' Shanter, fleeing a pursuing hag, crosses the Auld Brig at Alloway, losing only his mare's streaming grey tail.

Under milder English skies, Gainsborough's two young daughters gently pursue a white butterfly. Georgiana, Duchess of Devonshire, an ardent radical, sets the tone with free-flowing gowns and wide-brimmed hats. When she enters a room, all eyes turn.

Lord Hyde, lately returned from Italy, takes an evening walk with his son, aged nine, accompanied by the boy's tutor. They stop beneath a cloudy grey sky to observe children flying a kite over a meadow. He inquires of his son, casually, where might that kite's shadow fall. Without hesitating, without turning his head, the boy answers correctly. Which was enough for the enlightened father, and the following day he granted the tutor a life pension.

—Well deserved, cries Scheherazade.

Edward Gibbon sums up his magisterial *Decline and Fall of the Roman Empire* in nine words: *I have described the triumph of barbarism and religion*. Laurence Sterne sends an inattentive reader back through the pages of his novel. After which, having duly informed herself, the lady rejoins the party and is given a hearty welcome.

But later, put up at a French inn, Sterne finds he cannot release a starling, confined in a cramped cage and crying: *I can't get out. I can't get out ...*

—That cry still rings.

❦

The planet Uranus swings into view. From his winnings at cards, Squire George Ley builds Pack 'O Cards Inn, boasting four storeys, each with thirteen doors and fifty-two windows.

Attitudes differ. According to John Wilkes life can supply little more than a few good fucks and then we die. But James Lackington often goes without food to buy books.

He sets out bravely in search of a dinner, returning—to his wife's consternation—laden with nothing but Young's *Night Thoughts*.

In his Edinburgh studio, Henry Raeburn works a little grey into his pale blue. The Revd Robert Walker is elegantly skating on Duddington Loch, one hand held, like Goethe, behind his back.

An admirer writes:

> Iron and ice release a sweeter music than yesterday's psalms, and the effortless inscription of these rings round and round the centre of the loch is more persuasive than any sermon.

His fellow countryman, Adam Smith, grimly notes a skilled worker performing the many separate operations required to produce a single gleaming pin. Happily finds, by a division of labour, that willing workers with much less skill can turn out thousands more such pins during the course of a shining day.

> —Beyond even the needs of dancing angels, murmurs Scheherazade.

Johann Hamann, the Magus of the North, is always awaiting an apocalyptic angel: one with *a key to this abyss*.

Though his compatriot, Georg Lichtenberg, informs us:

> If an angel were to tell us anything of his philosophy, I believe many propositions would sound like, $2 \times 2 = 13$.

In the sleepy old German town of Wolfenbuttel, Gotthold Lessing gently blows dust from mouldering papers in the silence of the neglected ducal library. Baron Münchhausen, on a lengthy coach journey through Upper Austria, entertains Princess Schwarzenberg and her female companion with his amazing adventures.

We step lightly into a gently rocking gondola. Goethe enthuses:

> *We Northerners who spend our lives in a drab, dirty and dusty atmosphere, where even reflected light is subdued, cannot develop an eye which looks with such delight upon the world.*

Candles faintly crackle.

The Princess raises herself on her juniper couch.

Takes up the tale.

—Tiepolo, an artist whose very shadows are transparent, banishes darkness from the scene. His Apollo rises, triumphant against a spreading circle of peach and pale mauve, to greet his pawing horses.

His Cleopatra, a necklace of pearls wound tightly round her throat and wearing a sumptuous gown, releases an earring into a glass, while her ebony-skinned attendant, attired in a jerkin of crushed blackberry, tries to restrain a highly strung hound.

And, under tranquil southern skies, his blonde princess rests her soft, dark eyes on the infant Moses.

She pauses. Then concludes.

—Now our path lies North. Let us depart the shimmering mists of Venice. Leave Canaletto to reveal her late splendour—the soft muted light, pale blue skies and turquoise waters. Guardi to hint at an advancing decay, with tiny muffled figures and drooping fishing nets. A distant ritornello, fading away …

Across the glistening Alps we go.

At exactly half past three in the afternoon in the quiet Prussian town of Königsberg, the philosopher Immanuel Kant leaves his front door in a grey coat, a bamboo cane in hand, and goes for his daily walk to the lime tree avenue. He draws a vital distinction between the world as it is in itself, and as it appears to us.

Things in themselves have no spatial properties and are not located in time. And so, the transformation of reality occurs in our minds.

We do not draw our laws from Nature. Rather we prescribe them to her. We impose on the giddy butterfly, the silent sphinx: Space and Time.

Scheherazade's dark eyes rest on me.

But we can admit something does indeed lie beyond the scene. Meanwhile, our interior journey goes on. Man walks the grey streets. It is the idea of freedom that lifts him beyond.

Dark and hazel eyes meeting.

—Kant opened the gates to the stars.

Metaphysics is the bounds of the conceivable, as distinct from the limits of the actual.

—Soon we shall climb the starry heights of High Idealism.

We shall take that star-lit path.

—And look back to Kant.

Soon we shall hear that cry.

—He was fond of tulips.

A red petal on his grey prose.

She lies back.

The night is dark. The scent of jasmine hangs in the air.

This punctilious man, who sought to unite rationalism and empiricism in a grand synthesis, noted that two things fill the mind with new and ever-increasing admiration and awe: the starry heavens above, and the moral law within.

—Does, now, perhaps, only one remain.

A faint breeze causes the candle flames to tremble.

❦

We enter on turbulent times. In Paris the tricolore is raised. Blue for freedom. White for truth and purity. Red for the blood of liberty. The guillotine—the blade of eternity—begins to tumble.

De Maistre enthuses: *This earth, an immense altar soaked in blood, on which all that lives must be immolated ...*

Charlotte Corday arrives in Paris, purchases a knife, and brings it down on Marat as he sits in his bath where he was writing, urging further excess. Talleyrand sees the Revolution as a fall of snow on blossoming trees. No one who did not live before 1789 knows the sweetness of life.

Her low voice.

> —Caught up in these times, Adelaide Labille-Guiard portrays a lady writing what seems to be a last message to her children ... She paints herself, seated by an easel in a wide-brimmed feathered hat, under the admiring gaze of two girl pupils ... Elizabeth Vigée-Lebrun captures the delicate beauty of the Duchesse de Polignac and the vivacious Countess Golovin, her wild, dark hair escaping her head scarf. She too paints

a tender self-portrait, in which she hugs her daughter, Julie, to her.

The dark mirror.

Ten days before the Bastille is stormed a certain Marquis de Sade is taken from his cell under close guard and placed in the lunatic asylum at Charenton. As a young voluptuary, de Sade appears, attired in a grey coat and deep orange silk breeches. A long pheasant's feather dangles from his hat, while, idly, he turns a slender cane.

Prison makes him a writer. Those high, thick walls that surround convents, monasteries, and the like, always attract. Hidden behind those high walls is an organised life, all the more intense for being secluded.

One quality shines like a dark star from his voluminous writings: *Verité*. His vision of Truth.

> *It is only by sacrificing everything to sensual pleasure that this being, known as man, cast into the world in search of himself, may sew a few roses on to the thorns of life.*

He lays down his adamantine law: *Vice must always prosper. Virtue always suffer.*

Words of fire that will straddle the centuries to come.

A call to Women:

> *Have no other thought than your own pleasure. No other law than your own desire. Languish no longer under constraints and restrictions that wither your body, dry up your skin, dull your eyes. But answer the divine urges of Nature.*

On the dark mirror a candle flame, woven as of water.

> *Saints and martyrs to degradation and toil; hearts that are heavy, bodies that are worn. Yet, as they look up, faint*

wants and tremors appear on their thin, wan lips, in tired, sad eyes, and I see—How It Should Be.

He was to bury his heroine in a bower of jasmine—his favourite flower—and on her tomb was to be engraved the one word: VIXIT.

From his cell, on the brown paper he had to write upon:

I am alone. I am at the world's end. Held from every gaze. Here no one can reach me. No creature can draw nigh.

His hand trembles.

But I am free.

Out of the jasmine-scented night appear the glistening stars.

༺༻

A hush has fallen on the bewigged guests assembled in the courtyard of a *residenz* where a wind serenade is being played.

Under the stars, flickering torches fire the edge of a gleaming horn, cast a glow along an oboe, as the tender melody is taken up by the clarinet. A lady sighs. The harmony now winds through a minor key, casting an enchantment ...

Such carefree lightheartedness, deep ineffability, irresistible, infectious vitality. Music of playful exuberance, as Susanna scolds Figaro. Of tender melancholy, as Barbarina, in the gathering dusk, searches for a lost pin.

We enter Mozart's fairy kingdom.

I see the whole entire. It stands almost complete and finished in my mind so that I can survey it, like a fine picture or a beautiful statue ... What delight this is I cannot say!

Scheherazade's dark eyes shine.

The shadowy forces of the glittering Queen of the Night are vanquished, and vanish. The magic flute has triumphed. But its composer, nine weeks after its premier, lies silent, still, in a pauper's grave.

That last winter of his life, to keep warm in their cold, unheated rooms, there being no money for fuel, Mozart, who loved dancing, danced with his beloved Constanze.

X

During those long hours of my confinement I would take imaginary walks, turning the corner to come on Farquharson's where once, by the window, the young owner sat tinkling Noel Coward tunes at a white piano—to be replaced, in more utilitarian times, by chairs and tables—and on, past High Hill bookshop where, on warm summer days, faint whiffs of fresh print from newly-published paperbacks exude an intoxicating scent.

Up Flask Walk, perhaps pausing by the stationery shop or at an enticing display of review copies in the second-hand bookshop, before reaching—as the late October afternoon ebbs away—the beckoning green lights of the Wells Tavern, then to enter, by descending Hampstead's ways, shaded Keats Grove and its soft-lit lamplight.

Till a summons comes, and I stand once more before the Princess Scheherazade.

This evening she is attired in white. A slender band, the colour of a young alder leaf, runs round her throat. As woodland-green candles shed their light, I am invited to take up the tale.

We begin in England.

Writing within her little bit of ivory, Jane Austen: quite unmatched. A mind lively and assured.

> Let other pens dwell on guilt and misery. I quit such odious subjects. There is no charm equal to tenderness of heart.

Enter Emma, her sparkling, hazel-eyed heroine: active, concerned, contriving—until checked.

Fanny Price appears: gentle, unassuming, dove-grey. Her fine sensitivity appreciates the grace and repose of Mansfield Park—far from her family abode of noise, squalor and disorder.

A sadder note is struck with *Persuasion* where Anne Elliot and Captain Wentworth, many years estranged, draw together once more at Lyme in the subdued sea light.

Further along the coast, in the quiet cathedral hush of Chichester, sits John Keats, one leg thrown over the other. He begins *Saint Agnes Eve*—the sweetest of the year, where—*in the honey'd middle of the night, young virgins may have visions of delight.*

Winging her way across the seas to his brother in America, hastens *La Belle Dame Sans Merci*.

> Her hair was long, her foot was light,
> And her eyes were wild.

From the west coast of Scotland he writes to a friend: *Fancy is indeed less than a present palpable reality. But it is greater than remembrance.* Asks only for books, fruit, French wine, fine weather—and a little music.

A smear of blackcurrant jelly on a page makes him hesitate between describing it as purple or blue. So, in the admixture of fresh thought, writes, *purplue*. Which may be an excellent name for a colour.

At Winchester, in the mellow, late September light, he takes his afternoon walk along the water meadows. That autumn walk … held in amber.

A last letter. Heartrending. *I can scarcely bid you good-bye. I always make an awkward bow.*

Scheherazade closes her eyes. A slight tremor.

The sound of trickling water rises from the dark garden.

The German scholar, Grotefend, begins to decipher Babylonian cuneiform inscriptions. Things are no longer exactly as they stood when once Keats wrote of:

> *Hieroglyphics old,*
> *Which sages and keen-eyed astrologers*
> *Then living on the earth, with labouring thought*
> *Won from the gaze of many centuries:*
> *Now lost, their import gone,*
> *Their wisdom long since fled.*

ॐ

Coleridge watches a tiny water insect cast a dancing shadow on the sun-shot stream. As twilight descends into night, the window of his library at Keswick becomes a perfect looking-glass in which his rows of books appear; their spines spangled with stars.

Her voice.

—He believed, did he not, that happiness of life is made up of minute actions and reactions. A kiss, a kind look, a smile …

I incline my head.

She is silent.

Wordsworth, out walking with his sister at sunset by the shores of Loch Katrine, encounters two neatly dressed women. A soft Scottish voice asks: *What, you are stepping Westward ...*

Stirred by a soft breeze, the candlelight flickers.

Shelley is drowned off Livorno, a volume of Sophocles in one pocket and, in the other, Keats' poems, doubled back.

The cry of the peacock rises from the garden.

William Hazlitt stands in the National Gallery.

> *What signify the hubbub, the folly, the idle fashions without, when compared with the solitude, the silence, the speaking forms within. Here is the mind's true home.*

Byron assigns sixteen minutes—no more—to any passion: *I have a notion that gamblers are as happy as most—being always excited.* Poetry is the expression of excited passion—the *estro*: an inspiration, ardour, whim.

His heart is won by dark, languishing eyes; darkly, deeply-blue Mediterranean skies. By Venice ...

> *The greenest isle of my imagination. I like the gloomy gaity of their gondolas, the silence of their canals.*

The women, too, he finds, kiss better.

He enjoys a layer of port between his claret, *the company of my lamp, and my utterly confused and tumbled-over library.* Evenings spent in that calm nothingness of languor.

He has given up shooting.

> *The last bird I ever fired at was an eaglet, on the Gulf of Lepanto, near Vostitza. I tried to save him. The eye was so bright.*

A silent communion of eyes.

The poet and the stricken bird.

> *And I never did since, and never will, attempt the death of another bird.*

Thoughts of mortality.

> *As I grow older, the indifference ... not to life, for we love it by instinct, but to the stimuli of life, increases. Of the two, I should think the long sleep better than the agonised vigil. But men, miserable as they are, cling so ... probably would prefer damnation to quiet.*

On examining epitaphs on the tombs at Ferrara he pauses before:

> *Martini Luigi*
> *Implora pace*
> *&*
> *Lucrezia Picini*
> *Implora eterna quiete*

The dead have had enough of life—all they want is rest—and this they implore.

> *Implora pace.*

These two words, no more, put over me.

❧

We travel West. Towards the land of vespers. Spain.

Goya is invited by the Duchess of Alba to stay on her estate at Sanlucan de Barrameda in Andalucia.

She stands, dressed in low-cut black Maya clothing, her abundant raven-dark hair piled high beneath a black lace mantilla, a broad black riband round her slender waist. The painter's passion for her ends on an enigmatic note:

an inscription, long lost under oil, but indicated by the Duchess' lowered finger, reveals the words: *Solo Goya*.

—Is not the Duchess of Alba's riband a deep vermilion, remarks Scheherazade.

I have darkened it, Princess.

—Ah. *Todo es fingido*. Nothing is certain.

The candle flames flicker.

While held captive in the tower of Segovia, Diego Hervas conceives an ambitious plan to write a work on every branch of knowledge, running to a hundred octavo volumes.

He appears in *The Manuscript Found in Saragossa*. Its author, the Polish nobleman, Jan Potocki, rises from his chair in his castle's extensive library as the light fades one December day, and shoots himself—with a silver bullet fashioned from a sugar bowl that once belonged to his mother.

To return. Hervas is now free to pursue his audacious project. Of the one hundred subjects, the third part is devoted to Ornithology, the seventh to Lithology, the thirty-third to Physics. Uncertainty still reigns in certain circles as to whether a cryptic remark contains the first intimations of quantum theory.

—Really.

Yes, indeed.

Her fathomless eyes, dreaming.

I press on.

Aesthetics is embraced in the forty-first, Asceticism tripping lightly after. Unravelling Hermeneutics takes up the seventy-seventh, and in the tantalizing eighty-ninth—Magic.

After an absence on completing his labours, Hervas returns to his austere room to witness a voracious rat dragging the final pages of his manuscript—his life's work, conceived in rapture, born of pain mingled with pleasure, and now consigned perhaps to oblivion—down a large, dark hole.

The faint breeze causes candle flames to bend. Golden threads of gossamer, shed to cross Scheherazade's throat.

⁂

Shades of Romanticism are advancing. Colour is entering the pale pages of fiction. Chateaubriand writes tenderly of the blue haze on far horizons, of yellow and maroon butterflies encountered on his travels in America, whose descendants will later delight Nabokov. Victoria Regina, the Queen of the Night, is discovered fluttering over a decaying barque on the Amazon.

During the course of her novel *Corinne*, Madame de Staël observes that, in every genre, we moderns say too much. Madame Récamier, on her chaise-longue, wriggles her naked toes in agreement.

Thomas Bewick completes the engravings for his *History of British Birds*. While gliding through the North Sea, a school of herring casts a silvery reflection on a low bank of grey cloud.

But now, a Lorelei is calling from beyond the Rhine ... A fine mist descends.

So, let us climb the heights, the starry absolutes of High Idealism. Philosophy on its last winged flight.

We ascend.

Past Fichte, who cut Kant's one remaining cord to external reality: *Longing for the infinite and eternal is at the root of all finite existence* ... On, to Schelling where: *Art —the eternal sun in the realm of spirit—is the condition to which true philosophical reflection must aspire* ...

Reaching at last the town of Jena. Here, within the flash and roar of cannon fire, the Prussians, under Prince von Hohenlohe, are routed by Napoleon's *Grande Armée* and Hegel, master of German High Idealism, brings his *Phenomenology of the Spirit* to an epic close.

As battle rages, Hegel sees history coming to an end, even as he writes.

No more will the Owl of Minerva spread her wings at fall of dusk, grey on grey. Philosophy falls silent, as the universe moves towards realisation of complete self-reflection, in and through the human spirit.

Scheherazade's dark eyes flash.

Thought and being as one, encountering nothing outside of self. World Spirit, free from all objective existence, at last apprehending itself as Absolute Spirit.

The silent stars, limpid, moist, take up their stations in the sky.

We enter the Blue.

Scent of thyme and wild cumin on the air. Ruins of a Greek temple at rest, in harmony, on a hill.

All is open—pure—before us.

And now, the gentle descent; the return of the eagle to his nest. For finite existence, Princess—the here, the now—is as infinite existence, which is everywhere and always.

Of its passing, of the turning away, Martin Heidegger was later to write:

> *It was not that German Idealism collapsed; rather, the age was no longer strong enough to stand up to the greatness, breadth, and originality of that spiritual world—that is, truly to realise it.*

Softly, Scheherazade lets out a sigh.

❧

Hölderlin asks the fates for one more radiant summer, one more limpid autumn for mellow song.

Forced to become a tutor, he encounters a sympathetic lady of the house. Green ivy clings to its walls.

> *Green, too, the blissful shade along those high avenues, where often at evening we walked ... Still kindly lingering, the year departs, leaves your eyes. And, in Hesperian mildness, a winter sky pales above your garden ... The poetic, the ever-green.*

He mourns the passing of the gods; seeks to open a way for their return. Of our present age, born with the death of Christ on the cross, he sees only darkness and gloom. We are like water, hurled from rock to rock, downwards through the years towards a misty abyss.

Amber light glows through flesh; his fingers closing on a candle flame.

Yellowing pears hang waiting. Swans, dipping their bills in sombre waters. Winter approaching. Walls looming speechless and cold. In an icy wind, weathercocks clatter.

We are awaiting an epiphany, a *Helle Nacht* where, as silent lightning flashes, yonder the god—soft-stepping Apollo—completes our lives in harmony, eternal recompense, and peace.

Threads of gold, touching Scheherazade's slender throat.

❦

Art is where Goethe fuses the spiritual and the sensual.

> *I have often made poetry in her arms, and softly counted out hexameter beats on her naked back with my fingers.*

Scheherazade smiles.

> *The cosmic mission of the artist is to raise the world into the sphere of the spirit.*

The tips of her fingers curve out towards me.

He stands on classical soil, inspired and elated. On a whitewashed wall, a tiny prism of cut glass between his fingers, Goethe attempts to set free the seven-coloured princess Newton has trapped.

Germany.

Evening twilight.

Out walking in the gathering dusk he comes on a cloaked rider carrying a child.

The vision catches fire.

Who rides so late through night and wind: an anxious father and his son. The Erl King calls, *O lovely boy, come, come with me.*

I pause.

The Princess rests her slightly abstracted eyes on me.

We return to Faust, crouching in his dim study.

Thick, fat volumes spill along bending shelves. Spiders thrive, and spin their intricate webs in peace. Light grows wan as it falls through dull, dust-laden glass.

Her voice.

—All theory, my friend, is grey; but green is life's glad, golden tree.

Faust raises his pale watery-blue eyes from the close, black, angular Gothic type.

A candle flame flickers.

Mephistopheles apprehends that God alone can hold the whole entire, in a blaze of lasting light. Us he leads in chequered, shadowed ways.

Two strands intertwine. A clear-eyed classicism born under southern skies. A fevered romanticism, bred in cold and dark. From the Greeks, praise: for the world and ever-near gods. Close as breath they are.

Faust nears his end.

Then to the moment could I say: Linger. You are so fair. But time's flight is fabulous.

—As is our tale.

Water trickles faintly from the fountain.

༄༅

Franz Schubert's rejected lover trudges through the snow on his winter journey. Over fields lie tracks of fleeting deer. A black crow flaps overhead.

On the outskirts of a village he comes on an aged hurdy-gurdy man with numbed fingers, grinding away as best he can. *Stranger ... Old Man—shall I go with you.*

Trickle of water from the fountain.

Casper David Friedrich is haunted by a sense of immanence, approaching revelation.

On the barren dunes off the Baltic coast, beside a dark sea: a tiny figure—a Capuchin monk—stands alone, still, isolated, under a vast, sombre sky.

A funeral procession of monks crosses a monastery graveyard: tiny figures on the darkening snow carrying the coffin of one of their brethren. The trunks of leafless oaks stand in desolation. The ruined abbey soars beyond.

A pale moon climbs through a bank of purple clouds sending a serene light over the evening sky. Three figures —two women and a man—sit on a rock facing the sea, over which silent ships with stilled sails cross calm, gently glittering waters.

☙❧

Westward we hold our course, bound once more for England—where Luke Howard's classification of cloud formations has won Goethe's approval, as giving voice to the indeterminate.

Fishing boats are out on a cold, green, swelling sea. A moon fitfully sheds wan light. A hurricane lamp glows. Turner has painted his first canvas.

Lying on his back as skylarks outpour their joy, he sees constantly changing light reflected on passing clouds. Lashed to the mast in high seas, he opens his eyes on black, white, pale blue ... vying for possession in a whirling vortex.

He visits a Dutch harbour, towards evening. Limp sails. Hulls reflected in tones of warm amber on the calm waters, where a gull comes to rest on outspread wings ... Off Gibraltar, a setting sun casts a watery orange glow between black ships while, on the wind, an oystercatcher takes wing.

Pale opal visions of rivers and estuaries washed in ochre, touched by scarlet. In a diaphanous haze, traces of blue melt to a pearl horizon. Norham Castle emerges as a patch of blue in the morning light. Faint hints of yellow, pale blue, stain the delicate mists.

A watery sun of weak gold touches the horizon as a steamer sheds a long ribbon of black smoke approaching Staffa, a storm coming on ... On the Great Western railway, a speeding train burns and hisses through streaming veils of blue and gold ...

At Petworth, white dissolves a room; renders vague a mirror, approaching figures ... A sense of sadness lingers over the park. Lord Egremont, returning to the terrace where he has been sitting, is greeted by his dogs. A late golden splendour lights the sky. Deer, their long shadows falling, gently graze or lie at rest.

Memories of Italy swim before his eyes. A sun, flooding sea and sky in blinding light. His dearest wish as he lies dying: *to see the sun, once more, rise above the water*. He wrote—*the sun is God*.

XI

Light silently enters and retreats along the ochre walls of my cell. As Proust knew, the land we long to occupy holds a far larger place in our lives than wherever we happen to be. Subtle, iridescent colours, melting rainbows, fragments of texts, pale trembling shadows turning in silent, secret harmonies. Till the key rattles in its iron lock and I see the flickering torch in Yusef's dark hand, his quiet smile.

I have been summoned. The tale will go on. I rise and follow my silent guide.

Scheherazade reclines on her juniper couch. Tonight she wears a pale blue-grey watered silk, an amber ring on a slender finger. Beyond, the stars burn in an indigo sky. But now the apartment is lit by lamps—soft globes of silvery light that shine, softer still, on the dark mirrors.

She greets me with a smile.

I feel the warmth of Yusef's torch leave my side.

We are alone.

Her dark eyes shine.

She seems eager to return, post-haste, to France.

For Stendhal, the novel is a mirror travelling along a highway, at times reflecting an azure sky, at times the mire round puddles. Its chief charm: to induce reverie.

He avoids the dull dross of politics—*a pistol shot in the middle of Mozart*. His natural bent: *to live with two candles and a writing table in a room facing south, on the fifth storey of a Paris apartment*.

Like his handsome heroes, Julien and Fabrice, he is a lover of solitude, secluded heights, tender reveries. For Schopenhauer, who patiently awaits us, one effect of the beautiful is to calm the will. But for Stendhal, the promise is happiness.

He finds the pink tones on Van Dyck's *Eve* challenge the vocabulary available. Wonders if we can conceive of a shade of blue for which we do not have a name. He likes intelligent, well-bred, frivolous people—for whom he writes. His happy few.

Heartfelt feelings surface in a late letter: *I have two dogs to whom I am tenderly devoted. I was being saddened by having nothing to love.*

Ingres enters the drawing rooms of the *hautes Parisiennes*.

Encounters the voluptuous languor of Madame de Senonnes, attired in a low-cut burgundy velvet dress, rings on five of her fingers. At the edge of her mirror, the artist slips his calling card.

Introduces us to the melancholy Madame Marcotte de Sainte-Marie—one finger held in her volume of Pascal, she gazes out with sorrowful eyes. And, some years further on, to the pensive Comtesse d'Haussonville, her finger delicately touching her chin. She wears a blue-grey satin dress that complements her dream-filled eyes.

He conjures an Orient seen through Western eyes:

An exquisite beauty, a languidly-held peacock fan gently brushing her pale thigh; dark, enigmatically retreating eyes. A bluish-grey glazed vase softly shimmering over a scene of sequestered, sensual splendour where women relax, perfume each other, partake of sweet coffee or cooling ices; talk, caress, stretch languid limbs—all to an accompaniment on mandolin. They take their pleasure in an atmosphere free of men.

—Often agreeable, observes Scheherazade.

Delacroix walks along the beach at Dieppe. He notices that ripples made in the wet sand mirror the wavelets that have passed over them. Leaves for Algiers and Morocco, there to discover dignity and repose and, unlike the world of antiquity into which he also ventures, finds it still palpitatingly alive.

—An intenser light, she concludes.

An intenser light, inspiring elusive hues that seem to float. A shimmering haze. Vivid enchantment. Every reflection contains green. At the edge of every shadow hovers violet.

༄༅

Moonlight bathes the Queen's gardens, which overlook the sea. We enter Berlioz's opera.

Dido and Aeneas sing a rapturous duet to words once spoken by Jessica and Lorenzo, on just such a night, in a Venetian garden.

Her voice.

—Till Mercury, in solemn tones, adumbrates Aeneas' fate: *Italie!*

We follow that call to reach Recanati where Giacomo Leopardi, ensconced in his father's extensive library, looks up from his books. Black specks swim before his eyes.

He takes a meditative moonlit walk; passes a young girl who bounces a pallid green ball and smiles faintly at him. Lingers, looks up at an open window—an inviting, lit interior—before returning to his silent, darkened house.

Let us keep our lamp alight.

Cardinal Borromeo speaks to the vacillating Don Abbondio in Manzoni's novel, *I Promessi Sposi*.

Let us offer our hearts, wretched and empty as they are, to God, that he may be pleased to fill them with that charity which amends the past and ensures the future, giving of that virtue, of which we so much stand in need.

Hawthorne's sculptor, Kenyon, descends to Rome, gazing at the Colosseum, which is lit by moonlight—a nightly assemblage of melancholy ghosts looking down from tiers of broken arches.

Pius IX declares the dogma of the Immaculate Conception of the Blessed Virgin to be an article of faith. Neptune swings into view. The wedding guests at Lammermoor fall back as Lucia descends the sweeping stair to the candlelit hall—Donizetti's opera will later be seen in Rouen by an excited, sexually aroused, Emma Bovary.

We hold our course Westwards.

A drizzly November in Manhattan gives way to a dark December in New Bedford.

Herman Melville's narrator finds himself pausing before coffin warehouses and bringing up the rear of funerals. He signs on to a whaling expedition.

Casts off.

Jollity comes from the fo'c'sle, sombre and silent the stern. In the captain's cabin—dark Ahab. Dark as his ship. Seafaring: a noble craft, but somehow, most melancholy. All noble things are touched by that.

Under the stars the sea gently rolls. A thoughtful sailor climbs aloft to an upper yard. The binnacle lamp glows.

—Binnacle, inquires Scheherazade.

Close to the helm, a box to hold the compass and its lamp.

She nods.

Now Ahab takes down his charts, paces the quarter-deck. All round, as far as eye can see: the ocean. A trackless waste of water.

Melville reaches Chapter 85 just after 1.15pm on the afternoon of December 16th, 1850. His learning is part experience, part research, part sheer high spirits. It tends constantly to the scholarship of the imagination—the only kind, after all, at home in a work of fiction.

Scheherazade, slightly raising an eyebrow, smiles.

Becalmed in the South Atlantic. Enchantments creep over the waters, fall on the crew. Days pass. Trance to trance. Faint loomings appear on the far horizon. But who can say where blue ends and violet begins.

On a morning drenched in blue, the *Pequod* enters the Pacific, that mysterious, divine zone, the tide-beating heart of Earth. Here the great white whale, Moby Dick, in mighty mildness of repose, glides through the deep in a gentle joyousness ...

༺๛༻

Emily Dickinson, in her quiet room in Amherst, spends sequestered afternoons; the dusk comes early in.

> *My Hair is bold, like the Chestnut Bur—and my eyes, like the Sherry in the Glass that the guest leaves.*
>
> *Friday I tasted life. It was a vast morsel. A circus passed the house—still I feel the red in my mind.*

A winter's afternoon:

> *Enclosed in my gently swaying carriage*
> *as the steeples swam in amethyst —*
> *I first surmised the Horses' Heads*
> *were towards Eternity —*

Scheherazade's dark eyes rest on me.

Henry Thoreau sits in his boat at twilight playing his flute in the middle of Walden Pond, watching the perch, the moon, travel through water ... John Audubon completes his watercolour series, *Birds of America*. German sparrows, notably fierce, are imported as a defence against the ravages of caterpillars on crops.

Charles Darwin sails as naturalist on board HMS Beagle, bound on a surveying expedition to South America. Gold is discovered in California. Uruguay boldly declares war on Argentina—Simon Bolivar appearing, to much clapping and waving of fans, to valse, then vanish from the scene; and again valse, and work again.

We cross the Atlantic to disembark in London, where we witness a huge crowd of spectators gathered by Westminster, where the Houses of Parliament are ablaze. When flames burst through the roof, the people become so exhilarated that they break into applause.

—Such is their enthusiasm to be governed, observes Scheherazade with a wry smile.

I incline my head.

And resume.

Shall we accept an invitation issued by Thomas Love Peacock to visit his congenial fictional world.

In the extremely pleasant and agreeable surroundings of an English country house and its surrounding park he assembles his characters; then sends them out on excursions to picturesque views and ruins. From whence they return refreshed, to regale the company and convivially argue on issues of the day—and higher matters—over claret and port. As the urbane Reverend Doctor Folliott observes, through a brimming wineglass you see both darkly and brightly.

※

We travel North.

A snow-swirling night. Catherine's blood runs down a broken pane at Wuthering Heights.

Emily Brontë roams the Yorkshire moors.

At liberty.

A West wind blowing. Great swells of long grass, undulating in waves.

Wild with joy and passion she dares the final leap of the spirit. Till—heartrending—the soul begins to feel the flesh; the flesh, the chain.

Now, as stars begin to fire the dark mirror, we cross the grey North Sea.

An oystercatcher shrieks over Amalienborg Palace.

Søren Kierkegaard finds he enjoys reading fairy tales rather more than he does Hegel. Prefers to be a thinker who is like a bird, flitting from twig to twig.

He lights a tall white candle in his damp apartment.

Opens his New Testament at Luke:

> *He made as though He would have gone further. But they constrained Him, saying, abide with us, for it is towards evening, and the day is far spent. And He went in to tarry with them.*

Clatter of horses' hooves. A coach rumbles past.

> *Abide with me.*

This lingering: for us a need. For Jesus, patient suffering. Contemplatively, Kierkegaard writes,

> *After my death, no one will find among my papers (this is my consolation) the least intimation about what really filled my life.*

☙❧

Cigar smoke slowly swirls around a room in Berlin.

Anderssen quietly moves his white queen's rook along the back row, thus setting in motion, after queen and rook sacrifice, mate in three moves: the Evergreen.

Karl Marx has studied gold.

> *The less you buy books, show up at the dance hall, drink at the Green Huntsman, the more you save; the greater becomes your treasure, which neither moth nor dust can devour: your capital.*

Arthur Schopenhauer strokes his cat.

He offers only two alternatives to escape the strident tyranny of the will: asceticism or art.

> *We live in a constant fever, never attaining that blessed state prized by Epicurus as the highest good, closest to the gods, but scurry, caught between desire and boredom, knowing we cannot reach where the clouds touch the horizon.*

Woyzeck, a downtrodden soldier, proceeds to shave the Captain, opening Georg Buchner's revolutionary play.

> *Our kind is miserable in this world, Captain, sir. And in the next, I think, if we ever got to heaven we'd have to help with the thunder.*

By the edge of a slumbering forest, rime glitters in the moonlight. A tinkling of iron hoofs falls on the frozen ground.

Germany.

A winter's tale. Heinrich Heine's distant land.

> *When I think of you I almost weep ... a twilight feeling comes over me. I seem to hear from far, soft and low, a mellow horn; see a silent, darkened hall, where a silken banner—black, red and gold—hangs motionless.*

Stars on the dark mirror tremble.

Scheherazade shifts on her couch; leans forward and, extending a graceful hand, gestures to indicate that she will take up the tale. She does so softly.

—We tiptoe towards the magic realm.

As a white mouse tweaks her aristocratic whiskers, let us gently open the door.

The brothers Grimm listen intently to an old woman crouched by a juniper-scented fire. As the twelve strokes of midnight desultorily ring out, twelve slender, light-footed princesses steal forth and trippingly descend a winding, darkening stair.

It is a mild, still evening. A blood-red sun sinks silently through darkening firs. Hans Andersen wrings his fingers after removing a sizzling apple from the stove.

A little match-girl huddles against a doorway, snowflakes whirling down on her thin dress ... A vain, wicked queen is screaming, screaming: made to dance and dance in red-hot iron shoes—till she drops.

Kay encounters the tantalizingly beautiful Snow Queen, is taken in her lamp-lit sledge to the far North —the hyperborean realm—to her glistening, icy Palace, there to play in a vast, chill hall with myriad pieces of flat blocks of ice.

A pensive princess, golden hair gleaming in the sun, ties a green spotted scarf round her head and becomes, for a time, a goose girl; a poor princess tosses all night long on her feather bed on account of a tiny green pea placed beneath fifteen mattresses; a pale princess casts down her soft eyes—the loveliest—upon the rim of the world. She waits in trepidation as a milk-white unicorn with a mild blue eye slowly approaches.

Scheherazade lies back; turns her amber ring.

〜

Our tale runs East. We enter the cold seas of the Baltic. Pass lands that once rang—and will again—to Teutonic rule, travelling down the waters of the Neva to arrive at glistening Saint Petersburg.

Along the deserted Nevsky Prospect the pale buildings slumber. The bronze Tsar reins in his horse on a vista of wide squares and spacious avenues. The pinnacle of the Admiralty glints in the twilight as, in his room, without a lamp, Pushkin writes.

The bells of Saint Peter and Saint Paul chime; chime like breaking crystal. On the Neva the sun dances on bluish blocks of breaking ice, flashes over the glass of the Winter Palace, turning it to liquid gold. Pushkin writes.

Frost-dust melting on his collar, our hero, Eugene Onegin, arrives at the ball. Greetings and laughter as corks fly skyward. Outside, patient horses nod their heads. The twin lamps of the coupés shed pale rainbows on the Saint Petersburg snow.

We withdraw to the country. Gently hissing, the evening samovar sits. Tatiana stands at the dark window, pensively tracing with a meditative finger upon the bemisted glass the tender sign, the cherished monogram: an O and an E.

An affront. At dawn, as a yellow bunting quietly jingles, two duellists stand in a forest glade, their pistols—catching the sun's first rays—faintly glimmering.

Her voice is low.

—How Russian writers staked everything on the turn of a card, the roll of an ivory ball.

Onegin is first gently to raise his pistol. Lenski falls ... as his creator, too, will fall, fatally wounded, in the duel he will fight over a notorious flirt.

Eugene travels abroad. Tatiana visits his deserted home. Finds a cue stick reposing by the green baize table, an abandoned riding crop lying where it has been tossed on a rumpled sofa. Entering his silent study she runs a finger along his desk, sees its extinguished lamp, takes down and turns the pages of his books—dim and enigmatic. Some bear the trenchant mark of his nail, the dashes of his pencil.

On his return to Saint Petersburg they meet at a dull reception. Is this radiant beauty the woman he once spurned. He pours out his heart in a passionate letter. There is no answer. He drives unbidden to her door. As in a fairy tale, door upon door flies open—and there she is—alone, unadorned, and reading his letter.

Eugene falls at her feet. Pensive, Tatiana regards him. She speaks: *Happiness has been* (with a little gasp) *so near. I married. You must leave. I love you ... but I'm given to another.*

Tatiana leaves the room. Onegin stands alone. The clink of the husband's spurs is heard. Upon which note Pushkin abandons his hero for ever.

—Aaah ... breathes Scheherazade.

Haunted by hallucinations, Nikolai Gogol walks crabwise —his back to the wall—down Saint Petersburg's wide streets.

We encounter a certain lieutenant from Ryazen, trying on his gleaming boots by candlelight in the depths of a star-dusted night ... the ghost of Akaky Akakievich hunting through the dissolving mists of Saint Petersburg for his lost overcoat ... Chichikov clutching lists of dead souls to his heaving chest.

Now his troika is racing, racing, towards a distant, dissolving horizon. Mileposts sail past. Merchants cling to their hats. In a pearly haze, birch groves loom ... and fall back.

Rus! Rus! Rus! A tender voice is calling. *Rus! Rus!* The wind rips it away. *Rus!*

O troika, winged troika, you have wings, wings, wings ... Horses, horses, what horses—hoofs that hardly seem to touch the ground as you thunder past. *Rus!* Where are you racing so ... Bells trill as in a dream ... Roaring air drives into your eyes ...

XII

Alone in my cell my reveries return me to Wiltshire. Still, hushed, late November days. The last burnt yellow beech leaves hardly stir. Long, slanting, pale gold threads cause a faint gleam. Tranquil drift of blue wood-smoke, the incense of nostalgia. Soft failing light. Beat of wings. A flight of greylag geese, straggling out in a long V, one a little behind. Pale grey clouds sink earthwards. A low mist, like spilt milk, curls along the Kennet. A sedge warbler quietly wheets from the reeds.

The key grates in its iron lock.

The tale goes on.

Tonight, Scheherazade wears a sea-green silk flecked with gold. She holds out long slender fingers. I touch them with my lips.

She smiles and inclines her head.

The night is dusted with stars. Lamps shine—now they are golden globes of light. Shadows besiege the outer edges of the apartment. Glasses of green peppermint gleam upon the worked brass tray set on a wooden stand before us.

We return to France, where Flaubert has set out his ideal: to live like a bourgeois but think like a demigod.

He is tempted. Torn between the life of an urbane Jesuit perusing his breviary, and smooth perfumed flesh.

Boredom—that silent spider—spins her web in a dark corner of Emma Bovary's heart. She has a rendezvous at Rouen cathedral where, before Monet, Flaubert has noticed how slanting light makes the grey stone glitter.

His style came slowly.

> *I would rather die like a dog than hurry any sentence of mine. The greatest events of my life have been a few thoughts ... reading ... certain sunsets.*

He dreams of a book, one which would have almost no subject, would be pure form, pure style.

> *What seems beautiful to me, what I want to write, is a book about nothing. A book dependent on nothing external, held together by the strength of its style.*

His castle of pure form recedes before us.

On rue Dauphine, Baudelaire is passed by a slender, fugitive figure ... dark blue eyes that promise enduring tenderness. Slipping away, never to be seen again ...

> *You whom I could have loved; who saw me as a lover ...*

Returning, an ancient clock wheezes out the hours.

On the chintz-covered table the handsome Knave of Hearts and the sinister Queen of Spades review their defunct amours while a black cat—lover of silence; sphinx intent on empty distances—blinks. In her eyes, flakes of gold finer, more glittering than sand, shimmer like evanescent stars.

Dusk falls.

Lamps along the boulevards flare.

His ideal is the dandy, dressed in sombre black; a touch of colour, maybe, at the cuff.

A disinterestedness, in life and action. Heroism in an age of tinsel. A last radiant beam of human pride, before the onset of night.

By the fire, his amber dreams ... images ... A longing to depart. Raise tent. Set sail. Enter a pure, unalloyed blue.

There, where all is Beauty, Joy, Tranquility.

But always, after absinthe—the green fairy—forced back.

Scheherazade, lightly touching her peppermint.

Paris changes, but in my melancholy, nothing moves ...

A peacock screams.

Verlaine conjures a pale moonlight where birds dream in the trees. Enters through a gate, leading to an old deserted park, where two figures pass, recalling days of long ago:

Do you remember our ecstasy ...

To Rimbaud: that rarest thing, a young master.

White on Black. Above. Below.

A cold dark pool where a wan moon lies and a child squats, full of sorrow, launching a boat frail as a May butterfly.

Faint tinklings.

In the dying days of the Tokugawa era, in the old quarter of Osaka—the floating world—a geisha, wearing a magnificent scarlet obi of old brocade, opens her fan and begins to dance.

Poets praise her.

She is lighter than a dragonfly, a rainbow. She moves like morning mist through sunlight, like the waving shadow of a willow-branch, reflected in the river ...

※

We cross the Pacific.

The final track is being laid down at Promontory Point in Utah, linking Union Pacific and Central Railroads. Over Chicago, the first skyscrapers will soon be roaring into the blue.

Light glimmers through muslin curtains in Baton Rouge as a young girl turns to her smiling maid:

> *Oh lace me up tight*
> *I've a big date tonight.*

Charles Peirce puts forward an All-American philosophy: Pragmatism—*Truth is what you can do with your statements.* Or simply, when examining each idea ask, *What is its cash value.*

The first printing of Charles Darwin's book, *On the Origin of Species,* sells out in days. Léon Foucault successfully measures the speed of light as it passes through water and, while blue dusk descends over the Mediterranean, ivory balls begin to roll and click in the casino at Monte Carlo.

Paris.

A young dandy clad in grey passes an elegant woman crossing the Pont de l'Europe, exquisite behind her flecked veil. He appears to address a brief remark to her.

Under the protective gaze of her governess, a little girl wearing a dark blue cloak enters the Luxembourg Gardens holding her wooden hoop and stick.

Men turned out in black, like stuffed beetles, escort ladies shimmering in satin and silk through the scented air. Ladies, on whose flesh glittering diamonds cool; who hold, by the tips of their long, gloved fingers, trailing, rustling dresses and bear, on their coiffured hair, gently nodding aigrettes. Languorously—bored but alert—they mount cascading flights of stairs to pass, resplendent, before the long mirrors that acknowledge their glory, to take their place at the Opera.

The Blue Danube waltz sweeps Vienna, where psychoanalysis will soon take its first tentative steps.

The Orient Express glides out of Paris.

—All quite dashing.

Indeed, Princess.

In Rome, Leo XIII opens the Vatican archives and library to scholars. They begin to turn over crackling parchment pages, releasing clouds of greyish dust, to reveal—it is not certain—gold. Stonemasons at Cologne cathedral, who seem to act through a constant grey dust in an eternal golden realm, see their work, begun in 1248, completed.

And, in Prussia, Von Moltke, chief of the General Staff, envisages the need for orders, rather than detailed instructions, on the vast battlefronts of the future.

Saint Petersburg looms through the mist.

The former engineer, Lieutenant Dostoyevsky, convicted for participating in certain criminal plans, is brought out at first light before a firing squad. As he waits—not yet knowing of his reprieve—he gazes intensely at a golden spire that catches the first rays of the sun.

A pale lilac, fading from the sky. Stars softly wink. Turgenev's sympathetic hunter comes on a group of peasant boys near a faintly gleaming river. He settles down for the night and listens to their talk of water fairies and wood demons, whispered by firelight.

Freed from the prison camp—the House of the Dead—Dostoyevsky resumes writing.

A dark and stifling night in Seville. The Grand Inquisitor lowers his lantern and addresses his prisoner.

> *I will burn you for appearing among us, to hinder us, for if anyone deserved our fire, it is you.*

The prisoner approaches the old man and softly kisses his bloodless lips.

Stars gleam on the dark mirror.

The prisoner has gone.

But that kiss still burns—on the old man's lips; in his heart ...

Splash of water, rising from the garden.

Steam escaping along the station platform.

Vronsky encounters Anna Karenina. Her bright grey eyes seem dark, framed by their black lashes. Tolstoy's heroine enters the pages of supreme fiction.

While staying at a neglected old Italian palazzo, Anna and Vronsky visit an artist's studio and admire a painting of two boys fishing by the shade of a willow. The younger, his fair tousled hair in his hands, gazes with dreamy blue eyes at the dappled water.

Days. Skies. Blue ... grey ... passing ...

Anna, alone in her carriage, looks out on the animated Saint Petersburg scene. Murmurs, *The zest is gone.*

Gathers herself, as the train approaches, to throw herself under the wheels of an oncoming truck. The candle, which had witnessed all her anxieties, her sense of deception, her grief, flares for a moment; lights for her all that had been dark. Begins to flicker. And goes out for ever.

Scheherazade's eyes gaze through me.

☙❧

An amethyst ring is faintly reflected on Dietrich of Freiberg's dissertation, *On the Rainbow*. John Henry Newman has been received into the Catholic church: *Out of the shadows, into realities.*

Beyond the Catholic Church, all things tend to atheism.

> *Thou alone, my dear Lord, art the food for eternity and thou alone. To see Thee, to gaze on Thee, to contemplate Thee; this alone is inexhaustible. In Thy presence are torrents of delight, which whoso tastes will never let go. Thou indeed art unchangeable, yet in Thee there are always more glorious depths. We shall ever be beginning.*

James Joyce will come to regard his prose as the most felicitous in English.

Her voice interrupts softly,

> —Though ... Newman wished the Arabian Nights were true, did he not ... His imagination ran on unknown influences; on magic powers and talismans.

Robert Browning, rummaging through an oddments stall in the Piazza San Lorenzo, comes on a faded volume that tells of an old murder trial. Eight years later, the story is re-told: *The Ring and the Book*.

His Bishop Blougram pours out a glass of claret for his guest. Browning's cleric muses on the dangerous edge of things, and confesses to doubt. Another of his bishops, one from the Renaissance, decides to have depicted on the bas-relief of his tomb both the Saviour, preaching his Sermon on the Mount, and Pan, eager to divest a nymph of her garment.

The Princess looks pensive.

All on a golden afternoon—though it may have been overcast—comes the gentle drip of water running from a suspended oar as a boat drifts down river.

Alice, moving under tranquil skies …

Takes tea with the March Hare and the Hatter, where it always seems to be six o'clock in the afternoon. Encounters Humpty Dumpty, master of words: *There's glory for you!* And, at the last, the mild blue eyes and kindly smile of the White Knight. Lewis Carroll.

Scheherazade smiles.

Low in the sky lovely blue Vega burns. And still blue: the approaching shadow: Impressionism.

❧

This earth as paradise is what Renoir paints. A Sunday afternoon in Montmartre. Sunlight dancing over young couples under the trees—hardly a trace of black. Even the men's jackets, like the shadows, belong to blue.

We approach the less lighthearted Manet, who shows couples physically near, yet emotionally distant. A dark-haired, pensive girl leans on an alder-green iron rail that echoes the slender silk band round her throat. A silk-hatted gentleman clutching his cane admires a frisky young lady clad in a white, transparent slip.

In Venice he passes palazzos where washing hangs from windows, catching the light. Sun-tanned children on crumbling steps, their faces smeared by watermelon. As the light fades, ash grey falls on facades, faces. A violet shadow which, just before his death, begins to appear.

Standing sadly at the bar of the Folies Bergère in her dark blue dress, a barmaid, her distracted eyes lowered and slightly to one side, rests her palms on the edge of a long, marble counter displaying bottles of beer, champagne, and one of *crème de menthe,* this last playfully reflected in the green boots of the trapeze artist who appears in the far corner of the mirror behind. She looks out, without hope, waiting to serve.

On a summer's day, Berthe Morisot takes us to the Bois de Boulogne, where two elegantly dressed ladies are out on the lake. While one leans on the edge of the boat looking at the ducks, the other, her folded blue parasol on her knee, seems lost in her own quiet thoughts.

Dégas is creating his magically beautiful world, bewitching the truth.

On a Normandy beach, a young girl in a black and white striped blouse rests under the green shade of a parasol. Her hair is being combed out by her maid. After they have gone, and as the sun casts its last rays on the water, three young peasant girls shed their clothes and join hands in an ecstatic dance by the edge of the sea.

Back in Paris, darker notes.

At a bar table a hunched man sucks on his pipe. His dowdy companion seems absorbed by maudlin thoughts; a glass of cloudy, green absinthe waits before her.

Scheherazade runs a long finger round the rim of her glass.

A bare-armed laundry girl presses down on an iron; her companion, one hand resting on a bottle, yawns. As they wait, a young dancer in ballet costume bends over, massaging her ankle while her anxious mother leans forward, dangling the tip of her black umbrella on the parquet floor.

At the café-concerts he notices, reflected in mirrors, the varying degrees of opal tones from lit globes. How rouged flesh is further coloured by harsh stage lighting.

Queens are made of distance and dyed flesh.

He enjoys accompanying his lady friends on their lengthy visits to the milliners. The first faint, assured, smile to the mirror, a slight nervous touching of the hair, the questioning, graceful turn of the head.

Once, as he attends a fashionable dressmaker in the company of Mme Strauss, she notices his close attention during a fitting and inquires what could possibly interest him. Dégas gravely replies: *The red hands of the little assistant who holds the pins.*

He considers writing an essay on women: *their way, during the course of a day, of comparing a thousand visible details that pass men by.*

—A fine observation, she interjects.

Becomes absorbed in a series on women at their toilet: sponging a back, emerging from a zinc bath, bending almost horizontally to pick up a towel, drying round the nape of the neck with solicitous care.

He lays plans for a series in black aquatint. On mourning: black veils floating over faces, stiff black gloves being pulled on, black carriages gathering. On smoke: billowing from trains, puffing out from barges on the Seine, grey-blue threads from cigarettes; a cigar's more expansive flow ...

—And always, the ballet.

A dancer holding the sole of her foot evokes a memory.

When asked why he returns to the ballet so often, Dégas replies that it is all that is left to us of the movement of the Greeks. At rehearsal in the practise rooms, dancers are caught stretching, yawning, scratching, working at the barre, adjusting tights, tying a slipper, resting—their feet spread apart.

He enhances the gossamer lightness of their tulle skirts with pale yellow, dark green, sky blue sashes; winds a black riband round their swan necks.

Their grace, poise; their compact inward gestures; rising, reaching, backing on tiptoe with outstretched arms ... all seen in the dusk, the gas-lit, perfumed atmosphere.

Her voice, a shade triste.

—Till ...

Till it seems that everything is ageing in me. My dancers have sewn this heart of mine in a pink satin bag; a slightly faded pink, like one of their ballet shoes.

In his dusty studio he models dancers out of wax. As he moves their slender figures to catch the light, they perform a silent ballet for their master.

—Such a beautiful scene, exclaims Scheherazade.

I sip a little peppermint.

—What ideal ballet did he create, for himself, alone.

Scent of lemon and laurel hanging in the air.

❦

Brooding dark chords.

An overcast, humid evening in Madrid. Philip II, alone in his study, sits at his desk surrounded by state papers, petitions, reports from the Indies. His saddened eyes drop their gaze on low, burning candles. Then—the Grand Inquisitor is announced. Giuseppe Verdi's unique scene for two bass voices.

Sunset lingers on the panes of the Garter Inn where Falstaff is staying. A letter is brought to him. An assignation at midnight has been arranged beside an old oak in Windsor Park: *Come disguised.*

As midnight faintly chimes from a nearby church tower, Falstaff counts away the strokes—but is destined not to have his sweet way after all with Dame Alice Ford. Unmasked, he bears it all bravely and calls on the company for a final chorus.

Evviva!

In Venice, Richard Wagner is dying.

From the green depths of the Rhine, the Rhinegold shimmers. Bound by inexorable wedlock vows Wotan cries: *Gods, have grief! Have grief!*

In forest depths, Siegfried begins to understand the song of the woodbird. In the dark hall of the Gibichungs, Hagen grips his spear and broods on absolute power, attained through possession of the ring.

Dawn breaks over the domain of the Grail at Monsalvat.

Parsifal.

> *With this last work I must have absolute freedom, for I have no other to send after it.*

At Monsalvat, realm of order and light, is supreme spiritual fulfilment.

Gurnemanz sings:

Time here becomes Space.

As the Good Friday music gently unfolds, Parsifal becomes aware, almost for the first time, of the flowering meadow sparkling with dew before him. Gurnemanz smiles. That is the magic: the world, as it can be—as indeed it is.

The Grail bells begin to toll, summoning us to prayer. Amfortas raises the Grail cup.

I believe in doom to those who have polluted and degraded the Earth. I believe that the true be blessed. Granted grace.

Water laps stone as Wagner dies, cradled in Cosima's arms.

To the West, a low vermilion sun touches banks of dark-grape clouds with fire.

XIII

Late afternoon in the courtyard.

A narrow band of shadow runs out from the western wall. A thread of water from the fountain glistens in the last rays of the sun. The old man, the former storyteller to the Princess Scheherazade, rests on the ground under the faintly rustling palm leaves, worn orange wooden beads loosely held between his slender, moving fingers.

We greet each other, my hand on my heart.

—Peace be with you.

And with you.

I join him beneath the undulating shade. Flashing light clings to the palm leaves above.

He begins, as is his way.

—The universe is an immense book and we are each but one letter in a work of many pages. We cannot discern the beginning. Nor the end.

This pronouncement seems to give him much pleasure.

—How goes it with your tale, your enchanted journey.

I advance through the gardens of the past, breathing their roses.

I have slipped into his mode.

He observes my pensive response.

—You are troubled, my brother.

I wonder if I shall ever depart these shores, see again a long line of wild geese stretch across a grey sky.

—Ah. Grey skies. To travel is to seek. And you travelled to our lands, where destiny waited in a moonlit square on the edge of the sands.

His black eyes shine.

—All is fleeting. All is passing. The life of man glides by like a shadow. Hangs on a single thread. It is told of a seller of perfume from Samaria who, in the market of Nablus, encountered Death looking at him curiously, that on his return home, arriving towards evening—the sky robed in dark clouds—he found Death waiting, a faint smile on his pale lips.

The worn beads held between his slender fingers hang loose, stilled.

—In the darkened house of the perfume seller, the pale gold of frankincense, the honeyed gold of myrrh, await their master.

He sighs.

—Were it written with a needle glimpsed in the corner of an eye, it would still serve as a lesson to the circumspect: corruption waits for everything save the diamond.

Scheherazade's dark eyes flash before my mind.

I inquire:

What became of the others.

—Others.

Those who entertained the Princess Scheherazade ... once their tale was told.

He did not answer directly.

—Scheherazade, she says, eyes blazing like the blades of Isfahan: if what you have to say is not more eloquent than silence, then preserve silence.

He smiles.

—They fell silent.

A shadow edges out from the western wall.

—Man's pleasure is like the noonday halt in the desert.

Together we watch the thread of glittering water rise and fall.

—Only silence is great. All else is weakness. Without stirring, we can know men's hearts. Without looking up, we can see the stars.

I see my question means little to him. Did he not say, *Freedom, that Western word.*

—As I approach the gates of death, I swear they are better than the portals of birth. A living cat may be better than a dead lion. But the grave is better than poverty.

He laughs, showing his fine teeth, and raises a slender finger towards the sky.

—If desire still holds you by a single hair, the end of all your toil will be despair. What matters where you dwell, what you are at. To go unburdened is to possess the world.

We sit on as water faintly trickles and light slips along the palm leaves, till Yusef breaks his dark reverie and slowly approaches. At which point, the former storyteller to Scheherazade raises his hand in valediction.

꩜

Silently, light advances and retreats along the ochre wall. Till …

Once more I stand before her.

Once more, the cry of the peacock, rising from the darkened garden; the faint trickle falling from the fountain. Once more, Scheherazade. Tonight she wears a dragonfly-blue and peacock-green silk. A turquoise opal glows on a slender finger. Low-lit lamps burn beneath myrtle-green glass.

Her dark eyes rest on me.

—We have travelled far, Gabriel.

My name like liquid honey on her lips.

—A thousand years ago, when Sylvester II sat in his study, five minutes were forty ounces of fine sand running through a glass.

She smiles.

—One for each of the thieves in the famed tale.

I incline my head.

—The world is a once-upon-a-time tale, is it not. It never ends. Or rather, one narrative draws to its sunset close, maybe becoming a star, an iridescent text that causes others—already formed—to quiver a little before settling into a new constellation.

And so, as the moist stars climb an indigo sky, calling the caravan drivers from their fires, the way shimmers ahead through the setting nineteenth century—the turquoise and mauve *fin-de-siècle*.

Lady Guest's translation of the tales of the *Mabinogion*—a ripple from an earlier age—circulates in polite drawing rooms. Hugo von Hofmannsthal notes the spirit of the time: the musical element. Secure in their front stalls, heavily-scented, slightly foreign ladies reveal pale, bare shoulders; incline abundant, elaborately coiffured hair, and surrender to Wagner.

As sea mists drift in over the skerries, Ernest Chausson evokes a green and gold Celtic world. A mystic forest in Brittany where Viviane, a beautiful, beguiling siren, encounters a knight who has lost his way. Coyly, she lowers her eyes, so as not to dazzle him ... Erik Satie lets clear, cool notes from the piano induce reverie, late lingering dreams ... Gabriel Fauré offers up a gentle requiem, promising peace.

Seated at the piano under the melting gaze of Marcel Proust, Reynaldo Hahn sings in his melodious voice—one of his Venetian songs, in which the beloved need not fear dust from carriage wheels.

Nicolai Rimsky-Korsakov, an ex-naval officer who has sailed around the world and wears blue-tinted glasses, brings out fairy-tale operas: *The Snow Maiden—The Legend of The Invisible City of Kitezh—The Golden Cockerel.*

A peacock screams.

—And *Scheherazade*, murmurs Scheherazade, raising an eyebrow, coy.

Acknowledging her remark, I bow.

Therein, Sinbad's ship on the capricious seas ... My own uncertain voyage ...

I hesitate.

Her eyes opaque, she makes no sign.

And so ... we approach *Swan Lake*. Tchaikovsky's *ballet blanc*.

By the lake the white swans flit, bending long arms over their feathered hair. Coming to rest—white, still, ethereal. An arabesque of ice on glass.

Odette, on tiptoe, weaves among them, raising her arms to her breast; gazing, imploring, folding her hands. Sinking down—heartbreakingly—she expires.

Scheherazade shakes her head, her long hair tumbling.

❦

We hold our course as further North we go. North, where sombre pines descend to the still waters of the fjord. A low arctic sun burns between the dark trunks where a girl in a long white dress stands listening. Couples dance on the shore beside shimmering waters. As the sun drops down, three young girls lean over a bridge. They look into the dark, flowing river.

Edvard Munch portrays his three stages of woman: a young girl stands dreamily looking out to sea; a naked woman, her legs firmly apart, stretches up her arms and smiles; a pale woman in black stands lost in yearning.

Mrs Helseth brings in the lighted lamp, shaded under its green glass.

We enter Ibsen's soft-lit rooms. Rebecca West stands by the darkening window watching John Rosmer return from his late afternoon walk. He takes the long way round, avoiding the rushing mill stream.

The lady from the sea waits—the fjord ... still ... beyond. She longs for the return of the sailor whose eyes change colour like the sea. Hedda Gabler—beautiful, intelligent, and terribly bored—gazes at the fallen yellow leaves as she plays with her late father's pistols. Two sisters confront the truth: perhaps being starved of love preserves love's power. Standing over the body of John Gabriel Borkman, the dead man they both desired, they take each other's hands.

The air is pure. Danger, near.

We feel an icy wind on our cheeks, the bright sun high overhead. Our boots crunch through snow, leaving bluish holes behind us. The peaks glisten. We have reached the land of Nietzsche.

Living dangerously. A re-evaluation of all values. Possibilities above and beyond actualities.

> *I swear in two years the whole world will be convulsed. I am sheer destiny.*

> *My ambition is to say in ten sentences what others say in a book—what others do not say in a book.*

The idea of eternal recurrence catches fire.

> *Six thousand feet beyond man and time. I shall return ... as this sun ... as a leaf ... that gliding eagle. The moment is eternal. This life is your eternal life.*

A moth flutters near the lamp.

> *One can see what came to an end with the death on the cross ...*

The Princess, attentive.

> *Happiness on earth.*

A madman lights a lantern in the bright day at noon, searching for God. Nietzsche admonishes us:

> *God is dead. But there may be caves where his shadow lingers ... And we—we must conquer his shadow too.*

The sun shines through the grape, dances in the leaves, turning the green fruit to watery gold.

He responds to the siren call from Greece. Pure. Sovereign. Eternal. A fine wire tension between the calm, clear restraint of Apollo; the extravagant, ecstatic frenzy of Dionysus.

> *I tell you, one must have chaos within to give birth to a dancing star.*

Nietzsche dances.

The man who nears his goal, dances.

The spirit of the philosopher—a good dancer. For the dance is his ideal, his art. Philosophy must be light.

Light.

> *I should only believe in a God who knew how to dance.*

For everything god-like runs on light feet.

A faint trickle rises from the fountain. The little moth flutters near the terrace.

His best readers—aristocratic radicals, like himself—read him slowly, deeply; a delicacy in their eyes, their fingers.

Together, we aeronauts of the spirit, brave birds, fly further. Where everything is blue, blue, blue ...

—Blue.

He senses a sea-change in perception: *The world has become, for us, infinite.*

—Open, declares Scheherazade.

Yes, open. The world lies open before us. No certainties—only interpretations.

All may be transcended in a realm of aesthetic illusion and play. For only as an aesthetic phenomenon is the world—and the existence of humankind—justified.

On the dark mirror the moist stars tremble.

His last serene autumn days:

> *I have never known such an autumn; every day the loveliest.*

Transparent. Glowing.

A mellow note. The true aristocrats of the spirit are not too zealous. Their creations appear in due time, and gently fall, on quiet autumn evenings, imperceptibly.

He travels South.

To Turin: *My proven place, my residenz henceforth.*

An old market woman finds the sweetest grapes for him.

> *One receives as a reward for much ennui—despair. A solitude without friends, duties, passions ... But still remain quarter hours of insight.*

He sighs. Leaving his room on Via Carlo Alberto, he witnesses a horse being beaten with a whip. He goes up to the silent, suffering animal, puts his arms round his neck and bursts into tears.

As he once said, no artist can tolerate too much reality.

Shadows invade pools of lambent light.

Raising a hand, Scheherazade touches her lip.

The little moth dances away.

My pen, poised above an A4 pad.

A blackbird settling in the apple tree.

Fading light.

The eternal flame, soaring upward, unseen so long by the gods, is visible once more. At last, the Olympics return to Greece.

—And will do so again, the Princess whispers.

༄༅

A stormy night in Genoa. Paul Valéry wrestles in his mind and decides in favour of an exploration: the act of writing poetry. André Gide sees clouds dissolve in the blue sky, melt into azure over Vincigliata. Count Ferdinand von Zeppelin builds his airship. Across the Atlantic, the first comic strip characters take their bow.

By a shaded pool, a dragonfly's wing shimmers. Cardinal Vaughan lays the foundation stone of Westminster Cathedral, raised as a proud and triumphant assertion that Catholics are ready for—and expect—the conversion of England. While walking in the grounds at Bly in the fading light of a June evening, a young governess feels her eyes drawn to a tower.

Paris.

In the Moulin Rouge Yvette, searching for an elusive flea, begins to remove her clothes. The Prince of Wales admits he plays Baccarat for high stakes. The Dreyfus affair rages.

Louis Lumière, suffering from disturbing dreams and a migraine attack, invents the cinema in one night. The Metro opens. Gustave Eiffel sees his elegant iron tower rise over the city.

—Paris, breathes Scheherazade.

On the afternoon of 16th February 1899, the enticing Mme Steinheil is admitted to President Faure's private study. An hour later his secretary, hearing loud screams from the lady, breaks in and finds his master lying in a coma, still clutching for his dishevelled companion's abundant, flowing hair.

Dusk descends as, returning late from their afternoon calls, a few lamp-lit carriages enter the exclusive Faubourg Saint-Germain. The Comtesse de Noailles turns to her friend:

> *The soul we have this evening shall never be ours again.*

Comtesse Greffulhe envisages a book that would portray a woman from high society: her feelings, her impressions. Celebrate the wild joy that sweeps over her, knowing herself beautiful. How can one live, unable to arouse an eye's caress ... Those ardent glances, among which one passes impulsively.

In the main reading room of the Bibliothèque Nationale, green-shaded lamps cast tranquil pools of lambent light. The reflection of rows of gas lamps quivers on the darkening Seine. Huysmans' hero, des Esseintes, sits alone in his silent study. After writing *Á Rebours,* its author had to choose between the barrel of a gun or the foot of the Cross. He chose. *Ad Majorem Dei Gloriam.*

From his chill rooftop garret, Villiers de L'Isle Adam sends his hero, Axel, down the stone steps of his ancestral castle, deep in the Black Forest. His blue eyes come to rest on his beloved Sara.

> *To die out is distinguished. As for living, our servants will do that for us.*

Scheherazade raises an eyebrow.

And now. Those mysterious symbols of the *fin de siècle* descending ...

Dead, forgotten queens ... dead, familiar voices ... dead, mottled leaves ...

Pale-cheeked madonnas ... pale, nodding roses ... pale, gliding swans ...

Silent, darkening lakes ... silent, still parks ... silent, burning stars.

Hegel proposes that, by sublation, an object is simultaneously cancelled and preserved. It is Mallarmé's concern not to name an object, but rather, to suggest it. That's the dream. He becomes the poet of deferment and absence, set against the vulgarity of possession and plenitude. Evokes a lady's presence by her shadow—which he seeks not to disturb.

His pen poised over the chaste, white sheet, site of every possibility, he attempts to raise a dazzling page to the power of the star-swept sky. The haunting insistence ... Everything in this world exists to end in a radiant book.

෧෴෨

We cross the cobalt strait.

From within the Jesuit Order, Gerard Manley Hopkins refashions English poetry.

Soars aloft with the heroic graces of the dapple-dawn falcon as he glides, sweeping, in the windcatching late vermilion light, on his wing. His flight is transmuted into spiritual ascent, bringing us closer to Christ: *O my chevalier!*

Her voice,

—All nature rings.

All nature rings. Aspens, dear before felled, hold the leaping sun among their leaves. Glorious, glass-blue days, when every colour glows, each shade and shadow shows. A great stormfowl by a seabeach, opening plumed, purple-of-thunder wings. Clear, fresh world, clouded, with Christ's blood suffused, with hues of sacrifice and redemption.

Holds, maintains, a delicate balance. An aesthete within the Jesuit Order, both muse and master. Not always opposed—yet in conflict through his last posting. Dangerous. Dark: *I can no more. Send my roots rain.*

Till shines God's better beauty—Grace.

He sits supervising examination papers. Senses sudden zest of summertime joys. Off with woolwoven ware! Dive into the flake-flecked pool. Laugh. Swim. Frolic in kindcold waters.

He raises Man.

Flesh fades. Leaves but ash. Yet, *this Jack, joke, poor potsherd, patch, matchwood, immortal diamond …*

Her voice,

—Is immortal diamond.

Stars, blazing in the dark mirror.

༄

At Lord's where, in the ebbing light, a spectral batsman plays to the bowling of a ghost, Francis Thompson hears a soundless, clapping host as the run-stealers flicker to and fro, to and fro …

Andrew Lang brings out his *Blue Fairy Book.*

—But fails to warn his young readers that a bluebell wood is an extremely hazardous place, admonishes Scheherazade.

Ernest Dowson finds *V* the loveliest letter in the alphabet. It can never be brought into verse often enough.

—Vaguely voguish.

Oscar Wilde collects blue china and peacock feathers. Defines an aesthetic: *to reveal art and conceal art is art's aim.* At her bidding, winged lions creep from their lairs in the Lydian hills. Pale, phantom kings pass in dim procession across a misty Scottish moor. Art can draw down the moon with a scarlet thread.

We listen. And hear,

a Blue Bird singing of beautiful and impossible things, of things that are lovely and never happen, of things that are not and should be.

He regards his masterpiece, *The Importance of Being Earnest*, as a modern drawing room comedy with cream lamp shades.

We wing our way North, passing through a limpid rainbow over Lammermuir, to arrive in Edinburgh.

That keen air, tinged by salt. An indigo twilight, starred by lamps that stand round Georgian squares, becoming blurred as silvery beads of sleet glimmer in their light.

As a boy, Robert Louis Stevenson, at that magic never-to-be-forgotten hour of winter twilight, dusk seeping in, watches, entranced—as did I, ninety years on—while the lamplighter silently raises his pole, bringing the pale globes to flickering life.

He loves lamplight, maps, creaking inn signs. Writes atmospheric tales of mystery and high adventure. A flash of blades by a candlelit shrubbery. A ship under sail, wind straining in the rigging, dark murmurings below deck; thud of waves, a running surf on an unknown shore ... Scent of wild lime and vanilla where, from his South Sea Island home, he takes tender leave, as Archie clasps Kirstie to him, their soft Scottish voices drifting away ...

We enter cooler waters, off eastern Maine.

Sarah Orne Jewett, whose pages are fragrant with wild herbs, discovers that some ink purchased from a landing store in the village—where pointed firs descend to the shore—is scented with bergamot.

The voice of the sea is seductive.

At the century's close, Kate Chopin's heroine walks slowly down the deserted shore, the gleaming waters of the gulf stretching out before her. A bird with a broken wing beats the air.

She removes her prickly bathing suit and stands naked under the sky by the edge of the whispering sea.

Wades in.

The touch of the sea is sensuous, enfolding in its hushed embrace.

She swims out.

Does not look back. Recalls a green meadow that has no beginning nor end. Faint hum of bees.

The waters rush in, fan out, over a darkening shore ...

The Princess. Triste.

Wheeling grey-white gulls merge to fluttering grey-blue pigeons.

Paris.

Dissolving clouds of blue and pearl rise to the glass roof of the Gare Saint-Lazare as trains streaked with green, rose and gold pull out.

Air and light are the most elusive elements known to Claude Monet. It is the surrounding atmosphere ... the air and light varying continually ... which gives the *motif* —his subjects—their true value. Before slender poplars, quivering and trembling, he has seven minutes till the light leaves a certain leaf. Monet pursues his fabulous prey—the play of light.

Light, held in spray, seconds before it falls. Slipping through upper branches; silently undulating on lower leaves. Flashing on water. Breaking. Forming.

Absent realities are evoked. Gentle, rippling masts stretch out towards an unseen sky. Invisible cliffs extend their dark shadows over the sea.

Moments held, suspended, in his series on the West facade of Rouen Cathedral. From an early morning misty blue shadow to afternoons flooded in shimmering drops of diamonds and sapphires that, by sunset, take on a fabric of burnt orange and blue.

Veils of lavender haze lie over the Seine near Giverny, blurring green foliage. As light advances, trees and their reflections appear, creating a greening blue opalescence. All is light, water, atmosphere, seeking—*ce que j'éprouve*—what he feels: awareness and emotion. To paint, as a bird sings.

Colours rage, burn, in Van Gogh's rooms. Blood red. Dark yellow. Nature convulses. Forms contort. Seem to split. Cypresses swirl upwards to exploding stars of gold that set the waters on fire ...

Paul Gauguin abandons his broad stockbroking desk for the South Seas.

—The charmed land. Perfumed land. Softly beating surf. Pain. Poverty.

Her voice, breaking in ...

Henri Toulouse-Lautrec becomes a *habitué* at a salon on rue des Moulins where, on quiet afternoons between customers, his accommodating lady friends in their cream chemises relax on wide, red velvet sofas.

In his Paris studio, from the tip of his brush, Seurat releases a tiny drop of blue.

A bow on the end of a kite string becomes a butterfly. By wan gaslight, a mysterious, tightly clad trombone player wearing a magician's cap plays, backed by two bowler-hatted musicians.

He passes still summers on the Normandy coast. With the tip of his brush sets down drops of colour that become sand-sea-sky. Jetties. Pale lighthouses. Distant sails. Evocations of the tranced atmosphere that lies along the channel coast. Those somnolent ports. Calm haze. Grey-blue skies. Mauve and violet dusks.

The *Salon de La Rose + Croix* is founded. Down an avenue where lilies seem to fall from clouds, descending from a bottle-green sky, comes Carlos Schwabe's pale virgin. Fernand Khnopff locks the door upon himself and paints his sister, a sphinx from another world: her inward-turned, aquamarine eyes. Gustave Moreau's bejewelled dream women—hair of floss silk, pale blue eyes, flesh chilled white as milk—seem hardly able to stand.

Scheherazade introduces a note of sadness:

—The tide is on the turn. A last lingering butterfly, a slender blue—paler now in autumn—struggles in the long grass. A low vermilion sun sinks towards a limpid green horizon. The *fin de siècle* draws towards its silent close.

A lady touches her hair in an oval mirror. Writes:

To the garden at fall of dusk. I cast a grey pebble into the dark pool. Silent ripples, till all is still and I return to the house. Stand in my room, till it is time to dress.

She turns her opal ring.

A cardinal walks alone in his garden. Deepening dusk. Beside a bed of deep red roses, he appears almost pale. Brightens by the marble statue of a pensive Hermes. Then, as the evening light fails, his robes sink back to black: to the ardent priest he was at the beginning of his vocation. So many years before.

White clouds pass across cool grey skies. Two little girls in white muslin dresses with broad black bows are playing by an almond tree, its blossom drifting to the ground. James Whistler sees warehouses along the Thames transform, become palaces, as twilight falls. Tall chimneys metamorphose into campaniles. The city seems to hang in the heavens, pierced by a golden web of light. Fairyland lies before us.

Art Nouveau. Wandering arabesques, delicate as the wings of a blue dragonfly. And fated, as the blue dragonfly, not to live long.

Aubrey Beardsley is master of the swirling black line, enclosing lakes of white space.

Charles Rennie Mackintosh ushers in its late phase. The whiplash line becomes straight. He brings to houses his *Amor Vacui*: love of a refined spareness. Designs a poster for Miss Cranston's Buchanan Street tea rooms, where ladies sit, sipping Earl Grey with extended finger; discussing, in muted tones, how nice the hot buttered scones are.

Marries one of the beautiful Macdonald sisters. She draws, in faint pencil, mysterious wan gardens where pale maidens in long dresses become entangled in briars, or muse gently, before a fading rose.

And now, as the stars fall, fade ... From Paris, *Au revoir*.

On their leek-green, cast iron stems, beneath dragonfly-wings, the Metro's lamps shed their last mother-of-pearl glow into a watery, saffron dawn.

—For centuries must draw to a close and silence come down.

Streaks of watered gold fan out, tinging the low edges of oyster-coloured clouds with incandescent fire. The twentieth century attained.

XIV

Light silently drains from the walls.

My reveries carry me to the edge of the desert.

A seductive wind blows. Paths seem to invite, open onto the sands. Realm of abstraction, dazzlement and wonder.

Long wisps of silken sand stream out like banners from the high dunes; wind hisses over the shimmering waste. Infinite distances unfold. A mysterious, far, trembling horizon, forever receding. An allurement, calling ever onward.

The desert is darkening as, over the city, amber lights fire the white walls. Air is laden with santal and cooking oils. Shadows float out, merge, in the engulfing darkness. Merchants rub a little myrrh between their fingers, make calculations. Old men waft frankincense over their silver beards. It is approaching the hour of the tale.

 —Is time.

A murmuring, sweet voice.

A soft-stepping youth has entered my dusky cell and released the magical words. I must have appeared bemused, for he smiles, wriggling his slender fingers along an invisible bar.

The Princess has sent for me. The tale will advance into the twentieth century, summoned by my nova messenger —player of the trembling flute heard rising from the dark garden.

He seems an annunciation angel, wafted from another world. Clad in a robe of fine, white linen, a fabulous embroidered bird—a brightly glittering hoopoe—nestling near his throat.

A gust of wind blows at our garments as we traverse flickering corridors, lit at intervals by bending brazier flames that straighten as we mount the low, wide stairs towards the Princess's apartments.

There Ayaz—I have learned his name—inclines his head and, with lowered eyes, takes his leave. I feel a pang as he turns and softly descends the stairs, the hushed glow from his lantern melting away ...

As I write.

Tranquil fall of light.

Blue fine-point pen, poised above an A4 pad.

Max waiting for his walk.

Time to begin ...

The twentieth century comes in on the flutings of a song thrush: frail, gaunt, and small. Thomas Hardy, who bore witness to disappointed aspirations and crushed hopes, hears her in the gathering gloom.

Low lit lamps burn beneath their cream shades, release a honey-coloured light.

Scheherazade reclines in an olive green silk, edged with nacre.

Beyond, at deep majestic intervals, the stars.

Albert Einstein announces his special theory of relativity. Energy is equivalent to mass. Light travels at the same speed, however fast you go.

Beyond our galaxy, he brings in general relativity, where gravity slows down time, warps space—and light bends. Always the democrat, he maintains that space and time are relative to where you happen to be in the cosmos.

Mount Wilson telescope is completed near Pasadena. Observations of the eclipse of the sun bear out Einstein's theory. Edwin Hubble observes distant galaxies receding into deep space …

Rutherford demonstrates that the atom is not the final building block. Max Planck formulates quantum theory. Where Einstein describes the vastness of space, Planck elucidates the effects of the infinitesimally small. Niels Bohr advances the theory of atomic structure. The atom is exploded—no indivisible, fundamental particle exists. The world of apparent substance has no absolute reality.

Sigmund Freud discovers the secret of our psychological life: the unconscious. He coins the term 'psychoanalysis.' The aim is modest—to turn common unhappiness into neurotic misery. But, by talking, the unconscious may release its secrets, a personality may heal. The movement may even bring about social change.

The human mind is irrational. Reason is not something given. It must be struggled for.

Hegel had believed that reflection and speculation constitute the life of philosophy.

Not so.

Science and Psychology, giant mice, nibble away at the Grand Design.

The Princess, inscrutable.

Zinfandel, the French favourite, is at the tapes, running in the Gold Cup at Ascot. That day in Dublin turns out to be quite fine and breezy—no less than four hours of constant sunshine. Not too bad for Ireland. A clear night following. The sands of Egypt begin to reveal hidden treasures. Tantalizing fragments from Corinna, a lyric poet who flourished in Boeotia in perhaps—it is not certain—the sixth century B C.

As she measures out tea into a glazed green pot—a sapphire bracelet slipping over her wrist—Lily Bart, Edith Wharton's splendid heroine, observes: *We are expected to be pretty and well-dressed till we drop.* But an impulsive Uruguayan visitor to Yantony's shoe shop is told in no uncertain terms that her shoes will not be ready for a further two years, at least.

Harry Gordon Selfridge creates the department store. Shopping must no longer be a chore, is to become an entertainment. No more will sales assistants clamber on steps reaching for boxes stacked on upper shelves; rather, they are to wait on customers as they inspect goods for themselves, attractively displayed around the store. And the customer is always right.

But in Paris, a woman accused of stealing two silk bodices from a department store explains: *It's so exciting, stealing. You feel wet. A climax is stronger when I've stolen ... Silk attracts me. When I feel it rustle, I have this tingling under my fingernails, then it's useless to resist—I just have to have it.*

Two poles of art—abstraction and empathy—are set out by Wilhelm Worringer. From Milan, the Futurists proclaim: *Space no longer exists.* Pavements soaked by rain open—to reveal the centre of the world.

Frank Lloyd Wright creates the Prairie House. Long, low brick walls. Gentle, sloping roofs. Quiet skylines. He calls his own home, Taliesin. Peter Behrens designs the first steel and glass building: A E G Turbine Factory, Berlin. In Vienna, Adolf Loos preaches an extreme functionalism, where ornament is almost a crime.

Roald Amundsen reaches the South Pole and plants the Norwegian flag. A tiny touch of colour in the white desolation, set there to await Captain Scott. At full steam on her maiden voyage, her lights burning on the dark waters, R M S Titanic is ripped open by an iceberg, and goes down.

☙❧

The foxtrot is all the rage.

Georg Simmel believes that once money exists, all it comes in contact with is bewitched: appraised according to its monetary value. Be it a long pearl necklace, a long funeral oration, or fast sex.

Paul Poiret frees ladies from the maddening constraints of the corset. They abandon them with glee. Among the paper and orange peel, empty champagne bottles, silver and tissue wrappings, smiling Parisian dustmen cart away pale whalebone shapes, bereft of their tender flesh.

Champagne is creaming, foaming over glasses as Franz Lehár's merry widow gracefully inclines her aigretted head. Arnold Schoenberg ends his *Gurrelieder* in an ecstatic apostrophe to the sun's streaming locks of glorious golden light—*strahlenlockenpracht!*

In Dresden, Salome loosens her seven silken veils: coral, hyacinth, sunflower-yellow, watered-emerald, midnight-blue, gold-flecked violet, black. Creamy surf rushes in over the gleaming sand on Naxos, wetting abandoned Ariadne's polished toenails. But soon, out of a hazy blue sky in Richard Strauss' opera, a white sail appears.

Take me away ...

Gerontius is granted a blinding vision that burns ere it transforms. Edward Elgar sets to music words by Cardinal Newman. At the end of the score, writes: *This is the best of me.*

The fan gently slips from view, ever so quietly wafted away. The long Edwardian summer winds towards its close. Blue smoke—that incense of nostalgia—drifts over Sussex woods ... An elegiac cello concerto mourns the passing years. A way of life—grand, imperial, expansive—dying. Never to return.

⁂

Scott Joplin's syncopated rhythms are being played, warmly appreciated in the liquor bars and sporting houses of the Midwest. In New York a woman is arrested for smoking in public. Charles Ives distils the mysterious stillness that emanates from Central Park in the dark.

All over America, teddy bears are being tucked up in bed at night. At the Ziegfeld Follies, girls show off long legs to warm applause, while along Broadway blue neon lights flash their urgent message. Wearing his bowler hat and carrying his bamboo cane, Charlie Chaplin sets off bravely to find work—and, perhaps, true romance.

Gleaming automobiles, shining in the sun, glide over Manhattan Bridge. Grand Central Terminal opens.

We sweep South to Buenos Aires where—sad, sobbing, nostalgic—the tango is being played in louche street corner bars.

I pause.

Her voice breaks in.

> —Now let us bend our steps East.

Faint tinkling of bells.

A geisha in a violet-and-white patterned kimono trips along a side street in Kyoto.

And Masaoka Shiki is the modern master of haiku:
> *A scarlet berry*
> *splatters*
> *on frost-white grass*

As suddenly as she had spoken, the Princess leans back.

Silent, her dark eyes rest on me.

༺༻

A hushed November afternoon.

Captured images.

An urn. An *allée* of trees. The water-stained cheek of a nymph.

A new art is being born.

Atget carries his heavy camera to Versailles. Deserted now, in the late fall. Stone horses lost in equine meditations silently regard him. He enters the gardens quietly and sets up his camera.

Shadows run from a fleeing Daphne, fall from a fleet-footed Diana as she brings an arrow to her bow. Dark trees, reflected in a still expanse of water ... Dead leaves strewn on the ground ... Isolated stone figures on their pedestals look out over long avenues, melting into mist, their tranquil gaze remote from the cares of humankind.

At Sceaux, as the light slips through overgrown hornbeams, illuminates wild flowers, a robed statue seems to float in the long grass: forlorn, pensive, abandoned.

In the absolute stillness and silence of his photographs of bare branches, drifting leaves, silent stone, we wait—perhaps for a god to descend that broad flight of stone steps, rising there.

Water faintly trickles.

☙❧

North we go.

By the lake, Masha, wearing black, wanders disconsolate, mourning her life.

Someone touches a guitar. There goes Yepikhodov.

Russia in amber. A distant sound seems to come from the sky; a breaking string, dying away.

Anton Chekov is the compassionate observer of a small group of landed gentry and their dependents who, in the dappled shade, drink tea from the eternal samovar in glasses clouded with raspberry.

Fog drifts in on the glimmering Neva. Buildings vaguely loom and disappear back into mist. Rippled amber lights undulate on the waters. A spire gleams, melts away. Over the vast, deserted square, the enigmatic bronze horseman holds out a green, patinated arm.

Andrei Bely conjures racing clouds, deception, the magic of space. A door flies from its hinges. A dark room is suddenly engulfed by a vast moonlit expanse. On the threshold, bathed in a green-hued light: the bronze horseman.

❧

On top of a cliff edge facing the Atlantic, John Millington Synge is lying, looking out to merging sea and sky. Shafts of sunlight break through the sea-mist, sending down soft rainbows.

On other days, on the Aran Isles, high deep blue waves break over dark, dank rocks. Leaping spray spatters his pages—wild, scented as the blackberries ripening on hedges. His plays: flavoured as a gleaming nut.

Clouds of yellow dust rise as a horseman comes riding out of shimmering sage against the golden glare of the sun. Zane Grey's lyrical Western, *Riders of the Purple Sage*.

His heroine, Jane Withersteen, cherishes two material things: the cold, sweet, amber waters; her fleet-footed racers, Night and Black Star.

As she leaves her land to start a new life she looks back one last time.

Oh, but look! Oh, look, so you will never forget!

Drifting golden veils mingle with low, purple shadows as the sun sets on the sage.

Raymond Roussel travels the world in some comfort. Devotes several pages to charting the progress of a soap bubble, but rarely leaves the cabin of his yacht to watch the passing scene. He devises a difficult rook ending to which, in the Belgian international, *L'Echiquier*, grandmaster Tartakower devotes no fewer than three separate articles.

On a luminous summer evening, as his Princess Yolande wanders along shady paths by her ancestral castle, she spies slender wisps of cloud that curl strangely in the sky, vaguely forming the potent word: *NOW*.

A low wave turns on the Lido.

Thomas Mann sends his writer—Gustave von Aschenbach, on whose face art has engraved adventures of the spirit—to Venice.

At the hotel, subdued foreign voices. A tolerant atmosphere of wide horizons. From his bedroom window, the beach ... Faintly flapping canvas. A slight haze.

Encounters Tadzio, faintly smiling in his blue English sailor suit, honey-coloured locks of hair, twilight-grey eyes. Watches as, far out, alone on a narrowing sand bar, he turns and stretches out an arm ... Pale and lovely summoner.

Scheherazade's dark eyes rest on me.

Henry James creates his house of fiction.

Newly arrived from Albany, grey-eyed Isabella Archer finds England as sweet as an October plum. But a rich expectation is dashed. What promises to be an infinite vista becomes a dark, narrow alley with a dead wall at the end.

The hapless butler, Brooksmith, is ruined for the common round of domestic duties by good talk and the beautiful growth of his powers of appreciation—a theme dear to the writer's heart. Ralph Limbert wakes to a radiant morning. The voice from the market, trash-triumphant, faint and far, in the blest country of the blue. Hugh Vereker, James' *alter ego*, gently smiles. His secret runs like a thread, a figure in the carpet, through the writing.

Settled at Lamb House in Rye, James returns in late, resplendent fiction, to favoured, much-loved, settings: Paris, Venice, London.

Against the bright intensity of Paris, Lambert Strether's mission falters. Having missed his train—its faint, receding whistle miles down the line—he turns to his young friend: *Live all you can. It's a mistake not to.*

Milly Theale, passionate pilgrim from New York—a gentle, grey-habited dove—rests on a bench in Regent's Park where she has taken herself after a visit to her specialist; who may have suggested she try the milder climes of Italy. She sits, aware. She would live, if she could.

In the gathering dusk on the terrace at Fawns, Charlotte Stant and Maggie Verver stalk each other. Meanwhile, in a soft-lit room, Adam Verver and Prince Amerigo consider their cards.

Charlotte asks,
   Is there any wrong you consider I've done you.

Maggie is ambiguous.
   I accuse you ... I accuse you of nothing.

Fine inward adjustments of sensitivities. So slight. Barely perceptible. The delicate shades and subtle nuances—in conversation, in manner—of a leisured society. Now irrevocably lost.

The trembling flute, rising from the darkened garden.

Édouard Vuillard shows a corner of a room where a figure seems to emerge out of the patterned wallpaper. Quiet interiors, where his mother and sister sit sewing. A friend reading a paper by lamplight after supper. Turn-of-the-century girls, wearing striped or spotted dresses.

The bringing in of a lighted lamp, a crease in a blouse, a patted, tea-dust-green cushion, set his eyes dreaming.

Young girls stand on the jetty at dusk, their faces reflecting that soft Midi light Pierre Bonnard so loved. His fruit soaks up the sun, leaving just the essence of its flesh on canvas.

Light slips through the slats of the shutters. A chair throws a white shadow. By tiles of iridescent yellow and sky-blue, bathed in light, his nude glows, floats, in a tub of nacre and opal.

Wassily Kandinsky, growing up in Odessa, buys his first box of oils and marvels at the colours emerging smoothly from their tubes. Jubilant—sumptuous—reflective—dreamy...

From Germany, he creates a glistening vision of a Russian fairy tale: a loving couple locked in a tender embrace on a noble white horse whose raised hoof echoes a dancer's graceful toe. Tranquilly, they ride through a landscape where birches are covered in a mesh of golden leaves that glimmer like stars, while a calmly flowing river becomes a watery mosaic of blues, greens, lilacs, gliding past shining domes and butter-scotch towers.

His most cherished memory is that magic hour, the sun already low in the sky, transforming Moscow to a reddish stain ringing with bells, running like music: pinks, yellows, whites, lilacs, blues, pistachio-green, flame-red.

To depict such moments seemed to me the greatest, scarcely attainable, happiness for any artist.

An evening in Munich, 1910. An extraordinary beauty awaits Kandinsky as he returns to his studio in the bluish dusk.

Standing the wrong way up—one of his paintings.

This revelatory moment will lead him on to pursue the mystical apprehension of the spiritual, through abstraction, to abstract painting. Colour and form liberated, in harmony. Every radiant work tranquil, giving out the quiet phrase: *I am here.*

In Sinaelsdorf, over coffee in a leafy garden, is born the Blue Rider. Franz Marc loved blue, his favourite colour. Kandinsky too. And the image of the rider. So, the name came.

Little whiffs of dust rise into the lamplight.

New heavens, new constellations, being formed, as the motes whirr and dance.

☙❧

From his darkened box at the Paris Opera, Diaghilev scrutinises his dancers through a tiny mother-of-pearl lorgnette. Brooding strings announce Koschei's enchanted garden, where the shimmering Firebird flits. Igor Stravinsky's triumphant entrée.

The *Ballets Russes* returns to Paris.

A star-dusted Saint Petersburg night. Snow whirls down softly covering the lifeless rag puppet, Petrouchka.

Paris sighs. Waits ... until ...

Suddenly, the violent Russian spring ...

Erupts—the whole earth convulsing. *The Rite of Spring.* Sweat-soaked dancers pound the stage. Greet birth. Renewal. Strengthened sun.

In the mid-day heat of the Midi, the flute of Claude Debussy rises.

Where the white and gold mists of Parsifal once drifted across the Rhine, now they are tinged blue-green in the forests of Allemonde. Melisande lets her long, honeyed hair tumble down the castle tower to brush Pelleas' lips.

At the piano his delicate notes fall, fragrant, still. Nostalgic, poignant, shot through with colour ... and light.

Watery ripples extend, disturbing reflections. A west wind weaves over wild, heathland grass. Abandoned, an ancient Egyptian city sinks back into the sands. Sails—or maybe veils—appear out of mist. Sea-green chords raise the legendary, submerged cathedral of Ys. Bells tolling, rising from the waves ...

Puck. Minstrels in top hats and tails raise a white-gloved hand, begin to dance. Leaves gently fall by the edge of a still lake. In a grey dawn, fairies flit without seeming to touch the glistening dew. An oriental terrace. Glimpses of the moon.

Ondine. A hushed, chaste dance at Delphi. A firework display, ending in falling droplets of gold and green light.

Scent of jasmine mingles with santal. Hangs in the air.

Scheherazade. Smiling.

A copper-haired woman—Klimt's vision—stands naked above a legend exalting the artist.

Many society women ask to be portrayed. Margaret Stonborough-Wittgenstein, cool and serene. Fritza von Riedler, confident and refined. Adela Bloch-Bauer, a highly strung soul, trapped in her sumptuous, encrusted dress of gold.

Down a winding spiral—the staircase of good-byes—Giacomo Balla sends his enigmatic, smiling ladies.

Downward, waving, they go, turning upward their smiling faces. We can almost hear their low, lingering, melodious—*Ciao!*

A peacock screams.

Lights burn in crystal orchids in the capitals of Art Nouveau: Paris, Brussels, Glasgow, Chicago, Munich, Vienna, Barcelona.

We advance ... to reach a Provence where red apples sing, their sheen of blue and green flowing on to the white, ruffled tablecloth.

Paul Cézanne lays out his apples, placing them carefully; weighs each in his hand.

He analyses form by colour. An exact shade to make an apple appear round. As Rilke wrote, he knew how to hide his love for each apple and lodge it in the painted fruit for ever.

He smiles.

Apples like having their portraits painted. They come with their delicate scent, speaking of fields they have left, the rain that has nourished them, the daybreaks they have seen.

He pours some red wine into a tumbler.

> *Look how the curves on this bottle change when it is placed near a round dish. The more oblique the edge of a table is, the more the bottle will seem to slant. Seem to stretch towards us.*

He coughs. Wipes his mouth with the back of his hand.

A ray of light falls on some fruit, strikes the wine.

Light cannot be captured, it must be shown, by colour.

> *When I painted my Old Woman with a Rosary, I seemed to be in a bluish, russet atmosphere. Only much later did I realise the face was russet hued, the apron bluish.*

In the late afternoon he sets out with his painting equipment strapped to his back, reaching the forest above Aix on a path strewn with slippery pine needles. It leads past the abandoned Chateau Noir.

Shadows cast by clouds tremble on the rock. *I imagined a shadow to be concave—like everyone else who fails to look. But see, it is convex. It flees its centre.*

By six, the air is limpid, deliciously scented. His favoured hour of harmony and peace. Mont Sainte-Victoire, thirsting in the sun during day, sinks back, her strength returning to earth.

In hues of blue-green, ochre, rose-violet, she rises. In all her changes: her permanence. These masses were made of fire, and fire is in them still.

His art, an attempt, an assault, towards a moment of perfect possession.

> *Whoever lacks a taste for the absolute—that is, perfection—is content with placid mediocrity.*

Yet, he remains aware:

We are makers of fragments.

His last wish, all but granted: *I want to die painting. I feel washed by all the colours under a rainbow. I dream, hazily…*

His work endures, like rock.

⁂

Winter.

We set out over fields covered by a glistening frost, on our search for a lost land, a lost love.

A grey heron rests on a wooden post before flapping away. A vast vermilion sun sinks slowly through the bare branches. We are on a quest for Alain-Fournier's lost domain.

At the end of a beech-lined avenue, the smoke-blue spires of an ancient château rise. A fête is being held. We approach. Are made welcome. Eager-eyed children. Mild old folk. A piano, being played in a distant room.

The author will fall in the coming carnage. As also, on the other side of the tangled barbed wire, the poet, Georg Trakl. Not in combat. Rather, unable to bear the suffering of the silent dead.

His sense of impending dread. Dark fear. Gold, fading from a distant cloud. A helmet, rolling from a bloodied forehead.

At evening the grain bends lower in the silent fields. A candle splutters in a bare room. Stretched out on a narrow bed, the body of a young girl. Her pale face floats through the village, drifts out over silent woods where her yellow hair waves, extends, from bare branches.

At the forest edge, blue deer nibble at peace. Lovers, their bodies yellowed by candlelight, intertwine. The hunt comes down. Trembling gaze of the stricken deer.

Stars softly go down. Blood darkens the undergrowth. A deer bleeds in a thorn thicket, quietly.

Scheherazade brushes her cheek.

Far off, the distant guns, preparing.

On a visit to Paris, Franz Marc walks among the Impressionists for the first time. Like a roe-deer in an enchanted forest.

Four young foxes sniff the air. He posts magically painted postcards to Prince Jussuf, to K.

Vermilion greetings!

Images of searing pain. Terrified animals cower among the trees, attacked by revolving and intersecting rays. Inscribed on the back of a canvas:

And all being is flaming, suffering.

Images of tenderness and peace. Blue deer emerge from woods to nibble at leaves, nestle together in unconscious grace.

An aim of modern art: to create symbols for our time but which belong to the spiritual religion of the future. *Der Geist bricht Burgen.* The spirit breaks down castle walls.

His last painting. A forest glade. An alert blue deer on watch. At rest, a russet-red female looks at her young fawn, who returns her gaze.

In the gathering dusk, his pure vision ... receding ... vanishing ...

Pain grips my heart.

BEING BURNED OUT OF HIM.

Scheherazade's dark eyes flash.

August 1914. Marc volunteers. Kandinsky visits to say *Auf Wiedersehen*. But Marc replies, *Adieu. I know we shall not see each other again.*

Shortly before his death, a victim at Verdun, he wrote: *The world lies pure before us. Our steps tremble.*

XV

The night is dark.

Scheherazade wears an indigo blue silk.

We have arrived at the month of August, 1914.

Gardeners with long rakes slowly advance, tending to the gently winding gravel drive. Fiona runs slender fingers through half-falling ash-blonde hair. The sky is an incandescent blue.

Down by the glittering river an archery match is in progress on the long meadow. A boy wearing a chocolate-coloured jacket, yellow edged, narrowly watches the flitting arrows.

Amber-coloured tea becomes clouded. Tinkle of bone china. By the late afternoon, the yew-tree shade, quite blue. Quiet voices. Some talk of Germany, the Balkans. Across the meadow, a red butterfly pursues a blue.

There will be no war, the young man studying at Freiburg asserts, laughing, showing his fine teeth, his flaxen hair forming a blonde aureole against the sun.

An evening haze descends. Mist rises in layers on the far meadow. A speckled trout breaks water. Melting voices ebb away in the fading light. White dresses glimmer in the dusk.

From his Paris apartment, a pensive Marcel Proust gazes at the sky. How slowly the day dies on these interminable summer evenings.

As a glorious harvest draws to a close, the corn in, doomed young men forgather before the searing dawn.

❦

World War I

Mons. Tannenberg. First battle of Ypres.

August Macke has completed his last lyrical painting. In the games of children, on the hat of a coquette, invisible ideas gently assume material form. Girls in inky blue, white, wine-coloured dresses saunter beneath beautiful dark green trees. Following Macke's death in action, Franz Marc paid him this tribute:

> *With the passing of his harmonies, colour in German art will pale by several degrees and take on a duller, dryer tone.*

James Joyce has already made his appearance with *Chamber Music*, a slim volume of verse, sweet to the ear. Now he brings to the light of day *Dubliners*, a collection of limpid vignettes of closely-observed life in that Georgian capital by the Liffey.

World War I

Second battle of Ypres. First battle of Isonzo. Tetanus rages in the trenches. Second battle of Isonzo. Third and fourth battles of Isonzo.

Karl Kraus opens his morning paper. Side by side on the same sheet: a fulsome account of the glittering opening of a new café in Vienna, and a harrowing account from the front:

> At six we went into battle. Barely light. In the silence, no one speaking. The guns open up. A comrade, his mouth all shot away. While being bandaged, half his tongue falls out.

Proust writes of these sad days that remind us how the years return, laden with blossom. But they cannot bring back people.

World War I

Verdun. Fifth battle of Isonzo. Somme. Sixth battle of Isonzo. Seventh battle of Isonzo. Eighth, ninth battles of Isonzo.

Franz Marc writes to his wife, Maria, from the front:

> 4th March 1916. Yes, this year I will be coming home to you and to my work. Amongst the boundless, horrific pictures of destruction, the thought of returning home has an aura which cannot be sufficiently sweetly described.

He is fatally hit by shellfire that afternoon.

Scheherazade's eyes, opaque.

A breath from the world of dark stars and deep space, reaching us.

Water faintly falling.

☙❧

Swallows fly through the sea-dusk, the darkening tenebrous blue, over the slow-flowing waters of the Liffey. Stephen Dedalus paces the streets of Dublin, not yet an exile. Returns to Saint Thomas Aquinas for another pennyworth of wisdom.

At Jutland, the British Grand Fleet and the German High Seas Fleet engage. But it ends inconclusively as Admiral Scheer slips away into the gathering dusk.

World War I.

Torrential rain. A sea of mud. Passchendaele.

A pale turquoise sky lingers over Saint Petersburg. Some *Roederer Cristal Brut* trembles in a crystal glass. The Provisional Government now meeting in the Winter Palace will not be there for long. Outside, even now, muddy feet come clambering over ornate iron gates.

Nothing will ever be the same again.

Rome.

As darkness descends, Hans Pfizner's opera *Palestrina* ends quietly, as the composer plays low, meditative notes on his chamber organ; the acclamations he has received, left far behind; the anguish and joy of creation, stilled.

His long fingers rest gently on the keys. Everything, he believes, inclines us towards the past. *There reigns in it a compassion with death.*

World War I ends.

Egon Schiele works on his last canvas, *The Family*. Himself, his wife Edith, and their longed for, but unconceived, child.

Weakened by privations of the war, they both succumb to the pandemic. As Edith lies racked with fever she manages to write: *I love you so much. My love for you is beyond all bounds, beyond all measure.*

Silently, the stars take up their stations in the sky.

Zurich.

While working out the 'wandering rocks' episode of *Ulysses*—where, in some twenty sections, Dubliners move around their capital city—James Joyce buys *Labyrinths*, a board game which he plays with his daughter, Lucia. He goes on to list seven errors of perception one might fall into, seeking a way out of the maze.

—One cannot get lost in a labyrinth, observes Scheherazade.

I incline my head.

Die Frau ohne Schatten opens with a nurse crouching on a flat roof overlooking the Imperial Gardens. The Empress casts no shadow. Light passes through her body as if she were made of glass. Ringing out from Richard Strauss' sumptuous score, a falcon cries his warning lament. The night watchmen exhort couples to love and cherish one another.

Hermann Hesse calls for an acceptance of chaos, where every idea may have its valid opposite. Hannah Hoch carefully cuts a bloated face from a Berlin newspaper. Ezra Pound observes that the sale of half-hose has long since superseded the cultivation of Pierian roses.

Walter Gropius founds the Bauhaus in Weimar, preparing the way for those who will one day bear the name of architect, Lords of Art. Those who will create gardens out of the desert raise wonders to the sky. In Russia, fired by his vision of the new society following the Revolution, Vladimir Tatlin conceives his ambitious monument to the Third International. A symbol to high aspirations and youthful ardour.

It is not built.

Visitors to an exhibition of Dadaist art in Cologne are invited to smash the paintings. Adolf Hitler, to much tankard-thumping, makes known his twenty-five point program in the Hofbräuhaus. Arnold Schoenberg announces his discovery—one that will assure the supremacy of German music for the next hundred years: serialism.

To thunderous applause, *The Three Codonas* becomes the only circus act in the world to perform a triple salto on the flying trapeze.

Her voice.

—Edna St Vincent Millay offers us a fig.

Safe upon the solid rock the ugly houses stand.
Come and see my shining palace built upon the sand!

Pens *An Ode to Silence*—a goddess long fled.

Only her shadow, once upon a stone, I saw ... I tell you, you have done her ill, you chatterers, you noisy crew!

Cries,

Flat upon your bellies ... Read me ... Do not let me die!

Max rushes in from our walk, looking for his green ball.

I pour out a glass of port.

It is quite dark outside.

༺༻

Seated at a table in the Café de la Rotonde Amedeo Modigliani draws, in the blue sketch-book he always carries, a single, supple, aristocratic line—a face.

Against a grey-blue background he portrays swan-necked women with inward-turned almond eyes, closed in anticipation of joys to come. His nudes recline, firm-breasted, wide-hipped, sensuous, aware. Carried to a haunting beauty on his pure Tuscan line.

A dark-haired beauty—smoke-grey almond eyes, smooth carmine lips—wears a thin black tie on a pearl-shaded silk blouse; gently inclines her rose and peach oval face. A vulnerable little girl in a washed-out lilac blue that mirrors her sad eyes holds her reddish hands clasped over her dress.

On an easel, as he lies dying in a freezing cold studio, stands the still-damp portrait of Varvogli—his tired drinking companion. One blank eye is turned inward; the other looks out, without hope.

Scheherazade's dark eyes, blurred.

We move to print. Ludwig Wittgenstein's *Tractatus*, written in the Austrian trenches during lulls between shellfire: *The limits of my language, the limits of my world*. A whole world of philosophy, condensed to a single sentence.

Language, seen as a city possessing an old quarter, a maze of bewildering alleys—a little like your witching city, Princess, where I became lost, not so long ago ...

Her enigmatic smile.

—Always, the difficulty, not to say more than we know. In the world, everything is as it is, and everything happens as it does. In this, no value exists. Any value that does have value must lie outside the sphere of what happens.

Indeed.

Giving up philosophy, for a time he tends vegetables in a monastery garden.

If God entered our minds, would he recognise his image; indeed, be bound by our knowledge.

Philosophy leaves the world be. What we cannot speak of, we must pass over in silence.

But now ...

Descending ...

Beating wings ...

Hovering over us gently ...

An elegiac angel, touching our lips.

Water falling through the air.   Stars cool in the dark mirror.

It is not *how* the world is, but *that* it is ... That is the mystery.

☙❧

Now ...

Raised finger on lip.

The year: 1922.

Annus Mirabilis.

Quivering radiance of noon.

Paul Valéry stands near faintly creaking pines, by shadowless graves, in the cemetery at Sète overlooking the blue Mediterranean. He raises his eyes from clear, dark thoughts, to gaze on a dazzling diamond-backed sea.

Her voice, reflective.

—Ah, what recompense after thought. A long regard.

Under grey skies, a hurrying crowd on Waterloo bridge.

Unreal city.

T S Eliot is with Lloyds Bank in the City of London. An unshaven Smyrna merchant, his pocket full of moist raisins, turns over sheets of dry bills of lading.

Rainer Maria Rilke touches a rose with the back of his finger. Living in silence, endlessly opening out into the world ... yet wrapped within.

To have only the stars resting before you, who from their vantage see everything at once. They bind nothing—rather leave everything free. Yet, in our lives, too great a weight forever overwhelms our gaze.

Animal and flower are in the world, while we stand apart. And the clever animals see that we are not very securely at home.

Boys—don't be too swift! See how rested all things are: shadow, and fall of light; blossom and book.

At the castle of his friend, Princess Marie von Thurn und Taxis, Rilke opens his *Duino Elegies*.

Who, if I cried out, would hear, from among the angelic orders.

The stars on the dark mirror tremble.

During the war, attached to an archives office in Vienna, he meticulously rules black lines across blank sheets of paper. Advances towards an inner world, on the heart's cliff, exposed—as if, within him, an angel encompassing all space were blind, and gazing out.

This he carries, secret, budding, till February 1922, when the angel—his dear angel—close as breath to him, so long contemplated, desired, waited for ... descends.

—Wings touching skin, breathes Scheherazade.

The past lies pristine before him; the present, dented. Already invisible.

On the gleaming white sheet where all may yet be possible, the little rust-coloured sails of the *Sonnets to Orpheus* appear. Swell the *Duino Elegies'* vast white canvas, released to sail, and sail forever ...

Earth, is this not your wish. To rise up in us, invisible. Is that not your dream. What, if not transfiguration, is your pressing need.

But for us ... a petal falls on the polished oval table.

We live our lives forever taking leave. Each thing, but once. Just once. Once and no more. And we, too: once, and never again. But having been once, though only once; having been once on earth—can we ever entirely be forgotten ...

   —Only within is near. All else is far, murmurs Scheherazade.

On his tombstone:

Rose, O pure contradiction, delight
to be no one's sleep, beneath so many lids

☙❧

From flower to star.

What spectacle confronts two figures, a lingering, wistful host and his departing guest, emerging silently from a dwelling in Dublin, causing a deeper darkness momentarily to fall upon the garden one mild summer's night.

Scheherazade answers:

   —The heaventree of stars, hung with humid nightblue fruit.

1922. Paris—City of Books, according to Gregory IX.

Among the yellow-backed volumes exuding a delicious scent of print, fragrant as lemons but bound in blue, dazzling as the Aegean: *Ulysses*.

The fabulous voyage undertaken by Leopold Bloom, advertising agent, through the streets of Dublin on 16th June 1904. Ascot Gold Cup day, the weather holding up quite well, all things considered.

James Joyce, the not so jejune Jesuit, wearing a Borsalino hat which he favours, and carrying a malacca cane, sees the world awash with signs; the world anew. In which, the Catholic Church—founded irremovably, because founded, like the world, upon the void.

Paris has for Joyce an atmosphere of spiritual effort. Racecourse tension.

I wake up early, often at five o'clock, and start writing.

Stephen Dedalus paces Sandymount strand, blacksuited against the blue. Without a God, he sees only the ineluctable modality of the visible. At least that, if no more.

Leopold Bloom, darkbacked figure, purchases a bar of lemon soap. It will rest, content, in his pocket all day. Ensconced in a slowly rocking cab on his way to attend a funeral, he passes an old tramp—forerunner of Estragon—shaking grit out of his boot after life's journey.

Round noon he partakes, moderately, of a glass of burgundy and a cheese sandwich; selects a potboiler from a rundown bookstall that contains few glories, for Molly, his beloved but unfaithful wife.

The shopman lifts eyes bleared with old rheum.

—*Sweets of Sin,* he says, tapping on it. *That's a good one.*

Joyce declines the use of quotation marks on the page to indicate speech, finding it most unsightly. Prefers the elegant dash.

Day progresses.

A wise tabby blinks from her warm sill.

The Very Reverend John Conmee S J re-sets his smooth watch, his thinsocked ankles tickled by the stubble of Clongowes field. Time. He opens his breviary. An ivory bookmark tells the page. From a gap in the hedge appears a flushed young man with his blushing companion who holds in her hand a bunch of wild, nodding daisies, and now, with slow care, detaches from her light skirt a clinging twig. Father Conmee blesses them gravely, and turns a thin page of his breviary.

Bronze by gold, Miss Douce and Miss Kennedy stand at the bar of the Ormond Hotel. Their slender fingers move silently to and fro, proffering a pint of dark Guinness, or —a rarer sight—reach up, satin blouse stretched tight, and briskly splash a little amber Jameson's into a glass.

Afternoon wanes.

Evening advances.

Lights, beginning to twinkle, floating out over the slow-flowing Liffey.

Stephen has moved on to the night-town district, where Bloom shows up and kneels before a well-laced madame, oozing sweat. Stephen shatters the scene with the Wagnerian cry—*Nothung!* Masonry crumbles. There is a general exeunt. He has already observed—echoing Sir Thomas Browne: *assuefaction minonates atrocities.*

The chimes of midnight ring out.

Bloom and Stephen turn their steps towards a cabman's shelter close by Butt Bridge, narrowly watched by an ancient mariner who turns out to be a bit of a literary cove—*The Arabian Nights Entertainment* a particular favourite. Bloom offers Stephen an antediluvian bun and invites him home.

Two figures, blacksuited, one full, one lean, pass beyond ebbing lamplight which extends their shadows. Emerge into brightening lamplight, to recede again. Draw on towards 7 Eccles Street, there to consume a cup of nicely warmed cocoa before Stephen takes his leave—with some reluctance on Bloom's part.

Outside, mutely, they urinate out of the shadows into faint light and, with upturned eyes, gaze on a shooting star falling from Virgo, passing through Berenice's streaming hair. Meanwhile, on firm, everchanging, neverchanging earth, Molly, like Penelope, waits.

Scheherazade's dark eyes rest on me.

Once, briefly, the two masters of the modern novel met and, in the shared immobility of their taxi, exchanged a few desultory remarks on truffles, among other things, before Joyce alighted, and turned to watch the dark vehicle bear its pale passenger, Proust, into the night.

XVI

Approaching evening, I am taken by Yusef to the courtyard. A wide rim of shadow runs out from the western wall. The glancing fire has left the high palms, and the thread of water falling from the fountain no longer holds such glistening light.

The old storyteller sits cross-legged as before, occasionally flicking the faded wooden beads he holds in his left hand; his dark eyes, a clear dream.

After salutations and exchanges for peace, my hand on my heart, I take my place by his side. Yusuf withdraws to the southern wall. As though we had never parted—as though in fact we have our own time—he begins.

—Sa'adi, whose roses never fade, tells of a slender, honey-eyed youth who swam the Tigris each night to be with his love. Till a night advanced when he became aware of a dark mole, a blemish, on her pale cheek. *Do not swim back,* his love implored, *lest you drown.*

His gentle smile.

—He has abandoned the realm of pure spiritual love. Entered our dust-laden world.

Translucent shadows float out beyond the dark rim of the wall.

—We have travelled far since first we met, my brother, to tread as on a silken carpet, though it be but sand. To reach towards the abode of modern man, where restless activity resides—assisted by his two viziers, Greed and Fear.

His eyes soften.

—All has been spoken to us in holy words, and wisely told. He who does not know the Qur'an by heart is like a lemon without its scent.

He pauses, having evoked in me a memory of Anna in Saint Petersburg sadly looking out of her carriage window: the zest, gone.

He continues.

—Once, a companion asked the Prophet what virtue was. He answered: *That which brings peace to your mind and tranquility to your soul.*

A blue-backed swallow swoops low.

—The perfume of flowers does not drift against the wind. No, not even the perfume of jasmine, of rose. But the perfume of virtue travels against the wind. It reaches to the ends of the earth.

The swallow rises, dripping water from her beak.

—He walked for a time among us. Said, *Three things have caused me to love this fleeting world. Tender sex. Fragrant perfume. The beauty of a soul in prayer. The delight of my eye, the cool of my eye, comes by prayer.*

He asks that the night be divided into three parts: for study, for sleep, and for prayer. True prayer lightens the heart, brightens the face, and brings us near the One God.

I remember an afternoon in a west-country churchyard, brushing dry leaves from a tilting slab. A scurrying spider. An epitaph: *Till the light breaks.*

His eyes shine.

—Do not be surprised that the dissolute do not heed the words of the devout. The music of a lute is drowned by the beat of a drum.

The old man, Scheherazade's former storyteller, tenderly regards me.

—Life hangs on a single thread. Only a breath stands between this world and what is to come.

It is the hour of advancing shadows, the hour when women pour oil from the jug, merchants rub a little myrrh between their fingers, old men waft frankincense over their silver beards. It is the hour of backward-beating rays, kindling the edges of clouds to liquid fire.

He rises.

—A thousand years ago Firdausi saw, unravelling before him, palaces soaring to Saturn; camels, laden with the many keys required to fasten locked treasure-houses. But for us ...

He gazes intently at me.

—For us lie beckoning gates opening to the Garden of Achievement. There, in cool green shade and by fresh running water we taste its fruits, enjoy its fragrance, that we may be enlightened and journey onwards, ever striving towards perfection.

He makes a valedictory gesture, almost touching my cheek with the tips of his fingers as Yusef slowly advances to lead me back to my cell.

Light ebbs and flows along the ochre wall. Images and reveries silently circle round. A little bright green beetle hurries along. And always, we return to—Time Past.

❦

Cornflowers and poppies, fluttering in the fields under racing clouds. The train from Chartres, stopping at Illiers: Combray.

Specks of dust rise and fall. A patch of light grows and fades, till once more Scheherazade's dark eyes rest on me. In her apartments, Carcel lamps now shed their tranquil pools.

She is wearing a violet-hued silk rippled by green turquoise. An amethyst—the colour of Time—glimmers on a slender finger.

Her smile is enigmatic, knowing.

I begin.

Paris has two saints named Marcel. One is still invoked at baptism in Notre Dame; the other gave up his life to art—as, perhaps, never before: Marcel Proust.

From a tiny crumb of *madeleine,* soaked in tea, rises the vast structure—a Gothic cathedral of recollection. Time Past.

Her voice,

> —Time that is past is not lost. For it is this very time that fills our hearts with contentment.

❦

Long summers spent reading in green shade. Threads of golden gossamer drifting into light, dappled on the magic page. An azure silence ... limpid, protective, endless.

For Marcel, so often under strain, intense release comes in the small, locked closet smelling of orris-root, where wild currant clusters at the narrow window. His refuge.

In the evening, the hesitant, ferruginous tinkle of the little oval bell announces a visitor at the garden gate: Monsieur Swann.

The moon, rising.

Voices.

Footsteps crunch on the gravel path. Smothered laughter.

Marcel, anxiously waiting to receive his mother's goodnight kiss.

Her voice comes, low.

—A kiss, my mother's heart entire, for me alone.

Afternoon walks along the river bank. Two ways. One leading towards the Guermantes Mansion; the other, into the blossom-scented countryside. In Paris, Marcel is by Madame Swann's side as she strolls negligently along, her pale cream cloak billowing out behind.

I kept eyeing her admiringly, to which she responded with a lingering smile.

—Loving helps us to discern, to discriminate.

Her dark eyes glow.

During the mists of a late November afternoon, he visits Madame Swann, the last flares fading from the sky; replaced, prolonged, on the flaming palette of her chrysanthemums.

Cool, unhurrying Madame Swann. The silken pennant of her parasol toning with the showering petals on her dress, open and outstretched. A nearer sky, round, clement, mobile—and blue.

   —Blue.

Sweep of blue.

⁂

Balbec.

Marcel stays at the Grand Hotel on the Normandy coast.

Encounters Baron de Charlus, sombrely attired, a spot of red on his tie almost imperceptible—like a liberty one dare not take.

He learns that Albertine—who attracts him—is one of a little band of girls whose supple bodies are unimpaired by any exhausting reflection, moral anxiety or nervous disorder.

   —That is their charm.

I raise my eyes; find hers, shining like stars.

They set out together to explore the surrounding countryside, travelling by motorcar—an intoxicating scent of petrol melting into the pale azure on scorching days. Arrive at a Norman church, there to be greeted by stone statues that rise—almost in benediction—through the warm haze, bathed in golden webs of sunset.

He visits Elstir's studio and, as he examines the painter's seascapes, where sea and sky seem to merge, becomes aware that art is metaphor. Reality—never really knowable, attainable—becomes illusion. And art—the artist's work—is a reflection of those illusions.

Deckchairs are being folded up. Put away. The reception clerks gaze wistfully at the departing guests.

The tide comes further in as summer draws to a close. Certain days which, at the time, seemed almost too hot, now take their place in us as the unalloyed essence of pure gold and indestructible azure.

He returns to Paris.

Attends the Opera. There, from her box, her grotto, leaning slightly forward, gently waving her white swan fan, the Duchesse de Guermantes—goddess turned woman—showers upon him the celestial torrent of her smile.

Alone, he seeks to fathom the ideal life of the people he has known; to know the people whose life he must imagine.

From a courtyard window Marcel witnesses Baron de Charlus—a plump bee seeking its welcoming orchid—as he makes his approach to the discreet tailor, Jupien. There within, where each of us carries inscribed a human form, he carries, not that of a nymph, but of a youth.

At a reception Charlus invites him to his house and late into the night confides: *We cry out for a man. We cultivate begonias, we trim yews, but we would prefer a plant of human growth.*

Scheherazade's dark eyes rest on me.

He is by his grandmother's side as she dies.

> *As my lips touched her face, her hands trembled, recognising through the veil of unconsciousness what they scarce need sense to love.*

He learns that the dead exist only in us.

Her dark eyes. The dark garden. A star, moistening the dark mirror.

At the moment preceding pleasure, a childhood innocence on Albertine's face. Similar, in this regard, to the moment that follows death.

Now she sleeps.

> Along a sunlit path in the Bois our shadows trace a pattern that is immaterial, but no less intimate than the fusion of our bodies.

Outside it is quite dark. No moon.

At the junction of her slim thighs, a curve as indolent, as hushed, as cloistered, as that of the horizon after the sun has set.

ઠ્ય૦ઠ્ય

Paris.

The Louvre.

Proust, looking at Chardin, at the hands of a woman setting the table. She has been feeling the gentle, firm resistance of those plates all these years, at just the same point between her fingers.

He penetrates the exclusive Faubourg Saint-Germain—all the more real, being purely ideal. When one is young, every drawing room becomes a fresh universe.

He hears his name announced and enters the salon. Moves towards what we have only glimpsed, towards what we have scarcely imagined.

A slight giddiness overwhelms him. The chestnut-haired Comtesse Greffulhe, laying a gloved hand on the arm of a guest, glides with that attractive grace to greet him.

The Comtesse Greffulhe, her dark eyes lit by agate lights, becoming blue, becoming Oriane, becoming ... the Duchesse de Guermantes, who smiles on Marcel just as she did once before, in Combray, on leaving the Church of St Hilaire. Or from her box at the Opera—and now, still radiant, still mysterious, still smiling ... advancing to greet him.

Scheherazade rests her slightly abstracted eyes on me.

Late at night, descending from a cab, he looks up at the luminous bars of light breaking through the shutters of Albertine's room. We love only what we do not wholly possess.

—And always, the past, she murmurs.

And always the past ... At the end of an allée, coming on a maiden, a stone finger raised to her lips, a shadow on the face of the sundial indicating it is already noon, he remembers how, at that hour, he would accompany Madame Swann, her stretched silk parasol throwing the pale shade of wisteria on to her face.

❧

A darkened bedroom at 44 rue Hamelin. Céleste gathers the fallen sheets of proofs together, helps Proust undress.

You are so gentle, Céleste. A treasure I did not look to find.

—*You should rest now, monsieur.*

Caressingly, he rests what she calls his Persian prince eyes upon her.

Dear Céleste, I must go on correcting. Adding grains of sand till the end.

—*Then I bid monsieur goodnight.*

Goodnight Céleste.

Softly, she closes the door.

Proust stands, quite still.

❧

His novelist, Bergotte, far from well, visits an exhibition of Dutch paintings, and sees, for the last time, Vermeer's *View of Delft*.

Murmurs, *Little patch of yellow* ... Balanced on celestial scales appears his own work, and that little area of roof, touched by sunlight.

Dizziness overwhelms him. He must sit down. He rolls from the settee to the floor.

Dead ... forever. Who can say.

Proust holds that certain acts, without sanction in our present world, belong to another. A world of kindness, fairness, self-sacrifice. A world infinitely different from the one we inhabit here, for a brief time, before—perhaps—returning there.

They bury Bergotte.

All through that night in the lit bookshop window his books lie open, arrayed three by three, keeping vigil, like angels with outstretched wings. The symbol of his resurrection.

❧

Albertine has disappeared.

> *I felt that my life with Albertine, when I was not jealous, was nothing but boredom. And when I was jealous, nothing but pain.*

He picks up her grey cheviot jacket.

We exist alone.

People are held as an image within. But outside us, they undergo change, move beyond our reach.

We all see the same universe. It is dissimilar to each.

On the inside seams, along the pearly grey lining ... such fine stitching. Like those parts of a cathedral rarely seen by the eye.

❧

A host of grey pigeons takes to wing and arcs over St Mark's square.

Marcel travels with his mother to Venice.

After dinner I set out to explore an enchanted, an unknown city.

At the corners of Scheherazade's lips, the suggestion of a smile.

He enters on a maze of alleys, a network of little *calli* that gives out suddenly on a sequestered square: a moonlit piazza where a thread of silvered water rises from a slender fountain, watched over by a silent stone lion, balancing a cannonball on his cracked paw.

Water gently falling through the night. Faint tricklings from the darkened garden.

The next day he sets out on a quest to rediscover that elusive piazza, wishing he were like a character from the Arabian Nights to whom, in moments of uncertainty, appears a genie—or perhaps a maiden of surpassing beauty—offering assistance. Now, as *calle* gives on to *calle* ... may it have been a mirage, conjured from Venetian moonlight and mist ... Abandoning his search, he enters the Accademia where, bathed in an amber glow, the serene beauty of Bellini's *Magdalene* banishes all desire.

Approaching the hotel by water he sees his mother standing on their balcony, releasing from the depths of her heart a love that only ceased when there was no more corporal matter to sustain it.

Scheherazade inclines her head. Her low voice.

—Becoming aware that all love, and everything else in this life, evolves towards a farewell.

The deserted Lido at noon. A shimmering haze. Far out, a honey-haired youth on the edge of a long sand bar, raising an arm towards the shore.

☙❧

The years pass.

War comes.

A last stay at Cabourg on the Normandy coast, distributing cigarettes and playing cards with the wounded soldiers.

Proust returns to Paris.

Paris—where a scrap of garden is more ravishing than a whole country park.

Paris: darker, then. And becoming darker still, with the war.

Paris—which Proust will now never leave.

Observes, at a male brothel, Baron de Charlus—chained to a bed, like Prometheus to his rock—being gently whipped. Considers that the brevity that lies on all things renders moving the spectacle of every kind of love.

Dines late at the Ritz with the beautiful Princesse Soutzo. *Her charms have enslaved me and I hardly stir from my room except to go to see her.*

The years pass.

The time we have at our disposal is elastic. Passions we feel, expand it; those we inspire, contract it. And habit fills up what remains.

November.

Walks slowly through the fallen leaves along the allée des Acacias where once, graceful carriages passed. Now it is filled with motorcars driven by chauffeurs with cheap moustaches. The dresses, too, do not seem as beautiful as those once worn by Madame Swann, so long ago.

He sits on a park bench.

Where has the past gone. Where have the years fled.

Comte Robert de Montesquiou, who has lent his person to Charlus, calls on Proust late one night, for the last time. Tells him: *I would like to go on a long voyage and come back with white hair.*

ॐ

After a long absence, Marcel decides to attend an afternoon reception being given by the Princesse de Guermantes.

On entering her courtyard he stumbles on an uneven flagstone, evoking sudden memories.

Blue.

—Blue, echoes Scheherazade.

Venice. A serene azure. Tripping in St Mark's square. Beating pigeons' wings.

Entering the mansion, he accepts the proffered refreshment. Brings a starched napkin to his moist lips. Memory floods in.

Balbec.

The sea.

—Blue, repeats Scheherazade.

A cool, saline air. Drying his face on a starched hotel towel.

He soars on the silent heights of memory ... the sky at Combray.

—Blue.

The true paradises are those we have lost. But lost for ever, who can say. Let a sensation arise—real without being actual, ideal without being abstract—and we are released, freed from the constraints of Time.

He enters the drawing room of the Princesse. Various people come forward to greet him, and he sees that they are greatly changed.

Old age, which of all the realities we preserve longest, a purely abstract conception.

He hears names redolent of an earlier era—*a time of which we ourselves have witnessed only the end.*

Now, advancing towards him, he sees Mademoiselle de Saint-Loup—slender, smiling, supple, eyes of a pale watery aquamarine. In her, the Two Ways of his childhood meet.

∽∽

Proust returns to his chilly flat.

To the domain of what is, for each of us, the sole reality: the domain of our own sensibility.

He becomes aware that the idea of death has taken up residence in him—as, once, love had. That memory is spiritual—for the world he perceives surrounding him cannot provide the state he seeks.

Figures emerge out of the landscapes of the past, where once they led a sequestered and secret existence. By a shaded stretch of water near Combray ... In the slanting light of the nave in a Normandy church ... Along a sunlit path in the Bois ...

Marcel begins his novel.

Proust, dark circles under his eyes, lies back, exhausted, drops his pen.

Style, for the writer: no less than colour for the artist. A matter, not of technique, but of vision.

True books come not from daylight and conversation but out of shadow and silence. The Thousand and One Nights of another age.

A late taxi passes.

An Aladdin's lamp conjures a last ethereal rainbow in Proust's bedroom. November afternoons muffled in mist. Hawthorn blossom spilling over a hedgerow. Dark cherries ripening. Cornflowers. A sky-blue ribbon drooping over the edge of a rumpled bed. Honeyed light falling from a Carcel lamp. A smooth, creamed shoulder, where a pearl earring faintly gleams.

Till a dark figure blots out all light, all colour, all ideas but searing pain. And then that, too.

Stars begin to fade, an amethyst softly glows.

Art—the only salvation. Art—the redeemer of this life.
      Art—creation ... breaks, shatters, stands ...
           through Time.

XVII

Time runs silently through the glass.

My tale—enchanting, elusive, enigmatic—has no doubt been contemplated by a scattering of meditatively inclined poets and scholars poring, in some sequestered library, over an evocative page. On raising their dazzled eyes to the darkening pane, they let their bright fictions fade.

So, as I wait for the Princess Scheherazade, ambiguous mistress of my destiny, to break my reverie, the *Annus Mirabilis* 1922 still burns. The fabulous tale is winding towards its close. Once told, the future lies open before me. Dark. Uncertain.

Now the key grates in its iron lock, the door swings open, and Yusef stands, a burning torch in hand and, almost smiling, slowly raises the leaping flames in an angled pattern.

The Princess has sent for me. The tale will go on.

Scheherazade reclines, clad in an olive-green silk. A moon of mint drifts among oyster-shaded clouds. Low-lit lamps release an amber glow.

Her voice. Its resonant *éclat*, subtly welcoming.

—So, Gabriel, time pursues its fabulous course. Slips merrily through the night. Ebbs ever away.

As you say, Princess.

—While within our warm circle of light ...

A coral necklace. A gleaming nail. Ourselves.

A faint smile.

—We are in the early twenties, are we not.

Her dark eyes flash.

—An exciting time.

Indeed.

☙❧

Jazz comes in from Canal Street down in New Orleans. It's even heard behind white porticos on well-bred St Charles Avenue. Duke Ellington is playing the piano in The Cotton Club in New York. And on a wailing train bound for Boston, George Gershwin conceives *Rhapsody in Blue*.

Cocktails are being sipped at six. Scented young beauties with creamed, smooth shoulders and carmine-painted lips sway to the swaying saxophone player ... Freeze, to show a sheen of silk on a long leg doing tango ... And far into the blue, blue night—at some late party it's not considered fast to come and go dressed in satin pyjamas.

Sleek, smooth legs stretch out confidently along rue St Honoré. Jean Patou has brought over six leggy American girls to model his new collection. Ernest Brauk creates *Chanel No 5* and the rarer, *Bois des Iles*. On a Caribbean cruise, Harold S Vanderbilt devises contract bridge.

Scott Fitzgerald's men and women come and go, their soft voices filled with money. In the delphinium blue of dusk, among the whispering and champagne and stars, a bare-backed brunette in black crosses the scene, followed by an admirer armed with fizzing glasses.

Lost romantics ...

Tender is the Night reveals Nicole reverently crossing herself with Chanel, mirrored by Dick, swaying a little as he raises his right hand and, with a papal cross, blesses the beach.

Gatsby tosses his silken shirts in clouds of coral, apple-green, and lavender before Daisy. She lowers her coiffured head into them, and weeps.

Another couple lingers. With them, life has left, not bitterness, but pity; not disillusion, but only pain. In the wan light, each sees a gathering kindness in the other's eyes.

The gentle murmur from the fountain.

Edwin Hubble, having verified that the universe is still expanding, leaves it uncertain whether, at some point, it may begin to collapse in on itself, leaving a dark void.

—Perhaps, as the Indian sages say, then to expand anew, remarks Scheherazade.

Niels Bohr finds that experience can be ambiguous. Two incompatible sets of scientific evidence may be complimentary rather than contradictory. Werner Heisenberg, now researching in Copenhagen, brings his uncertainty principle to bear on quantum mechanics. Atoms of elementary particles form a world of potentialities. Infinite possibilities, performing a never-ending dance ...

But Albert Einstein, believing the distinction between past, present and future to be illusory—however persistent—holds that all is determined. The beginning as well as the end is set by forces over which we have no control. It is so for the ant as for the star; for human beings, cherries, or cosmic dust. We all move to a mysterious tune, intoned from afar by an invisible piper.

A final entry in Aby Warburg's diary celebrates an apple tree in his garden that, in late October, suddenly burst into clouds of pink and white blossom.

☙

After forty years on his horse-drawn cab, Gustav Hartmann notices he is being overtaken by taxis. So, at almost sixty-nine, he sets out with his brave horse, Grasmus, taking many weeks to travel from Berlin to Paris, and back again. They are greeted with wild enthusiasm on arrival in Paris. And later, back in Berlin, where …

Erna Thaler distributes her poetry on Potsdamer Platz and reads from her work to those gathered around. And Marlene Dietrich sings, in her dark, husky voice, *Falling in love again … What can I do …*

Martin Heidegger feels the human race has been thrown out into the world. He asks what it means to exist. To be. For space, it seems, is nothingness. Yet, we must apprise ourselves. And choose—authentic existence.

Walter Benjamin describes the *flâneur* … Streets are his home. Walls become his desk; newspaper kiosks, his library. Benches are his boudoir … And the café terrace, a bay window.

Oswald Spengler regards the flowers at dusk.

Not a leaf stirs.

Only the little gnat is free. He dances still in the fading light.

'Western Faustian'—our present age—is journeying on, from a late autumn afternoon towards the onset of a winter night.

The wolves howl.

The great cultures form majestic waves. They appear, swell in splendour, flatten again and vanish. And the face of the waters will be once more a sleeping waste.

❧

The Art Deco ocean liner, *Normandie*, slips her moorings at Cherbourg.

Skirts shoot to the knees. Restless fingers twirl long strings of pearls, turn high heels up for the Charleston.

I'm dancing, you're dancing, he's dancing Charleston. We're all dancing Charleston.

How about you.

Brave attempts to lower the skirt are bravely resisted. And advice is given to the *nouvelles pauvres*:

To be poor, and to look poor, is to be damned poor.

In her quiet Croydon room, Cicely Mary Barker stirs her fine brush in a jam jar of water and bestows on her sloe fairy a purple and mud-green dress and plum wings.

At a Paris café Tamara de Lempicka exclaims—*There is an unforgettable light coming through the window opposite. Please move, monsieur, so that I can study how it bends the red and white lines on the tablecloth.*

She paints herself driving around in a green Bugatti.

The Leica hand-held camera becomes a treasured companion. Caught, by Jacques Henri Lartigue: poised in mid air above a flight of stone steps—a joyful, bounding, carefree Afghan hound; stepping out along the avenue des Acacias, a graceful, gloved lady, wearing a long dress and a wide-brimmed, plumed hat; a wet Irish setter by the sea, seeking further encouragement; Renée, on a sofa, extending her long, sleek legs.

Her voice, quiet.

—Shades of Proust.

Of love.

The 5th Earl of Rosebery has been granted his three wishes. He marries Hannah, daughter of Baron Rothschild, the richest heiress in England. Wins the Derby three times with his horses, Ladas, Sir Visto, and Cicero. And becomes Prime Minister.

—How little is required to be happy, murmurs Scheherazade.

※

The last silent film days. Lillian Gish finds herself cut off in a cabin as the wind rages outside. Louise Brooks, all bobbed hair and long dangling pearls, arrives in Berlin to star in *Pandora's Box*. And a final dusty chase for the legendary *Keystone Kops*.

Helicopters buzz between buildings and automobiles purr along aerial highways while, ensconced in his lair, Rotwang—the inventor in Fitz Lang's *Metropolis*—creates a new woman: one who incorporates all the sweetness of a Gothic madonna with the charms of a nightclub hostess.

Sergei Eisenstein sends Tsarist troops advancing down the Odessa steps, firing into a defenceless crowd. An abandoned pram, still with the baby in, bounces on before them.

The human face is a land one never tires of exploring.

A tender vulnerability radiates from Maria Falconetti as she clutches the wooden cross before the stake in Carl Dreyer's supremely composed *Passion of Joan of Arc*.

Joan slowly raises her shaven head, her tear-stained face, to her accusers.

Her eyes shine.

Antonio Gaudi, last master of *Art Nouveau*, guards a Spanish mansion with a wrought-iron dragon gate. His climactic work, the Basilica of the Sagrada Familia, is still rising over Barcelona. Stone angels bring long trumpets to their lips. High *Art Nouveau* spires soar on a final flight. A last imperial gesture from Catholic Spain. The last grand cathedral the Roman Catholic Church will attempt to raise in this world.

For now, a moor is like a church to R S Thomas. Breath held like a cap in hand, he finds God in the stillness of the heart's passions, in the movement of wind over grass.

Scheherazade's dark eyes rest on me.

☙❧

At Giverny, Monet creates a water-garden where *nymphéas*—his water lilies—silently float, reflecting an ever-changing sky. Delicate, misty nuances of lavender and blue. Soft morning mother-of-pearl clouds, tinged by rose ... Falling willow leaves, casting a deeper, darker reflection on a flood of orange and yellow ... Silent world of sky, foliage, flower, flowing over a canvas without beginning or end. Moments of light, conquering time.

By his bed a volume of Baudelaire lies open.

> *What do you love, extraordinary stranger.*
> *I love the clouds ... the passing clouds ... the wonderful clouds.*

Faintly, a quaking flute.

Green shadows.

Bare feet on blue tiles.

Opening, like a far-away fairy tale, to Paul Klee.

He is possessed by colour.

—Light.

Palms. Earth. Sea.

> *I do not need to pursue it. This is the moment. Colour and I are one.*

An immense full moon. Domes. Shifting shades of sand. Hieroglyphs. Tiny coloured flags. Fragments of Arabic script. Little flat-roofed houses. All find their way into his art.

Bands of watered grey, pale turquoise, green, yellow, violet, black, deep blue, rise above an overlapping lagoon city; a dream city in modulations of turquoise, sea-green, black, white, pinkish violet.

The attentive Princess.

He embarks on a series of magic squares ... magenta, to rose-violet, to vermilion, to peppermint-green, to reseda-green, to forest-green, to yellow, to sea-green, to ice-blue, to watered-pink, to juniper-blue, and—most magical—black, by violet.

His line has a Mozartian lightness and grace. An Ariel fantasy and wit. More than one blonde moonrise of the North casts its spell. But, like a blurred image in a mirror, merges with the rising moon of the South ...

A sheet of paper becomes a stage, a setting for an entertainment, a spectacle inspired by nature. He journeys into lands of greater possibilities, a seafarer in his little boat, crossing sea-squares of exquisite gradations of blue. A crescent moon hangs above as sailing ships move forward towards unknown destinies, on a sea without horizon.

On his grave is inscribed: *A little nearer to the heart of creation. But still too far away.*

༺༻

Scent of apples.

A Normandy manor.

L'Enfant et les Sortilèges. A magical, jewel-like score.

An elderly armchair proceeds to dance a lugubrious sarabande. A Wedgwood teapot and a china cup do a tea-time foxtrot. A shepherdess and her swain descend from the wallpaper to sing a haunting pastoral. Until a paler light falls and Maurice Ravel takes us out into the moonlit garden.

Water faintly trickles from the fountain.

No one must sleep, on pain of death, till the stranger's name be known. Giacomo Puccini—who likes English ties, tender heroines, shooting wild duck—drops his pen for ever at the glistening point where at last the icy heart of the imperious Princess Turandot begins to melt with love.

Attired in black, three students from Craców visit Doktor Faust in his Wittenberg laboratory to place in his trembling hands a strange and curious volume bearing the legend, *Clavis Astartis Magica*. They sing in unison:

For you are the master.

They vanish in vapour.

Now we enter a deserted street. Thick snow is whirling down. Ferruccio Busoni's opera ends as a nightwatchman —it is Mephistopheles—raises his lantern over the still body at his feet. This man, it seems, has met with some misfortune.

Alban Berg mourns Wozzeck, a common soldier. A searing orchestral threnody. In front of Marie's house, children are playing. They run off at news of the dead body, leaving Marie's little boy riding his hobby horse.

Hop, Hop! Hop, Hop! Hop, Hop!

Then he follows them, leaving the gently rocking horse.

A burning star appears in the dark mirror.

༄

Prague.

A dark November afternoon.

In the Accident Insurance Institution offices, the lights are all on. Franz Kafka sits at his desk, a sheet of office paper before him. In his left hand he holds a long, blue pencil.

Desks are our Procrustean beds, but we are no Greek heroes—merely suffering, tragic comedians. The world lies open, but we are imprisoned here, living in straight lines. In fact, in a kind of labyrinth.

K arrives at a snow-bound village to take up his post as land surveyor. But it is not certain that the castle authorities have offered him such a position, and it appears that they do not need one.

Franz Kafka smiles enigmatically at a friend.

The Talmud says that we Jews only yield our best—like olives—when we are crushed.

—And Christ.

K bows his head.

He is an abyss of light.

The Princess's dark eyes rest on me.

Lights undulate, crinkle along the Seine.

Now resident in Paris, James Joyce brings out *Pomes Penyeach*, a slim volume clad in the pale green of his favoured apple, the calville.

The following year—it is 1928—*Anna Livia Plurabelle*—or ALP, as Joyce liked to call his most melodious passage from *Finnegan's Wake*—appears, wrapped in a tea-coloured cover to match the chittering waters of the Liffey where, as night falls, two chattering washerwomen are turned into a tree and a stone. The idea came on a trip to Chartres, witnessing women washing clothes on the banks of the Eure.

—As, once, did Huysman, observes Scheherazade.

The night *Anna Livia* is put to bed, Joyce seeks reassurance and makes his way carefully, carrying his malacca cane—he has weak sight—down to the Seine, to stand by one of the arches and listen to the flowing waters.

He returns, content.

That same year his friend, Italo Svevo, is fatally injured in a motorcar accident after finishing a novel in which his hero is trying to give up smoking. His distraught wife asks if he would not like to see a priest. Svevo gently smiles, says, *It's too late,* and asks for a final cigarette. Fingers it tenderly, murmuring, *There's no doubt this will be my last.*

☙

Whiffs of grey-blue smoke drift from a select gathering in Mayfair.

Edith Sitwell, short bobbed hair, cut with some flair, raises a megaphone to her thin lips, declares: *Something lies beyond the scene.*

Beat, beat, thud, of waves on shore.

Swaying shadow of the acorn cord of a blind on the nursery floor.

Through half-closed eyes, white lace curtains fly. White foam lands, rushing over Scarborough's sands.

> *Now Pompey's dead, Homer's read,*
> *Heliogabalus lost his head.*
> *And shade is on the brightest wing,*
> *and dust forbids the bird to sing.*

Virginia Woolf pauses, her gleaming nib catching light, moving at an angle in the air before her. She watches rooks rise and fall, beat up against the wind ... *But what* little I can get down into my pen of what is so vivid to my eyes.

In the soft Hebridean air Lily Briscoe takes a little blue on her brush and makes her first quick, decisive strokes on the canvas ... Orlando, skating out over the frozen Thames on glinting blue ice, seems to be passing over fathomless depths of sky ... And Jinny enters the bright, perfumed room, arrayed and prepared, sensing the cool sapphire on her throat.

Katherine Mansfield writes her last short stories: *This lovely medium of prose—is a hidden country still. Coy to release her secrets.*

Adds: *By my bed is Shakespeare, an automatic pistol, and a black muslin fan. My whole little world.*

She admires *All's Well That Ends Well.*

—As do you.

Indeed.

From her bedroom window she watches a fine dusting of snow slip through the dark Swiss pines ... bars of sunlight, like pale fire.

—Echoes, intimations.

Returning to France, seeking a cure for tuberculosis, she sits in the Luxembourg Gardens. Leaves falling; footfalls, like gentle whispers.

She rises slowly, brushes a hectic leaf from her coat.

Little whiffs of dust rise into the lamplight.

New heavens, new constellations, being formed as the motes whirr and dance.

We slip back along the twenties.

Ronald Firbank, novelist, makes his bow.

Inclines to write in purple ink on blue cards: *I think nothing of filing forty cards to make a brief crisp paragraph, or even a row of dots.*

Dusk descends.

Tinkle of ice rolling into glass. The welcome splash of Gordon's. She leans, butterfly light, against his dark frame. A saxophone wails on the edge of anguish. Her warm breath, laced with juniper, dusts his powdered cheek.

Later in the sleepy rose of dawn, the tender, silken rustle of her dress yields to the soft frou-frou murmur of a clinging lace-edged petticoat.

> *It was very agreeable going to bed late, without the maid's aid, when one could pirouette before the brightening mirror in the last provoking stages of déshabillé and do a thousand and one interesting things beside.*

Scheherazade actually giggles.

—A very Firbankian thing.

Ensconced once more in fairest England, under the inattentive gaze of a coquettish Sèvres shepherdess and her demure swain, she lowers her pale grey eyes to begin a long meditative voyage of discovery on the sky-blue ribbons that adorn her oyster-and-cream striped gown, musing if perhaps, after all, marriage is altogether too excessive for such very light desires.

A peacock screams.

Beyond the window, in a secluded spot by ancient, spreading cedars, a Red Admiral pursues a Duke of Burgundy through slanting, honeyed beams. Sculpted gardeners in wide-brimmed hats lean languidly on their long rakes, reach out across the gravel paths, till their shadows begin to cast dark pools upon the verdant green.

Through leaded panes, the western sun fires pale Persian princes astride white Arabian thoroughbreds, ever pursuing fair French princesses fleeing on swift-footed unicorns over an azure sea—upon which her black high-heels rest. By taking down from the library a volume devoted to the early history of the Spanish Inquisition (with accompanying plates) she has caused Saint Thomas Aquinas and the Marquis de Sade almost to be rubbing together on the same dark shelf.

A pleasant evening, monsieur.

—*Indeed, by God's grace.*

Now, soothed somewhat, and seated in her lightly-scented drawing room, she holds her recalcitrant husband on the rack at figure 8, imploring mercy. How eagerly now, he proffers that diamond clasp that would go so well with her midnight-blue backless evening gown, that sweet cottage in the country dripping with bougainvillea, her own yacht.

Calmly she considers his pleas, before transposing him to the acuter agonies on figure 13, where she can almost hear his anguished cries rising above the bells ringing for evensong.

A slender spire soars beyond the trees, whence falls the saintly caw-cawing of the churchyard crows. An admonishing angel raises a stone finger to her lip as, caught in a last needle of light piercing the yew tree's shade, a tiny mouse trembles by a gleaming nut.

We tiptoe away ...

... Through the lych gate, over quiet fields sinking back into shade, to board a last slow train to London where, in the dark, heavily perfumed atmosphere of a West End theatre, James Elroy Flecker's camels sniff the evening air, and are glad.

The call is raised:

Open wide the gates, O watchmen of the night.

—*Ho, traveller, I open.*

For what land leave you the dim-moon city of delight.

—*We take the golden road to Samarkand.*

—*The golden road to Samarkand,* echoes Scheherazade, softly.

Gently tinkling camel bells fade into the distance.

※

We swing West.

Rattle of pebbles being sucked on the shore.

A wild swan takes to beating wing, rising over Coole Park.

In the still garden the daughter of the house, wearing a long muslin dress, lifts a white rose to her pale lips and breathes its honeyed scent.

While out collecting Irish fairy tales, William Butler Yeats encounters an old lady, a sapphire ring on her finger. Making it flash, she asks the poet if fairies' dresses were e're as beautiful.

He dreams he sees an illuminated page showing all the secrets of the world—so simply done, it could be written on a blade of grass with the juice of a berry. But we lose, as we age, something of the lightness of dreams, and the *Sidhe*—the Irish fairies—depart, ride out from his verse. Still, he clings to ghosts, believing that from the lees they can taste the wine's breath.

Attending an afternoon meet at Galway races, mingling with an ardent crowd, he bemoans the poet's loss: *We too had good attendance once.* Berates bent, snivelling scholars, annotating lines; young men tossing on beds, rhymed out to flatter beauty's ignorant ear.

Yeats has a liking for blue shirts, words, pebbles washed clean on the shore. The passing show. For high-stepping queens, the music of beggarmen. Dance. For a bone wave-whitened by the turning tide, the wind sighing among the reeds. A hare's fresh imprint in the long grass, a straggling line of ash-grey geese flying into a falling dusk. For the ever-turning wheel of Celtic legend …

Cathleen ni Houlihan steps out from a cottage door with the walk of a queen. Cuchulain, engaged all night long, wields his grey-edged sword against the raging foam. Deirdre and Naoise play out their last hour at chess, awaiting death.

Stars enter the dark mirror.

He sees the still point: eternity, on a hawk's wing. Every two thousand years brings the cosmic cycle round. The Classical world, swept in by the rape of a girl by a swan … The Christian world, coming in mutely, on a virgin birth.

Her voice.

> —And now, for you, Gabriel, another two thousand years have slipped out into the void since Virgo, carrying the star Spica in her hand, silently led the Magi out over the cold sands of our desert towards that

birth. Now, leaving behind Pisces—the fishes—you are coming under the sway of the water carrier: Aquarius.

At Coole, a sinking, late November sun. He watches a wild swan drift out on a last reach of glittering stream.

Now nettles wave among broken pots and urns. Saplings take root by cracked glass: an ancient house, in ruins. Does someone stand there, though all the floor be gone.

> I meditate upon a swallow's flight, an aged woman and her house, a sycamore and a lime tree, lost to shade, although that western cloud be luminous.

> We were the last romantics.

He turns from the sunless, beckoning waters.

But all is changed utterly. That high horse, riderless.

He mounts the winding spiral stone stair.

The swan drifts out upon the darkening flood.

Late-returning travellers on the road from market or fair pass his stone tower at Ballylee, see a candle gleam as the poet, like a long-legged fly upon the stream, moves upon silence, answering always to the siren call: Beauty.

> How can I my attention fix on the daily dross, that girl standing there ...

In Drumcliff churchyard Yeats is laid, these words cut in stone:

> Cast a cold eye
> on life, on death.
> Horseman, pass by!

A mist rolls in from the sea.

The sound of waves recedes.

༺༻

Faint trickle of water.

Soft sobbing blues, tender and beseeching, waft out over the Mediterranean.

—Blue, murmurs Scheherazade.

Sicily sinks from sight. The purple strip of Crete ebbs away.

—Blue.

We arrive at Alexandria, where Cavafy writes, keeping the Greek flame alive after so many years. Hellenic—no quality more precious. Everything beyond belongs to the gods.

—Blue.

Setting out for Ithaca, pray that the way be long, full of adventure, full of delight. Running a finger along an ancient stone inscription, a yielding back. Deciphering texts that offer other visions. Exploring bodies giving other joys. Be quite old when you return, without wealth or fame. Ithaca has given you the marvellous journey. Without her, you would not have set out.

—Blue.

But the poet remains.

Sips his coffee at a corner café where fragments of French, Arabic, Italian, Greek, mingle.

> *This city will never leave you. Here you will remain. You'll walk the same streets, pause at the same shop window, turn grey in this faded room.*

—Blue.

> *You're destined to end up here. There's no boat for you. No other shore.*

He gently smiles.

Now his poetry is on the lips of young men. His vision comes before their alert eyes. Their taut bodies respond to his paean of the beautiful.

—Blue.

Hurrying away from work, loosening his tie, a young shipping clerk is arrested by a face glimpsed at the window of a dingy shop. The cracked bell rings. The shop assistant comes forward. Hands touch over pink and purple handkerchiefs ...

A young Syrian from the Hellenic period has dangerous thoughts, strengthened by meditation and study: *I'll give my body up to the most audacious erotic desires, to the lascivious impulses of my blood.*

He runs his fingers lightly down his friend's heaving chest. *I'm not afraid. When I wish, at critical moments, I'll recover my ascetic spirit as it was before.*

Twelve.

Traffic rumbles by.

His tousled hair, honeyed breath. *Try to hold them, poet, when they come alive at night. Or in the noonday brightness.* His body, a little tanned ... Specks of amber in his dark eyes ... His adorable face, imprinted on a pillow.

Half past twelve.

How time has slipped by. How the years have slipped away.

Dying, his last gesture was to draw a circle on a blank sheet of paper and to place in the centre a black dot.

XVIII

Waiting.

Yusef. Approaching. Departing. A silent shadow. Has the Princess Scheherazade abandoned our tale ... The courtyard where I take my exercise remains deserted. Has the former storyteller taken gentle leave of this world and gone, to appear before another ...

Light fades.

Along a darkening shore, an incoming tide creams the wet sand. Lateen sails are released and boats set out, lanterns burning on the dark waters. Over a twinkling city men perfume their beards with frankincense before embarking on the evening meal, and a merchant rubs a little myrrh between his fingers as he calculates the day's takings. Out in the desert, rugs are being removed from the backs of camels, who stamp occasionally as they ruminate beneath the stars. Fires send sparks leaping, dancing, into the dark.

I wake to feel a flaring torch burn close to my cheek. Yusef's dark eyes ... The Princess Scheherazade has sent for me. The tale will go on.

It has been a long time, I tell him.

—Only Allah is eternal.

I follow Yusef, mounting the low, wide stairs that lead towards the Princess's apartments. Do I sense a certain regret as, with lowered eyes, he silently withdraws.

The night is dark.

Low-lit lamps cast an opaque, reddish glow.

Her voice.

My name, like rich red wine upon her lips.

She reclines on her juniper couch, wearing a smoky grey silk. No jewels, nor rings.

—Less. Less and less are the sands still to run in our glass ... our tale.

Indeed, Princess.

—And tonight, the stars hang back. They have abandoned us.

Unseen, they turn. Yet still, on fire.

—And our hearts still burn, still burn.

Soon we will enter the cloudy thirties.

A chill breath from the world of dark stars and deep space reaches us.

༺✦༻

Black Tuesday hits New York. On Wall Street, stocks crash. Money men look down from their high windows. Most step back.

A steel spire emerges from the Chrysler Building, making it the tallest skyscraper in Manhattan. But not for long. The

Empire State, growing at a rate of over four storeys a week, triumphantly soars past. Frank Lloyd Wright's design for the Johnson Wax Company in Wisconsin becomes a reality. Everyone wants to work there.

John Warde jumps, after spending fourteen hours on the ledge of the 17th floor of the Gotham Hotel in New York. Ten thousand people, waiting at the busy intersection of 55th Street and Fifth Avenue, watch him fall.

A wailing sax, a snarling trumpet. Duke Ellington's caravan is on the road. At Carnegie Hall, Benny Goodman's jazz band reaches an exhilarating climax, playing *Sing Sing Sing,* Jess Stacy on piano giving that marvellous solo.

Cole Porter is writing elegant, effortless songs. Fred Astaire and Ginger Rogers—*Oh, so silken, Oh, so chic*—tap dance their way with unfailing suavity through the decade, cheek to cheek.

Nancy Cunard enjoys the favours of Black lovers. Brings out, *Negro: an anthology*—a major contribution.

Diego Rivera starts work in the vestibule of the new Rockefeller Building: *Man at the Crossroads.* But a portrait of Lenin appears, centre right. Before the work is completed, it has been destroyed: lumps of hacked-off plaster, fragments of the master's brushstrokes, tossed into many bins ...

A white mist rolls in from the Pacific and drifts through the Golden Gate bridge in San Francisco. A red Russian balloon, Osoaviokhim, ascends thirteen miles into the stratosphere.

In the Soviet Union, at Magnitogorsk, a steel works is founded. Far into the night coke ovens and blast furnaces blaze. Rolling mills pound. Tin plating shops hammer.

Attempts begin to unite General Relativity Theory to Quantum Theory.

Georges Lemaitre believes that in cosmic radiation we may see glimpses of the explosions of matter caused during the formation of stars from the beginning of the universe, now ebbing into deep space.

Lost among the stars.

A tiny, moving white dot.

Pluto swings into view.

Étienne Gilson completes his magisterial survey of medieval philosophy. He regrets the fall that took place after the heights achieved by Saint Thomas Aquinas.

In England, a man sits with raised umbrella on a wooden bench. Others have sought shelter but he stays on, waiting for the rain to cease, the white-clad figures to emerge from the pavilion and take their place in the field.

Madame Yevoude is photographing society beauties attired as mythological figures. Lady Milbanke is Penthesilea. Lady Ann Rhys becomes Flora. The Duchess of Argyll appears as Helen of Troy. White telephones sweep into vogue.

An American hostess in Paris sometimes has to call on the services of her butler to make up her bridge four. Of course, he must remain standing.

Expecting a visitor, Anna Comtesse de Noailles exclaims to her maid, *For heaven's sake hide that jar of Vaseline. Monsieur Vuillard paints everything he sees.*

Schiaparelli's shocking pink lipstick sweeps Paris. Marinetti requires Italian women to add bands of green and white to the red of their lips and nails, reflecting the

Lombardy plains, the Alpine snow. As light fades on a green and rose afternoon, an enigmatic stillness reigns over the deserted piazzas, the silent, haunted squares of Giorgio de Chirico.

Encouraged by the Marquesa de Casa Torres, Balenciaga opens his first fashion shop. His colours: black, white, a brilliant red, turquoise, yellow, cinnamon, grey. His cut: an elimination of all excess.

Each night, during the summer of 1932, Alberto Giacometti constructs and reconstructs *A Palace at 4 am* —delicately made out of thin wooden sticks, glass, wire, and string—till a blackbird signals the approach of dawn.

Jun'ichirō Tanizaki—whose gentle heroine, Yukiko, recalls the forgotten ladies attached to the Heian court— will plead for a lost world of undisturbed shadows, its delicacy threatened by the glare of the West; for a shaded, withdrawn beauty, one that clings to high corners, attends a hara-kiri ceremony, leaves lavatories fit for meditation.

The Spanish Civil War.

Salvador Dalí proposes a monument to Fascism—at every kilometre between Madrid and the Escorial, a skeleton, gradually increasing in size, sculpted from stone.

Pablo Picasso responds to the suffering inflicted on Guernica. A mother rushes from a ruined house holding her dead child in her arms. She looks upward, screaming. A horse writhes in agony. A woman—fingers stretched wide apart—shrieks. An electric light bulb burns in an eye. A bird falls silent from the sky.

Yves Tanguy has squeezed and twisted whitened stones and bones into contorted shapes, casting bizarre shadows on a seamless plain and sky. Empty. Milky. Grey ... Broken, in one encrustation, by a tiny pool of blue.

—Blue, whispers Scheherazade.

✌

Reels are unravelling, releasing, in bands of light.

The silver screen.

Marlene Dietrich displays her long legs; Greta Garbo her devastating smile. Orson Wells lumbers on as Kane. Philip Marlowe fires a match in his dusty office. He leans back in his chair. No leggy blonde in high heels shows. He pulls a bottle of bourbon out from the back of a drawer and watches the light fade.

Busby Berkeley's mobile camera roams among a line-up of shimmering girls who dance on the wings of a fleet of planes flying down to Rio. The Marx Brothers romp through *A Night at the Opera* and then spend *A Day at the Races*. Caught in the sudden light of an opening doorway, Orson Welles is Harry Lime.

Lulling, soft-voiced Barbara Stanwyck, Queen of *Film Noir*, watches her dull husband sign away his life in *Double Indemnity*. Jane Greer leans back against a wall as Robert Mitchum, fatally attracted to her, tries to escape from his dark past. Gene Tierney, dark-haired star of *Laura*, holds back from throwing herself from the 57th Street window. *If I was going to die, I wanted to look pretty in my coffin.*

Scheherazade's eyes flicker.

Ice cracks under the weight of the iron-clad Teutonic Knights of Livonia. Ivan's long shadow creeps along the white walls of the Kremlin. Four survivors from an orgy at the Château de Sillery stagger out on to the thin snow.

Jean Vigo's schoolboys parade up and down on their dormitory beds as billowing white feathers slowly descend, falling upon their ecstatic faces. Flanked by outriders clad in black leather, Death—a beautiful, enigmatic woman reclining in the back of a dark limousine—is sent, by Jean Cocteau, to visit *Orphée*.

Dawn breaks over Paris. A workman, barricaded in his bleak room, shoots himself. As he lies dying, his alarm clock starts to ring.

Wearing immaculate pressed white gloves and delicately playing on a penny whistle, a French officer leaps across the castle ramparts, distracting the German guards as his men escape. Jean Renoir's requiem to a vanishing code of chivalry: *La Grande Illusion*.

Glamour descends from the North. Swedish movie actresses Zarah Leander and Kristina Söderbaum star in UFA films.

Back in Hollywood, slinky society vamp, Claire Trevor, displays her finely manicured nails while holding Dick Powell's hand steady as he lights her cigarette. Edward G. Robinson paints Joan Bennett's toenails. *They'll be masterpieces*, she breathes.

Gail Russell tracks Dane Clark down to a vacant plantation house—*You should have sent me away when I might have gone. It's too late now.*

Standing on the terrace in *Now Voyager*, Bette Davis murmurs, *Oh Jerry, let's not ask for the moon. We have the stars* ... A little later in *Casablanca*, white-jacketed Humphrey Bogart demands, *Play it, Sam.*

And Sam does.

◈

In Paris, James Joyce is still penning his wordspiderweb, *Finnegan's Wake*. Seventeen years in the making. Blessed be St Lucy, his eyes held out.

> *A lithesome lissome Irish girl lying on a stone causeway, one leg parted heavenwards, lacing up her shoe. Dandy all right, but when moonlight flits between her tits, Jesus Christ almighty ...*

We learn (twice) that the Liffey dried up in 1452 for the space of two, or a little more, minutes; that a cat chased a mouse into an organ tube in the crypt of Christchurch Cathedral. And could not then get out.

Anna Livia rushes out from her wet mossy bed, hitherandthithering her way back to her cold mad father, the Irish sea; then to be borne on blown, dove-grey clouds to fall, later, as rain. Back to source.

Her creator has the appearance of a superior lavatory attendant. Himself an ardent Vicoist, sees all: the same, anew.

◈

We travel East to Germany. To the dying Weimar Republic.

Berlin. Wreathed in smoke, figures emerging from blue-lit bars.

The stage darkens. A magic beam of light.

A priestess of pure joy floats on, followed by two handmaidens, lightly clad. *Zieh Dich Aus*—Take Them Off—is on at the Komische Oper.

Entering a pool of blue light, the cabaret artist, Werner Fink, smiles at his audience—*No, don't worry, I'm not Jewish. I only look intelligent.*

In *Mahagonny*—the city of nets—Jenny takes up with Jimmy till he is sentenced to death for lack of money. The greatest crime on the face of the earth. Lotte Lenya sings the bittersweet melodies of Kurt Weill to words by Berthold Brecht.

> *O moon of Alabama*
> *We now must say good-bye.*
> *We've lost our good old mamma*
> *And must have whiskey.*
> *Oh, you know why.*

Der Silbersee—The Silver Lake—becomes the swan song of the Weimar Republic. A witness remembers: *We met for the last time. I can hardly describe the atmosphere. It was the last day in the greatest decade of German culture this century.*

Slim, glossy, nylon-clad legs emerge from a purring taxi. High heels disturb a blue neon reflection as they trip over a shallow pool.

The female clientele of the Hotel Adlon are offered attentive male dance partners and discreetly attractive female companions. Soon, in the late afternoons, Hitler will go there to take coffee and flakey cream cakes, seated at a corner table.

But at the greengrocer's, a little girl begs her mother for some cherries. When told that fruit is excluded from the Jewish ration she runs out of the shop, crying.

Hitler wipes cream from his mouth.

Scheherazade remains absolutely still.

Lulu, free spirit, intoxicated by her own beauty, lives surrounded by an atmosphere of constantly ringing door bells, recriminations, tenderness, flowers. As her lover runs his fingers up her thighs, she cries ecstatically from an artist's studio in Alban Berg's second opera: *I can see all the cities of the world…*

Later, alone for seconds between lovers, lost before the mirror: *You… You… You…*

Murdered.

An anguished threnody.

Her female admirer, Countess Geschwitz, cries, *Lulu! My angel. Appear once more to me. For I am near, I'm always near. For evermore…*

༺༻

Begun some forty years before, Lazer Goldschmidt completes the twelfth and last volume of his German translation of the Babylonian Talmud.

Adolf Hitler assumes power in Germany. Books written by un-German and Jewish writers are burnt. A century earlier, Heinrich Heine had stated: *Where one burns books one ultimately also burns people … When at night my thoughts turn to Germany, sleep deserts me … I see a darkened land, ablaze with flags and banners.*

Deutschland. Ein Wintermärchen.

Berthold Brecht voices his concern. The laurel groves have been lopped down. Black smoke belches from the factories of arms manufacturers.

Walter Benjamin passes scraggy whores standing by dark tenements that open on to the edge of a void. His Angel of History—blown backwards into the future—surveys the wreckage behind.

Madam Kitty's, a Berlin brothel staffed by SS girls in kinky black, is doing brisk business. All conversations—grunts, groans, cries—are taken down by the Gestapo who work in the basement below.

For Hitler's first state visit to Rome, Mussolini has the last kilometre of rail track lined with fake apartment blocks: Rome of the Caesars, reduced to cardboard.

Edmund Husserl, whom Heidegger has succeeded at Freiburg, finds that the telos of science and philosophy set up by the Greeks has been abandoned; an ethical concern for the future has dropped virtually to zero.

An orotund beat of drums.

Hooded bronze eagles gleam in torch-lit processions. On display: Flaxen hair. Blue eyes. Fine-boned cheeks.

Germany's mystic dream.

Leni Riefenstahl films ecstatic, uplifted faces greeting the *Führer*, the sun catching his head in a halo. Each cheering face, raised arm, fleetingly consonant with the course of the world.

Her low voice murmurs,

—The music of a lute is drowned by the beat of a drum.

The brilliant mathematician, Emmy Noether, develops her theorem: *Where there is a symmetry there is always a corresponding conservation law.* She is hounded into exile.

On the streets of Vienna men and women are on their knees, scrubbing the pavement with toothbrushes. A Nazi spits. *That too, Jew.*

Sensing the coming war, Frida Kahlo leaves Paris—after exhibiting her paintings, where inside is turned out and every searing pain laid bare—and returns home, to Rivera, whom she loves more than her own skin.

We travel West, pass Tübingen—where Hegel and Hölderlin studied—to reach the Black Forest, where Heidegger finds a woodcutter, connected to his axe by a blue gleam.

—Blue.

Slanting rays slip through pines, dappling the path that leads to a clearing, bathed in light. Here Martin Heidegger stands: where pure space and ecstatic time—presence and absence—gather and enfold. For, *On the earth* already means, *Under the sky*: Before the divinity. Belonging to one another.

To what is most near.

Saving the Earth. Receiving the Sky. Awaiting the divinities. Creating ourselves. For Earth and Sky, divinities and mortals, are one. A mirror-play of simple onefold.

Scheherazade's fathomless eyes.

An oboe softly sounds.

The setting sun sheds its last rays, touching the pine trunks with a fleeting, fiery band. Richard Strauss's opera *Daphne* has begun.

Resin and rosemary drift in the air. We breathe again the Mediterranean world of *Ariadne auf Naxos*.

August, 1939.

A summer of exceptional radiance, drawing to a close.

Hitler adds to his Blue Seas fleet.

At Hamburg, Admiral Raeder thanks the *Führer* for naming a battleship after the Blacksmith of the Second Reich. Dorothee von Löwenfeld cracks a champagne bottle against the ship's bow—*On the order of the Führer I baptize you with the name, Bismarck.* At Wilhelmshaven, Ilse von Hassell hurls the champagne bottle against the bow of the battleship *Tirpitz*. At Kiel, Magdalena von Horthy de Nagybánya christens the heavy cruiser, *Prinz Eugene.*

We look back. Anno 1839: one hundred years before, from his Paris attic, Heine wrote, *Oh Germany, when I think of you I almost weep. A twilight feeling comes over me.*

The last sheaves of corn are being gathered in from the fields.

XIX

The night is still, as, summoned once more before her, I make my bow, raising my eyes to meet her attentive gaze. The flute player has departed. The peacocks are silent. Even the susurration of the fountain has been stilled. The garden seems to hold its breath, as if wishing to turn away.

World War II.

White horses attached to the Polish cavalry nod their graceful heads, their tails gently whisking, their tranquil eyes soon to be rent in pain. Rumbling German tanks approach.

A late fragment of Hölderlin: *9th March 1940. The meadows stand in their mildness. Clouds drift quietly. In higher regions, it seems, the year holds back its splendour.*

Children, playing among the rocks at Lascaux, discover prehistoric paintings.

1940 is the year when we approach the meridian of the first star in Aquarius, writes Carl Jung. *The war is the premonitory earthquake of the New Age.*

The German army enters Paris.

Walter Benjamin—student of Kabbalah, of High German Literature—finds himself unable to cross from France into Spain. Takes morphine to find, in death, the safe harbour that had eluded him in life.

His ideal text consisted of quotations. The writer as a swimmer who dives down to the sandy sea bed to gather loose coral and pearl, then carries them to the surface, where they undergo a sea-change, becoming rich and strange.

A banner flutters across the facade of the Assemblée Nationale; proclaims: *Deutschland siegt an allen Fronten.*

In Normandy, lamplight quietly gleaming on his insignia, a German officer talks of his love for France and her culture to an old farmer and his niece, both sworn never to speak to the invader.

Away to the north, on the Ythan, the shadow of an osprey falls.

❦

Louis Zukofsky hears announcements of baseball scores he still considers matter—*Or, do not matter a damn.* Song passes out of voices, as freedom deserts speech.

From her window in Brooklyn, Carson McCullers looks out on a late November afternoon. A soft fog veils Manhattan, drifting in from the Atlantic: the dark beyond.

World War II.

The stricken battleship, Bismarck, colours honourably flying, radios her last message. In the Fatherland, despite the radio victory blare, arises a creeping feeling, akin to dread.

Germany has invaded the Soviet Union. In Russia, a young girl treks forty miles through forests where wolves roam, to return with fifteen eggs.

Nora Joyce wakes.

> *ALP, then.*
>
> *Swiss lake is it, and creamy milk chocolate. But, with the war returning once more to Zurich ...*
>
> *Close my eyes. So not to see. Let it fall in its glory. I was sweet, when I came down out of my mother, all soft and sweet as the dew out of Galway—not buried under a hundred cares, laid low with a tithe of troubles. But enough, Nora, what is that, but lived life.*
>
> *You used to call me a strange beautiful blue wild flower, growing in some tangled, rain-drenched hedge. But now you've grown silent with me, bent over your pale wine, far away with Finn ...*
>
> *Now Finn's finished, and I remain. Still, for a little, humbly dumbly warm, Jim, in your arms.*

Pausing.

Eyes meeting.

Summoning the next phrase ...

Frost. Burning white. Burning blue.

Panic seizes Virginia Woolf.

> *Shall I ever write again one of those sentences that give me such intense pleasure.*

She forces a large grey stone into her pocket.

Blood seems to pour from her shoes.

This is death, death, death ...

She looks down. Running water, flowing water, crinkling up the light ...

❧

Werner Heisenberg visits Niels Bohr in Copenhagen. He believes Germany will win the war; hints it may be possible to slow down atomic research—which he would prefer.

The *Nacht und Nebel* Decree is brought in: by which those held to endanger the Third Reich must vanish into night and fog.

In the New Order, camp inmates are required to wear coloured patches: red for politicals, blue for stateless, violet for religious fundamentalists, green for criminals, black for anti-social, pink for homosexuals, yellow for Jews.

Resistance spreads. Chalked V's appear on pavements, along walls in Paris. On the Metro, tickets are folded into V's, as are broken matches. And fingers, too, proclaim the same sign.

A member of the French Resistance follows a German officer strolling along the streets of Paris, an attractive prostitute on his arm. He cannot bring himself to shoot—they look so happy and full of life.

In exile, St John Perse celebrates the curator who, in time of siege, still made the rounds of the great halls where crumbling papyrus rested under glass; who shone his lamp on an embalmed princess, her friable bones pinned with gold.

Held in a prisoner-of-war camp, Olivier Messiaen composes his *Quatuor pour La Fin du Temps*. First performed in a washroom there. Never has he known such an attentive audience.

Near the winged village of Rossitten, ornithologists continue to observe and protect the vast flocks of migratory birds that alight on that long strips of sand by the Baltic.

༄༅

World War II.

Poland. An apple drops from the hand of a young boy being swung against a concrete wall by an S S man. During the subsequent interrogation, the man starts munching it.

Over lunch and cigars in a villa at Wannsee, final plans are drawn up for a solution to the Jewish question.

A freight train stops briefly at Breslau. A nun appears at the door of a carriage—she is Edith Stein, Jew turned Carmelite philosopher. She tells a postal worker: *This is my beloved home town that I will never see again. We are riding to our deaths.*

At Auschwitz, two aspirins hang from a thread. Those with a fever under a hundred are allowed to lick them once; those with a fever over a hundred, twice.

Ash clings to blades of scraggy grass by gleaming rails. The wind blows charred letters—black, Hebraic—through the encircling wire.

Living skeletons gather in Bergen Belsen to celebrate Hanukkah, the feast of light. A wooden clog, together with string from a camp uniform and some black shoe polish, are transformed ... become ... Holy Light ...

A rabbi at Sobibor extermination camp picks up a handful of sand.

You see how I'm scattering this sand slowly, grain by grain, and it's carried away on the wind. That's what will happen to you. This whole great Reich of yours will vanish, like flying dust and passing smoke.

Pius XII consecrates the whole human race to the Immaculate Heart of Mary.

Smiling contemptuously, Goebbels reflects: *What a difference, between a smiling, benevolent Zeus and a pain-racked, crucified Christ; between a gloomy cathedral and a light, airy temple ...*

At Buchenwald concentration camp, the old oak tree, under whose shade Goethe wrote, is left undisturbed.

༺༻

T S Eliot completes *Four Quartets,* begun before the war after a summer visit to an abandoned mansion in Gloucestershire. Disturbing a dusty web on a broken flowerpot, he runs a finger along a loosened pane and moves on, to reach an overgrown rose garden, deliberate beside a stagnant pool.

The years pass.

He arrives at Little Gidding in Huntingdonshire, as light fades on a winter's afternoon. Kneels in a secluded chapel, where prayer has been valid.

In America, Wallace Stevens envisions the reality we see and touch as green, and what we imagine as blue—a delicate balance, held in his poem, *Notes Towards a Supreme Fiction.* What our eyes behold may be the text of life; but our meditations are no less a part of the structure of our lived reality.

In strictest confidence, Hitler tells Goebbels that air attacks on certain German cities, horrible though they may have been, had their favourable aspect. Streets that needed to be demolished have been demolished.

In this respect the enemy did us good service.

Love flowers in Berlin. A passionate affair between Lilly Wust, wife of a low-ranking Nazi, and Felice Scheagenheim, an intelligent, flamboyant Jewish lesbian. It ends after eighteen months, when the latter is denounced and sent to Belsen.

Scheherazade's lip trembles.

The massive tank battle at Kursk ends inconclusively. Cut off at Stalingrad, the German Sixth Army receives an air drop of boxes containing iron crosses. They are left to freeze in the bitter cold.

Whirling flakes of snow, each a crystal—a six-pointed Star of David—fall over Germany, melting on darkened panes, as the Christmas Eve broadcast connects all fronts.

Stille Nacht
Heilige Nacht

All is calm
All is bright

༺༻

World War II.

The widow of Andrei Bely compiles a list of colours her husband used in his fiction. Albert Camus remembers the sky over Tipaza. Tanned bodies on the beach.

Beauty is unbearable, drives us to despair, offering the glimpse of an eternity we should like to stretch out over the whole of time.

In America, Maya Deren films her fingers delicately resting on a window pane where leaves and sky are reflected. Calls it, *Meshes of the Afternoon*.

The American authorities draw up a list of those without a right to deferment from armed service: messengers, clerks, office-boys, filing clerks, hair dressers, milliners and dressmakers, designers, interior decorators, shipping clerks, sales clerks, watchmen, footmen, bellboys, pages, artists ...

Grey Atlantic seas.

Two convoys are attacked by forty-one U-boats, hunting in packs. The convoy loses twenty-one ships for the loss of a single U-boat.

Another convoy is under attack by forty-one U-boats. Blinding fog intervenes, but radar helps pick them up. The attack is called off—for the loss of six U-boats, and several others damaged.

At Stalingrad a stone sculpture of six children holding hands in a circle survives the destruction.

Addressing a party rally in Berlin, Goebbels calls for total war:

Now, people, rise up, and storm! Burst forth!

Albert Speer, like the Emperor Nero, enjoys spectacular light effects—now caused by night-time aerial bombardments. He advances a theory of ruin value: a configuration complete in itself. A kind of monument.

Ernst Jünger, serving in Paris, confides to his journal: *When all buildings may be razed to rubble, language will still persist ... Today that thought consoles me.*

A song is heard among those held at Börgermoor concentration camp. It is taken up by the guards.

Pius XII issues the Encyclical, *Mystici Corporis Christi*—the Church is the mystical body of Christ.

The Spirit Lives—proclaim leaflets released in the main hall of Munich University by the White Rose, a group of Catholic students led by Sophie Scholl. A rejection of the subjugation of the spirit by lies and brute force; a proclamation of faith in the power of conscience and truth. They are arrested for distributing subversive literature, taken out and executed.

In Paris during the screening of newsreels, the doors are kept locked, auditorium lights left on. Armed guards, stationed by the screen, scrutinise the audience.

Confined in a building used by the Gestapo, Pierre Brossolette jumps from a sixth-floor window to avoid speaking under torture.

Simone Weil, starlit thinker, member of the Resistance, refuses to eat while the victims of war suffer. She writes: *Even Kent and Cordelia attenuate, mitigate, soften, and veil the truth. Only the fool speaks it.*

༺༻

World War II.

Mussolini is strung up.

Pius XII describes him as, *The greatest man I have known and without any doubt a profoundly good man. I have seen too many proofs of his goodness to doubt it.*

While waiting off Jerusalem Strasse, a cultivated draughtsman blows into his woollen gloves. He pores over a street map of Berlin spread out on a heavy, Birdmeier table. Finds he can form a hidden Star of David by connecting the interlocking lines of invisible triangles formed from the points where once resided: Heinrich von Kleist, Rahel Varnhagen, Heinrich Heine, Mies van der Rohe, Arnold Schoenberg and Walter Benjamin.

While Brussels is being bombed, Paul Delvaux paints a calmly sleeping Venus lying before a moonlit temple, watched by a skeleton, a dressmaker's dummy and a woman with outstretched arms. In the background, kneeling women gesticulate in anguish.

On the last day he held a pen, René Daumal, suffering from advanced tuberculosis, stops writing his novel, *Mount Analogue*, in mid-sentence—its summit inaccessible—so as not to keep waiting the visitor who has knocked on his door.

An attempt on Hitler's life. The conspirators sound a doomsday roll call from the *Almanach de Gotha*. Stauffenberg ... Schulenberg ... Kleist ... von Wartenburg ... Lynar ... Dohna ... Moltke ... von Schwanenwald ... Trott zu Solz ...

Chartres is liberated! The bells ring out.

On that day, as the ospreys circle over the Ythan, a small, tousel-haired boy celebrates his third birthday.

Antoine de Saint-Exupéry fails to return from a last reconnaissance mission over North Africa. As, in *Night Flight*, his pilot, Fabien, flew above villages where soft-lit lamps hung, suspended over tables prepared for supper; climbed through a bank of dark storm clouds, to emerge above an endless white field of calm, reflecting back the light of the moon ... Allowed, for a time, to wander there, to fly in that remote splendour ... A little like a figure from one of your tales, Princess: infinitely rich, yet doomed.

The Third Reich has become true to itself: a primeval world of blood and darkness. News of the slow military collapse is finally released. Horror, the only stimulus. Goebbels tells his intimates: *A hundred years from this time a film will be made of what we must now go through. Gentlemen, would you not like to play a part. I can assure you it will be great and beautiful, worth standing one's ground for. Hold fast.*

☙❧

World War II.

Now Jung writes: *The Angel of History abandons the Germans.*

Soviet tanks cross the Oder and begin to trundle over German soil.

The ashes of von Hindenburg, reposing in the Tannenberg mausoleum among the standards of the Prussian regiments he commanded, are taken West.

Abandoning her vast estates near Königsberg, Marion, Countess von Dönhoff, mounts her grey and rides for a thousand miles West. She was to write:

> When I remember the woods and lakes of my native East Prussia, its wide meadows and old shaded avenues, I am convinced that they are still as incomparably lovely ... Perhaps the highest form of love is loving without possessing.

At Yarzin, the old Baroness von Bismarck refuses to leave her ancestral lands. She asks that her grave be dug.

The Berlin Philharmonic, under Furtwangler, gives a final concert: Beethoven, Bruckner, Wagner. At the end, baskets containing cyanide capsules are offered by members of Hitler Youth to the sunken, departing audience.

But Hitler is contemplating a model of Linz, transformed into the culture capital of Europe. He worries that the bell tower may be too tall. Must not eclipse the spire of the cathedral at Ulm.

Hanna Reitsch, who test-flighted the V-1 rocket plane, now flies in and out of the burning centre of the Reich on her last air mission.

Hitler foams at the mouth. If the war is lost, the nation will perish. But—those who remain are of little value. The good have already fallen.

The day before his execution by the Gestapo, Alfred Delp S J writes: *My crime is to have believed in a Germany beyond this hour of distress and darkness.*

Final Wehrmacht *communiqué*.

Since midnight, silence on all fronts.

☙❧

May 1945.

Berlin in ruins.

A woman pushes a battered pram filled with burnt pieces of wood along Prinz Albrechtstrasse.

For the years 1942-45, the surviving works of sculpture by Alberto Giacometti can be fitted into six matchboxes ...

Sheherazade shifts on her couch.

Brindisi.

The years are brushed away as Virgil lies, dying.

Hermann Broch, in exile, has given to the poet a final exchange with his friend, the Emperor.

> *There are tears in the very nature of things, and our hearts are touched by its transience.*

Virgil smiles.

> *Time is unrelenting, Augustus.*

The Emperor brings a beaker of water to the poet's lips.

> *Thinking has perhaps reached its limits ... Superficial perception may be increasing. But thought is diminishing.*

The poet attempts to sit up.

> *Oh, Augustus, everything was simple reality to Homer. That was his perfection.*

༄

Summer 1945. Paul Valéry, poet of the dawn thought, dies.

An angel resting on the edge of a well glances down and sees—to his amazement—his own reflection, in tears.

A strange-seeming grief, belonging to another world. A flaw in his diamond awareness: *There is something other than light ...*

A blade of trembling grass. A green dress worn in Marburg. A line of Hölderlin.

From his cabin in the Black Forest, Martin Heidegger writes,

> *We never come to thoughts. They come to us.*

> To think is to confine yourself to a single thought that one day stands still: a star in the world's sky.
>
> A few, perhaps, may rise up to become journeymen in the craft of thinking—so that one, unforeseen, may become a master.

The melodious sound of a musing horn rises.

A gentle fullness of strings, on which a beloved soprano soars …

Richard Strauss brings his life's work to a hushed close:

> O spacious tranquil peace, so profound at evening. Is this, perchance, death.

A winter's afternoon.

Evoking memories …

A tousle-haired boy by a blazing log fire cuts out characters for a play in a toy theatre. The set is an eighteenth century coaching inn. Snow lies on the ground. A lady and her pretty maid are seeking shelter for the night.

☙❧

Gathering ourselves in the face of all that has been lost, we look back to that which once we held to be of value. Colour, irradiated by light. The Past.

Before the war, when Henri Matisse journeyed South he found rooms saturated in light—flowers, palms, the dazzling Midi. Space had became flat, from the horizon to the interior of the room. A passing sail … shades of Proust … A plum, on the sill …

He embarked for Tangiers.

Greens, rioting by pinks and mauve, flooded his gardens with light. A ravishing blue window with a vase of red poppies, floating on deep blue, tinged with violet, melting against a turquoise roof.

Six Arabs clad in white rest on pale green before a bowl of goldfish: a harmonious state of being, when time dies. Shchukin, the rich Russian merchant who owned the painting, wrote to the artist: *It is the one I love now more than all the others. I look at it every day for at least an hour.*

On the French Riviera, he found calm and repose. A liberating release of colour expressing his *élan*—joy.

White stucco buildings soak in the sun.

Tanned bodies turn on the beach.

Scent of lemon and rose.

He visited Tahiti. Swam in the greyish jade waters of the lagoon where coral lies. A blond sky, honey-like—the light ferociously beautiful, as if immobilised forever, until ... a flamboyant sunset spreads into a sky that is turning blue ...

Her voice, very quiet; almost a whisper.

—Blue.

After many years, reveries from the South Seas became paper cut-out frescoes. A blue mermaid, a blue parakeet—floating, flying, through a magic space among pomegranates and trailing arms of algae; of waving seaweed, starfish opening like flowers, birds diving, soaring ...

—Enchantments of the sky ... the sea.

Cuts into pure colour—his scissors a Zen master's brush—where black, violet, magenta, yellow, blue, lime-green, red, orange, forest-green paper patches fashion a snail in motion.

Within the Chapel of the Rosary at Vence—his votive offering for the gift of life—quivering light magically merges the Orient and Chartres.

My chapel is not: Friends, we must die.
Rather, it is: Friends, we must live!

XX

A needle of light scintillates off the ice in my glass. Out, on all sides, to the shimmering horizon, a boundless blue. The white ferry, *Ariadne*, departing from the land of the gods. A last lingering scent of thyme and wild cumin on the air. Recalling an ending, drawing to a close. No more—no, never again to see those trembling shadows, floating on pools of lambent light ... Her enigmatic smile ... dark eyes ...

My tale ended, I had been taken to the coast, where the edge of the sea runs like white silk over the wet sands, and put on board a trading boat bound for Crete. Now, embarked again, and sailing to Brindisi, following in the wake of Virgil.

Land fades, sinks from sight. A blue swallow skims low, barely above the waves, and arcs upwards, away. The sun blinds, strikes slow diamonds off the waters.

On deck. Faint hum of engines. The splash of the prow, cutting through waves. Brightening circles of light on the waters. Wisps of cloud rising westward. Returning now, to England. Where fleeting cloud shadows dapple the downs. Gulls follow a lumbering tractor up a hill.

Late October there. St Luke's little summer. A tender blue sky fragrant with blae woodsmoke. Dank scent of damp earth. Rotting leaves. A low milk mist lying on the river.

Dusk, now. A silence—deep, enigmatic, verging on the spiritual—takes hold of the desert. Sands, softly running from the high dunes. The Empty Quarter, the Uruq al Shaibu, darkening. A diamond awareness, breaking through ... The last time I was summoned to narrate to the Princess Scheherazade.

Shadows, advancing and retreating along the flickering walls. The burning torch ... Yusef's naked back ... moist points of dancing fire ... resolving in ...

Her eyes.

—We near the end, Gabriel.

My name like liquid honey on her lips.

—Our tale of wonder to beguile the night.

Scheherazade in a sapphire blue silk, a slender gold ring upon her finger.

The stars were out. To the east the Pleiades softly glimmered and, far fainter, Aquarius beckoned.

Time to begin. And for the last time.

༺༻

Winter.

Cold.

Paris, a prey to sickness and despair.

Louis-Ferdinand Céline, off to see a patient, an old woman with no one to look after her, finds she has danced away into the night. The moment her music sounded, she took wing ... Most croak like rats; dancers vanish in ethereal rigadoons.

Wild about dancers, he has a passion for the dance.

A gold flash.

An arabesque in the air, traced by Scheherazade's ringed finger.

Accompanied by his wife, Lili—who was a dancer—and their loyal cat, Bébert, he fled across a Germany torn, going under. They pick their way through rubble. Berlin in ruins. Bébert in his bag.

After the war, and internment in Denmark, he returns to Mendon on the outskirts of Paris, overlooking the Seine:

> *The loops! I've got that view from my window as I'm writing to you.*

As a doctor he attends the little wants of the poor.

> *What remains ... I write. It is my life. This sheet of white paper, my tombstone. We are all croaking inside because we have no legends, no mysteries. We must become dancers. We must learn to dance. France was happy in the time of Rigadoon.*

He puts on his coat.

> *World has two anxieties: ass and bank account. The rest is fluff. So many vaginas, cocks ... But hearts—very rare. Too many cocks to count, but hearts ... on your fingers.*

From below deck. Low hum of engines.

Max, nudging my sleeve. Waiting for his walk.

Banged up in an iron cage in Italy at the end of the war Ezra Pound, taking a shit, comes on an anthology of verse by the jo-house seat. He's still allowed to look at beauty: the divine essence. Has in his pocket a eucalyptus seed he stooped to gather while descending the hill path from his home, accompanied by his captors. Observes—like Joyce before him—seven birds on a wire. Notes of silent music.

Works for fifty years—longer—on the *Cantos*. Luminous details: Lake Garda in sunlit mist; larks rising at Allègre; deer's feet making dust in shadow at the wood's edge. He turns dismal documents and junk mail the morning brought into poetry for the few who will follow him into the arcanum. And derives from this, an income that would keep a cat content for two weeks.

From the movement of the Cantos—fire and wind—we reach back through the years. How long since ... fifty ... sixty ... more ... Alighting from the Metro, when— suddenly—he sees a beautiful face. And another. Yet again ... Then a beautiful child's face. And yet another beautiful woman. Becoming: *In a Station of the Metro*.

> The apparition of these faces in the crowd:
> Petals on a wet, black bough.

Always ready to put ideas into poetry. Say, that in Italian painting—when usury increases, the line thickens. He embraced Plato's flickering shadows; Galileo's faint shadows on Jupiter; this morning's fleeting shadow of events at MIT.

All the soul needs is at hand. A lifelong theme.

There! No need to crave, to buy, to burden oneself. Hush, and look. Clouds process over a prison yard near Pisa. Autumn leaves descend on a madhouse lawn.

But … mental torture.

A world lost …

Grey mist …

Futility of what might have been …

Aiuto!

A final, slow, sea return to Italy.

> *Do not move*
> *Let the wind speak*
> *That is Paradise.*

☙❧

Jean Genet has sniffed the air of children's penitentiaries, oil seeping from cargo ships riding at anchor in fog-bound ports, low-lit bars, wax-polished cathedral benches, sweat-soaked mattresses in male brothels—and prison: a former monastery with tumbling, pale purple wisteria and climbing dark red roses, where chains seem to become flowers and prisoners move like mysterious, sensual princes.

> *I worship him. That prince, standing there. Guards kneeling at his feet, riveting an iron bracelet round each delicate ankle.*

Like Céline, on his travels he carries a sack, visits a beloved pissoir, corroded by the spray of hot, strong urine. Upon the rusting, stinking sheet-iron, he lays a dark red rose.

> *I told the court, the judge, I stole in order to be kind. To partake of that gentleness, ease, that largesse brings. I told the court, the judge, being destitute, alone, I searched in others for fleeting glances, that silken thread that unites us all.*

Fine gold threads of light running out from the candle flames.

He ends his days, like Saint Augustine, waiting for death.

The horizon rushing towards me, into which I shall merge; behind which I shall vanish, not to return.

Faint and tremulous from the garden, the sound of the flute.

Scheherazade's slightly abstracted eyes, resting on me.

❧

Fragrant fragments from the tenth century are discovered, preserved in your dry air, Princess. After so many years of silence they speak once more, Dinazed asking her sister, Shirazed, if she is not too tired to unravel a tale.

Her smile comes, long and slow. Dark and hazel eyes meeting, holding each other in a lingering gaze.

A breath's space. Then:

Cries of the guide.

Days spent in the saddle riding up the caravan trails towards a temple on the edge of the Gobi desert. The poet of incantation and high praise: St John Perse.

All the silent paths of the world, open. Glory at the threshold of the tent. The idea, pure as salt. Eternity, yawning over the sands.

Memories of childhood spent on the Leeward Islands, one leg dangling in warm, greenish amber water; the other heavy in a cool current. White sails appearing between the leaves of palms; starched petticoats rustling through the rooms of the house.

Dawn. His birds—robed in those dawn colours between bitumen and hoarfrost—come down to us. Strangers descending: the Dream of Creation, anew.

Pius XII defines the dogma of the bodily assumption of the Virgin Mary into heavenly glory. This, to Carl Jung, the most significant religious event since the Reformation.

> But any religious statements, without exception, have to do with the reality of the psyche, and not with the reality of the physis.

And now, along a country track towards evening, we approach a lamp-lit cottage, to find Gaston Bachelard, a phenomenologist for whom, frequently, a single word is the gem of a dream, a philosophy of the imagination.

Burning turquoise candles release their gossamer threads of gold round Scheherazade's throat.

—He opens the poetics of reverie, towards childhood.

Gentle fall of rain. A pensive child, forehead pressed against the pane. Only too often life disturbs us, summons us from this radical childhood melancholy. Gentleness of the past. Freedom to see sun slowly setting, smoke rising. Unhurried … Drifting … Blue …

For Samuel Beckett, words are all we have. A few words. Scraps. But less and less … Language at its limits. At the edge.

An old man sits before a low fire. He rubs his hands. Bitter cold. Beyond his gate, a white world. All still.

Not a sound.

Let us embark at Cherbourg, to board the Blue Star Line, arriving at that land where flutter pale yellow and dark velvety-maroon butterflies—so entrancing to Nabokov and Chateabriand.

Manhattan looms. Glittering blocks of gold and black stretch up into the night, ripple out over the dark waters. Dawn seems to start on the tenth floor as glass melts into light.

Rock'n roll thunders from gleaming chrome jukeboxes in downtown bars where young men with creamed hair and faded blue jeans feed voracious machines. Marilyn admits, *The only thing I wear in bed is Chanel No 5.*

Everyone goes to the movies.

Gene Kelly is *singin in the rain.* Cary Grant flees from a crop-dusting plane. Marilyn Monroe's skirt gets blown about by a hot-air grille. As *High Noon* approaches, Gary Cooper slowly walks down a dusty, deserted Main Street. And, tragically, Joan Crawford stalks through the haunting Western, *Johnny Guitar.*

Playing a corrupt sheriff, Orson Welles inquires of Marlene Dietrich:

> *C'mon, read my future for me.*
>
> *—You haven't got any.*
>
> *Whad'ya mean.*
>
> *—Your future is all washed up.*

As Harry Lime, he looks down from the Great Wheel in Vienna. Wonders if it really matters if one of those dots below were to stop moving, for ever …

Sheathed in satin and pushing smoke through her lips, Rita Hayworth, as one of the muses, asks to be allowed to stay on in New York.

> *It's much more fun. And Coca Cola's not available on Parnassus.*

Colours are running ... Blues, lilacs, greys.

Jackson Pollock drips paint on canvas. Dances round. Enters the painting. Blue poles sway with an airy grace through a mesh of threads and cords—white, yellow, red. The act of painting, an adventure.

Veils wash over canvas, hover in space.

Mark Rothko's blurred-edged rectangles float, as in a mist. The faded reds and blacks of Pompei haunt him, become deepening fogs of plum reds, blacks, dark purples. Tenebrous. Sombre. Brooding. Facing in towards the void. The long silence beyond ...

Scheherazade's dark eyes, resting on me.

We travel South.

Clarence Laughlin has been photographing New Orleans. A vanishing magic. Madewood Mansion is the only plantation house in Louisiana with Ionic capitals, carved in stone—but now in need of restoration. Billie Holiday sings: *You can be up to your boobies in white satin, with gardenias in your hair, and still be stripping sugar cane ...* In six states of the Union, a woman may file for divorce if her husband dare depart from the missionary position.

After leaving her analyst—a certain Dr F J A—a woman muffled by a long green cloak releases, from the tips of her fingers, her father's shrunken head. It falls into a small, circular well that may have been placed there for that purpose.

Remedios Varo conjures with Time and Space.

Her clockmaker is illuminated by a new vision of Time: delicate, serrated wheels slowly falling from his bench and rolling to the floor. Her astronomer seeks to prevent his model of planet and moon from slipping off into another dimension ...

The artist has by her side an old phone book, a twig of laurel, a thumbtack, a comb, a pot of green paint, a woman's shoe, a fake five pesos piece. She pursues her delicate, fantastic, starlit way.

Paints a thin, pensive girl wearing a long black jumper and skirt who feeds stardust from a wooden spoon to a sad-eyed crescent moon, held in a wire cage. Flaxen-haired girls in slate-blue capes with high, wide, white collars ride out on ghostly, ethereal bicycles under a mist-wreathed sky ... A star seeker in a gorgeous gown of creamy yellow and dark maroon has captured in her long butterfly net a pale crescent moon.

Scheherazade, twirling her fingers.

☙❧

Louis Zukofsky's firefly pages.

Clavichord notes, scattered on *A*—an epic poem.

His father, an *émigré* on the Lower East Side. Night watchman. By day, he pressed pants. Six days a week, from six in the morning to nine—sometimes even eleven at night. Or midnight. Except Fridays, when he left before sunset.

Ralph Ellison's anonymous African-American protagonist leaves the Deep South for New York—where he finds he is invisible. Those he encounters: *see only my surroundings, themselves, or figments of their imagination.*

In Virginia, the day is green. They said, *You have a blue guitar, you do not play things as they are.* The man replied, *Things as they are, are changed upon the blue guitar.*

Wallace Stevens has gone into business—it gives a man character to have this daily contact with a job. Catches breath at the sight of blackbirds in a green light.

On a quiet Sunday in New York he watches flocks of pigeons making ambiguous undulations as they sink downward to darkness on extended wings.

෮෴ඹ

Afloat on the Atlantic, the SS United States wins the Blue Riband for crossing in record time.

In Paris, Yves Saint Laurent shows his first collection.

> *Like Proust, I'm fascinated by perceptions in a world of transition, cutting those moments from cloth.*

Henri Cartier-Bresson, accompanied by his Leica—*my constant travelling companion*—has been photographing life in Paris for more than fifty years. He captures moments which cannot recur—but now endure. A young boy, proudly carrying home two bottles of wine, each one nestling under an arm … Lovers, kissing over a café table as a spaniel looks up apprehensively … A small dog, standing by his mistress and her young daughter. All are looking out over the Seine from the Pointe du Vert-Galant—before turning to walk away from that moment, forever.

Colette, who also described poignant Parisian scenes, hangs a sheet of the blue paper she always writes on to shade her lamp. It glimmers, beckoning to a young man who is just now crossing the park towards the Palais-Royale.

A late flourish from the Surrealists.

René Magritte paints men wearing bowler hats—he wears one himself. They stand motionless under a crescent moon, or maybe are about to take a walk through the sky. Dalí shows Velazquez' as a shadowy figure painting the Infanta Margarita—a vast, ghostly presence. Slanting bars of light fall through her, extending backwards towards a distant picture gallery.

An osprey, circling over the Ythan.

Two boys wearing deep blue shirts and navy jerseys sit at a long wooden desk, bathed in late afternoon light. One holds a green Faber pencil, the other a slightly longer, blue Staedtler pencil. They like glamorous cigarettes and their elegant packages. Green *Three Castles.* Pink *Passing Clouds. Balkan Sobranies* that comes in black and white tins. Slipping from sight, vanishing over the horizon, in a last whiff of smoke.

֍

Images appear, flowing along a beam of light.

Ingmar Bergman is captivated by light. Gentle. Clear. Misty. Bare. Sudden. Falling. Slanting. Sensual. Subdued. Calming. Pale ...

Death, waving his scythe, leads a dance along a bare hill. In a country mansion two sisters and a steadfast maid, in long, turn-of-the-century white dresses, wait in a deep, red-walled room, recalling the past. A third sister is slowly dying from cancer.

Images. An empty boat silently emerging out of mist on a Japanese lake. A mysterious white-veiled lady riding through a sun-dappled forest. Kurosawa brings to the screen Mieko Harada as Lady Kaede, slinking across the polished wooden floors of her mansion, her silk gowns rustling.

Late at night, a private eye drives into Alphaville ... In a bleak industrial landscape Monica Vitti stands disorientated by the side of a road ... Alain Delon, a professional hit man in raincoat and lowered hat, sits on the edge of his bed in a Paris apartment and looks at his watch ... A leper limps slowly towards Christ.

On a Hungarian plain, soldiers—a few on horseback—enact a choreographic poem ... After years of patient suffering, an ass is gunned down in a grassy meadow, where sheep quietly graze ... The captain of a U-boat raises pieces of potatoes he himself has fried to the lips of his exhausted engine room crew ... A hush falls as a Gestapo agent enters a classroom in a Catholic boys' boarding school in occupied France ... A steamship is hauled over a hill in a South American jungle.

A long tracking shot, down corridors, past motionless servants, limpid mirrors, out over a formal French garden, comes to rest on a woman in evening dress, leaning on a stone balustrade ... An angel drawn to a Berlin in need of hope watches a trapeze artist apply her make-up ... Her black dress billowing out in the wind, a dark-haired Scotswoman waits on a bleak, New Zealand shore with her young daughter and encased piano ... Thirteen beggars at a long table enjoy a late supper in *Viridiana*. Its director, Luis Bunuel, will later muse,

> If I have twenty years left, give me two hours a day of activity. The rest I'll take in dreams.

Images, flowing along a beam of light.

A lingering shot of a closed white door brings Carl Dreyer's oeuvre to a close.

෴

Faint rustle of palms.

We enter the bare, austere landscape of Sicily.

On a winter's afternoon, Tomasi di Lampedusa, author of *Il Gattopardo—The Leopard*—and last male descendant of the founder of the convent of the Holy Ghost, receives a sprig of jasmine from a gently smiling nun.

At Donnafugata, drenched in summer heat, bouganvillea cascades over the gates. The garden becomes a paradise of parched scents. The house, an intricate maze of guest rooms, state rooms, galleries, leather-tanged saddling rooms, sweet-scented drawing rooms, conservatories, corridors and dark back stairs that lead to a series of abandoned and neglected apartments which form a mysterious and complex labyrinth of their own ... Here, on a honeyed afternoon, through slanting light, Tancredi and Angelica flee.

Amid smothered laughter they blow dust off an old music box, releasing in clear, silvery tones a delicate tune. Gently they kiss, in time to those notes of disillusioned gaiety. Or find a far-flung room where dust-streaked mirrors hang extremely low, and a wide, worn sofa is studded by tiny nails, to which traces of grey silk cling.

Scheherazade's dark eyes, resting on me.

൙൚

Lying in the long grass on the island of Fanø a young man is watching passing clouds drift slowly, melting away into the blue. Sunlight dances on running water as the princess of modern storytellers, Karen Blixen, explores joy and sorrow in her pure, magical tales.

Memories of Kenya. Running a coffee plantation and looking up as the Ngong hills turning a deeper blue than the sky. Later, back in Denmark, at the family home at Rungstedlund, where the wind blows in from the Sound, sighing through the lamplit house.

Africa. A great wave building. Chinua Achebe, whose world straddles what is passing and what is yet to come, takes us to the homesteads and yam fields of Umuofia where, still, not a ripple disturbs a way of life rolling back into the mists of time … The wave breaks. Okonkwo rises, proud, only to be overwhelmed by the advancing flood. After some difficulty finding a publisher, Achebe brings out *Things Fall Apart*.

൙൚

The world to come.

As the first man steps out on to the Sea of Tranquility, a little moon dust rises. In an upper room an old man patiently picks fluff from between wooden boards with the point of a pin.

Grey skies. Rain in the air.

Intense young girls spill ash on their dark jerseys while struggling with existential texts. Freeing the slender strap on her high heels a young girl in a rented room in Paddington dreams of making love with her favourite movie star in a gravity-free space shuttle. In nearby Bloomsbury, a mild librarian laments the passing of those index cards which once carried diverse details that cannot be put on to the new electronic database.

To Devon, where Sylvia Plath stands near her kitchen window watching a wet blackbird shake himself ... *Black feathers can so shine.*

To London where, as evening falls on Primrose Hill, night-lit strings of lamps stretch up the hill, burning against the cold. White candles spill tears that cloud, and dull to pearls.

Her child lies awake. *Your clear eye is the one absolutely beautiful thing.*

Early morning. Milk lands softly on snow. *The blood jet is poetry. There's no stopping it.*

☙❧

It grows dark.

Paul Celan writes: *your golden hair Margarete ...*

He writes it and steps out of doors. And the stars are all sparkling.

Your ashen hair Shulamit ...

This Death is a master from Germany. His eye is blue.

The Poet and the Philosopher meet for the only time, at Todtnauberg, Heidegger's hut on the slopes of the Black Forest. A yellow star of David; a dimmed party badge. One, coming from Paris. The other, down a forest path.

Survivors.

At that meeting, only themselves present, what words passed between them.

> *Stouter boots required. Herbs of the region. The quality of light ...*

The poet falls silent. There has been a systematic suppression of silence. Poetry, being close to silence, tends towards silence.

The philosopher: *Only a god can save us.*

Turning in an arc in a limpid blue sky, a blue-backed swallow darts through a hilltop colonnade.

—Blue.

The sun—a burning pillar on the Aegean.

Martin Heidegger, at seventy-three, visits Greece for the first time:

> *We've lost our cosmic roots ... That first beginning, inaugurated by the Greeks.*
> *After the pre-Socratics, man stepped out of the light.*
> *Yet that beginning still is.*
> *It soars, serene in the sky, among the olive groves, out over the sea.*
> *It does not lie behind, as long ago, but stands before us. Pure. Free. Radiant.*

Her voice.

—We emerge out of the dust of stars, and to dust we return.

Her resonant voice, receding ...

Low hum of the ship's engines.

•

Va va voom!

Hair now cropped short, supermodel Linda Evangelista poses for her white shirt photo. Declares, *We don't wake up for less than $10,000 a day.*

The minimalists flourish.

Steve Reich takes us on a long train journey across America. John Adams has Nixon arrive in China. Laurie Anderson is performing *O Superman.*

With some trepidation, a dark-haired young woman enters an airy auditorium constructed to enable an audience to promenade, without intermission, for over five hours. Philip Glass mesmerises with *Einstein on the Beach* at Avignon. Later, he opens the double doors of the horizon on *Akhnaten.*

Thick black graffiti—congealed gestures of estrangement and assertion spread along subway walls, advertise wonder bras and power-driven wagons—surround a man descending an escalator, reading Dante. He has reached the lines where Saint Gregory, on entering Paradise, smiles to himself on realizing his error in the placement of the angelic orders.

At a conference on cosmology held by the Jesuits in Rome, John-Paul II warns it is right to study the evolution of the universe after the Big Bang, but not to inquire into the nature of creation, as that was the work of God.

A little whiff of dust rises.

New heavens, new constellations, being formed as the motes whirl and dance.

༄

It is implied that superstrings may offer a route to combining General Relativity with Quantum Theory, and so bring about a single, unified theory of all physical phenomena. A Theory of Everything—or TOE, for short.

In a gloomy apartment off rue Cardinal Lemoine, an old, reclusive bookseller sits before a nearly completed jigsaw puzzle. A last blank gap in the blue sky—almost the shade of this particular evening—in the shape of a U waits to be filled. But the final piece the old man clutches in his trembling fingers, before it wriggles free ... is a blue V.

By the site of the ancient library at Alexandria, as swallows dip and arc into the dazzling blue, a new library is emerging, inspired by the rising sun. Floor on floor cascading down. A bright beacon, beckoned by the flashing, diamond-clad sea.

☙❧

We approach Swiss lakes and mountains. Literature as a realm of magic, a game of intricate enchantment: Vladimir Nabokov.

Possessor of radiant, tender memories. Silver birches shimmering after rain ... A bar of Pears soap turning topaz. A large, mulberry-coloured cake slipping through Ada's wet fingers. A worn-down, much-loved, purple-coloured pencil. Intoxicating scent of vanilla and musk, of butterflies on fingers ... A pale lilac sky at *sumerki* ... dusk ...

Wrote his first novel—*Mary*—in the blue evenings in Berlin during the early twenties. Already, due to the Bolshevik terror, an exile.

Rus ... *Rus* ... In the melting distance—as gossamer threads float, gleam, through the dusk—the beloved estate at Vyra. Mushrooming in the gossamer dusk there. Time, suspended as an olive and pink hummingbird moth, beating its wings against a kerosene lamp.

Departs in the long, romantic, auburn carriage of the *Nord Express,* bound for Paris and beyond—to Biarritz. Takes leave of a delightful seaside companion who tap-taps her glinting hoop through light and shade, round and around a fountain choked with dead leaves. Till she, too, dissolves amongst slender shadows ...

Swept by the war across the Atlantic, he arrives, in the lilac mist of a May morning, in America. Pursues native butterflies over more than forty states with his big green net. Translates Pushkin, *con brio*. Gives to the novel, in his new-found language, colour, *élan*, enchantment ...

His dancing pen sends Lolita crisscrossing America on a fantastic, state by state car trip. Prelude to his return to Europe, where he remains, in the Montreux Palace Hotel, with a view of the lake from his sixth-floor apartment. But never, except in late fiction and radiant memory, to ... *Rus* ...

In winter, he writes standing at an old lectern, on crisp, cool cards. In summer, under the shade of an old cedar, spangling the serene skies of his novels with limpid magic.

Writes *Pale Fire*.

A wandering snowflake alights on a thin, Swiss watch ...

Crystal to crystal ...

John Shade, his ageing poet, carefully transcribes an image to his winter poem. His commentator and would-be friend and intimate, Charles Kinbote, raised as a promising prince in a castle in Zembla—a distant, northern land—cannot contain his glee at discerning a link between his own life and that of the poet.

A fritillary frolics round resplendent Ada. Our tantalizing heroine explains her system of metaphysics while carefully licking translucent honey from her fingers.

☙❧

A blue dragonfly sways on a long, green reed over a windswept pond. Coffee cups scatter across broad, executive desks on upper floors during stormy weather in Chicago. And, as the wind sweeps South, a group of convent girls in Louisiana can be seen running before a dust storm, holding on to their hats.

Cockroaches scurry over wooden floors in the music rooms of South American mansions while, on the white sands of Copacabana beach, all is relaxed and beautiful as tanned girls in tiny lemon and pink bikinis soak up the sun.

Strange, unknown constellations swing into view. For our tale now takes us South ... to Argentina. To Buenos Aires. To Jorge Luis Borges.

The sun is sinking, darkening the blue-washed walls of an outer district. A tango, sobbing, nostalgic, louche, emerges from a corner bar. A peeling poster slits an attractive blonde's slim, silk-clad legs up to her short, black leather skirt. A detective with sad, hazel eyes, who has read all the books and acquired a taste for metaphysical speculation, parks his dusty, maroon Buick and, pushing back a grating gate, enters on the overgrown garden of a seemingly deserted villa. He bends low to avoid disturbing a gleaming spider's line, slung out across his path. The faint scent of eucalyptus hangs in the air.

It's very quiet.

He finds a side door left unlocked. The evening light is retreating from the walls. He senses a trap. A sort of endgame. Gently he touches a rose in a tall blue glass. Almost abstractedly he watches a deep red petal silently fall.

He stands quite still.

With a certain weariness of spirit he climbs the spiral stair, coming, almost as expected, on the wan blue eyes of his killer, whom he recognises from a former encounter, patiently waiting, a ·45 in his left hand.

They almost smile. Almost apologise.

The detective, without too much sadness, realises he has been on an intricate labyrinth of his own, woven since childhood days. It has led him here, to this deserted villa, to this still evening and setting sun.

But, for us all …

There is a mirror in which we will not appear again, a nearby street we have walked down for the very last time, a favourite book we have closed for ever.

Now, Borges seeks mornings, the downtown, peace.

He stirs his coffee.

A passing man touches the rim of his hat.

> Back in the early days, I sought out sunsets, the city's outer limits and, yes, sadness. Now, gradual darkness —a slow summer dusk—overtakes me.

What will die with me ... A sorrel horse whisking his tail in a vacant lot ... my mother's voice ... an elusive smile from Elvira de Alvear ...

Scheherazade tilts her head; her eyes, enigmatic.

☙❧

Gertrud Voss sets up her installation, *Germania,* in Berlin.

We enter down a long, steep ramp where, on either side, the bronze busts of nine spiritual masters of Germany stand on dark green plinths: Kant, Goëthe, Friedrich, Hölderlin, Heine, Hegel, Wagner, Nietzsche, Heidegger. They gaze out with tear-stained cheeks. Before them stand wide metal bowls in which burn honour flames.

Proceeding, into a low-lit, plum-coloured room. To one side, three paintings. Two women walk by a deserted shore under wan moonlight. Hitler stands before a mirror, sniffing his immaculate, ironed underpants. A woman, holding a green can in her hand, waters some wild cornflowers growing in her garden.

To the other side, three paintings. A woman places a hotpot on a table before her subdued children. Among the ruins of Berlin, Hitler tweaks the cheek of a young boy soldier. By the edge of the sea, two women dance on a deserted beach by the light of a full moon.

We move on, to a dimly-lit chamber where five central screens show slowed-down close-ups of German actresses from Rainer Werner Fassbinder films: Petra von Kant, Maria Braun, Lili Marlene, Lola, Veronika Voss.

Exit is up a steep ramp. The walls are bare.

Ending …

The poor tread lightest upon this earth. A tribe from the vanishing rainforest of the Amazon elects not to exist. They quietly turn from their ancestral lands, and walk away.

Ending …

On the white snowfields of Hokkaido, red-crested cranes perform a slow dance. An ancient Thai instrument has almost become extinct, its gentle tones abandoned as too delicate for our loud world.

Ending …

Olivier Messiaen takes his green notebook out into the French countryside to notate the cries and songs of the greatest musicians—the birds.

A black-eared wheatear's chattering gives way to a melodious orphean warbler, and is answered by a high, chirruping corn bunting, followed by a descending, melancholy note from an ortolan bunting.

By the glimmering ponds of the Sologne, a reed warbler greets the dawn, joined by a clear-voiced, liquid-fluted blackbird. As sunlight dances along the Charente, a sedge warbler releases rapid notes; a yellow bunting makes his rhythmic, insistent call. And—travelling upstream—a grey wagtail hops and hops from stone to stone, as sharp cries come from a coot.

Off the coast of Brittany, while fog drifts in on the night tide, grey plovers, kittiwakes and an oystercatcher can be heard. And, over the darkening moors, the prolonged purring churr of the nightjar; the pure ringing cries of the curlew.

Faint rustle of silk.

Scheherazade murmurs ...

> —A night comes in *The Tale of A Thousand Nights and One.* A night of nights when the secret gates of the sky open wide, birds fly through us, water in the jug tastes sweeter ... On that night, an attentive, amazed Caliph hears from the lips of Scheherazade of a Caliph—amazed, attentive—hearing again a once-upon-a-time tale ... It never ends ... Or, perhaps, it does. A narrative draws to its sunset close.

And now ...

Her low voice.

—Another whispers ...